Praise fo[r]

'*Thirsty* is a frisky, campy para[...] your blood pumping. With a [...] swoony set of heroes, it's an essential spooky season read for those of us who like our monsters best when they're making community and making out'

Timothy Janovsky

'My all-time favorite kind of vampire: surprisingly soft, adorably grumpy and sizzling hot. *Thirsty* is charming and downright fun, showcasing a vibrant community of supernatural creatures trying to get by in the modern world, with a crackling romance I couldn't wait to sink my teeth into'

S. A. MacLean

'*Thirsty* is an absolute blast from start to finish! I came for the clever worldbuilding, stayed for Lucy Lehane's wry, hilarious voice and was fully swept away by Charlie and Lorenzo's spicy and soulful romance'

Ava Wilder

'The grumpy-sunshine vampire romance of readers' dreams! Fast-paced, clever, sexy and fun – *Thirsty* is a delicious confection you don't want to miss'

Emily Ohanjanians

'Lucy Lehane has a true talent for crafting deliciously unconventional love stories. With all the sexual chemistry of *Boyfriend Material* and the humour of *What We Do in the Shadows*, never has a romance between a mortal and a vampire been more irresistible. I devoured it'

Merren Tait

THIRSTY

THIRSTY

Lucy Lehane

BRAMBLE

First published 2025 by St. Martin's Griffin,
an imprint of St. Martin's Publishing Group

First published in the UK 2025 by Tor Bramble
an imprint of Pan Macmillan
The Smithson, 6 Briset Street, London EC1M 5NR
EU representative: Macmillan Publishers Ireland Ltd, 1st Floor,
The Liffey Trust Centre, 117–126 Sheriff Street Upper,
Dublin 1, D01 YC43
Associated companies throughout the world

ISBN 978-1-0350-7739-7

1 3 5 7 9 8 6 4 2

A CIP catalogue record for this book is available from the British Library.

Designed by Gabriel Guma

Printed and bound in the UK using 100% Renewable Electricity by CPI Group (UK) Ltd

MIX
Paper | Supporting
responsible forestry
FSC® C116313
www.fsc.org

Visit **www.panmacmillan.com** to read more
about all our books and to buy them.

for Chris

whose magic powers include listening,
stubble, and always being right

Chapter 1

Charlie Wever's inbox was overflowing with tales of yearning, delusion, and despair—letters from people who needed his help. Normally he loved perusing the inbox for his advice column, *Wise Old Crone*; poring over the toxic drama and ridiculous entitlement and confused longing that people sent him, and thinking of how he could help. But right now, when he looked at all the many letters, all he could think was *I can't use any of this*.

His editor, Ava, did not agree. Emails kept leaping to the top of his inbox as she forwarded them back to him, searching for the very best ones. Each forward came with a little note of her commentary, like OMFG this can't be real and dyinnggggggg. do this one! He tried to ignore her; he had a draft column going already, responding to a woman whose children had ruined a family wedding with their squabbling over entrée options and now wanted her to pick which one of them to blame. It was . . . incredibly boring.

is this even possible??? Ava wrote on top of another email, and he hissed with annoyance. It echoed in the empty coffee shop; at least there was no one but a bored barista to witness his encroaching mental breakdown.

He clicked away from his terrible column to the warm embrace of his DMs, where he found his thread with Ava. I can see the letters. It's my inbox. Stop.

She responded to him instantly. then pick one!! and write something!!!

I'm writing right now. It was essentially the same column he'd already written dozens of times before, but at least it was something.

The dots of her drafting appeared, and then she sent back: ,,,another wedding meltdown?

It hit him like a punch to the gut—like she had somehow peered over his shoulder and seen his trash writing all the way from New York. Thanks, he wrote, his face burning.

I'm sorry! He could hear it in her voice, warm and sincere. He missed the days when he and Ava had worked almost shoulder to shoulder in their tiny cubicles, when she'd been more than a message box in the corner of his screen. I'm just trying to help! I want to get you PAID

He ground his teeth. Yeah, of course, he said, while he clicked back over to his awful column and deleted it without saving.

He had been good at this at some point, right? He wouldn't have landed *Crone* in the first place if he'd been a shitty writer from the jump. He had to hold on to that thought or else he'd give up completely.

He'd been proud of his writing, and his column—once.

When he'd first gotten into it, as a staff writer at his college paper, he'd called his advice column *No Cosmic Lover*, after a line from his favorite track off *Hedwig and the Angry Inch*. He loved that name, but when he'd graduated and been lucky enough to land a full-time position at *Midnight*, the after-dark, counterculture online mag, they'd said the name was too niche.

So he'd picked a new persona: the Wise Old Crone. He'd meant it as kind of a joke—y'know, your fat gay friend who never gets any actual dates but listens well and gives great advice. He might as well be a decrepit old woman in the village, handing out bowls of possibly magical soup and quests, probably. It was just his kind of self-deprecating humor—trying with all his might to turn a weakness into a strength, and getting the feeling he was only half pulling it off.

But *Wise Old Crone* did take off, and he got plenty of dates, thank you. Truthfully, it was kind of nice using a proper pseudonym—it allowed him to feel like there was at least some separation between his real self and his advice-giving persona. It made him feel like a real writer.

Now he was just one more real writer who'd gotten fucked over by the media industry's death spiral. A VC firm had bought *Midnight*, and one of their "innovative" cost-saving moves had been to shift him from a salary to a pay-for-clicks model that meant he couldn't make rent anymore. The stress made writing feel like pulling teeth, which just made him more stressed, causing a vicious spiral of writer's block and misery.

His last few *Crone* columns had been aggressively mediocre, both in actual quality and *engagement*, much as he loathed that word. He was getting so sick of posting the links online and watching the numbers barely gurgle in response. His next column was due after the weekend, and he was starting to seriously contemplate whether it would be worse to get fired for not submitting anything, or for sinking beneath some mysterious click threshold they'd never stoop to actually explain.

If he couldn't manage to write something in the next few days, the choice would be taken out of his hands completely.

Tension flared in his gut like a firework, and he ground the heels of his hands into his eye sockets to try to dispel it. When he blinked his eyes open, Ava had DMed him again. you know I hate this. fuck the new owners! let's make them choke on all your clicks!! and on all the money they'll be paying you!!!

He ignored the gross and seemingly contradictory metaphor. Of course Ava wanted him to write something scathing and sensational that would break the internet and force the new management to keep *Wise Old Crone* going and pay him more than a pittance. She'd probably get a raise too. He took a sip of his tepid coffee and typed: Ava, I can't just wish my column into going viral.

I know! but you need to pick juicier letters

He sighed, dreading this next part. Like what?

Another dozen emails flew to the top of his inbox as Ava re-forwarded them. Grimacing, Charlie opened the first one.

Dear Crone,

I am a cis male werewolf married to a wonderful human man, but my mother-in-law is testing my boundaries on the issue of kids. Specifically, she's been reading a lot of 2010s-era Teen Wolf fanfic and as a result seems to believe not only that mpreg is real, but that I have been holding out on her by, in her words, "refusing to let her son get me pregnant." Crone, I don't have a uterus, and my husband and I have no interest in having kids, whether via fantastical pregnancy, adoption, or any other means. How do I talk some sense into her, or at least draw a reasonable boundary?

Sincerely,
Wolf With No Womb

He stared at it for a few seconds, then clicked to the next one.

Dear Wise Old Crone,

I am a middle-aged mother of two. In my youth, before
having kids, I had a one-night stand with a man named
"Diego." Recently, I met my older daughter's new
boyfriend and was shocked to learn that it is Diego
himself. Apparently he is a vampire and has not aged
since our encounter. (Also, he did not seem to remember me at all.) How do I broach this subject with my
daughter? Should I be concerned that he seems to be
working his way through our family one generation at
a time?

Sincerely,
Vampire DiCaprio's Ex

He clicked quickly to the next one.

Dear Crone,

My fiancé "Zara" and I got engaged a few months ago,
and it's been nothing but nonstop fights between our
families ever since. My family wants a live band, hers
wants a DJ. I want to get married at our local synagogue,
but Zara's family is insisting that the venue be the eternal
wellspring of Braxl'thar the Forsaken, which is lovely but
can only seat 66, and my cousins alone—

He stopped reading mid-sentence and clicked back over to
his messages with Ava. I can't do any of these.
why not??? she demanded. they're weird and messy and cool!

and it's such clickbait, Ask a Manager did a whole series on hexes in the workplace last week and it was everywhere

He stared at her message, trying to think of how to respond. Ava wasn't wrong—supernatural stuff was all anyone was talking about these days.

When the vampires, werewolves, faeries, and such had first "come out" a few years ago, they'd been more or less ignored; the world was a dumpster fire being carried away by a tornado, and the whole *magic is real!* thing had kind of gotten buried. Charlie thought he might have posted something like NOT NOW, MYSTICAL CREATURES and moved on.

But over the last year or so, people seemed to remember that it had happened, and interest in the paranormal had grown until this summer, when it'd finally tipped into a full-blown frenzy. All his competitors were doing pieces on dating the supernatural, working with the supernatural, and rooming with the supernatural. (The consensus was to *not* steal their food.) There was a strange sort of push and pull going on, where the public had never been more interested, but the paranormals themselves seemed highly reclusive, as if maybe they regretted coming out of the shadows. Or maybe that was just something inherent in being a creature of magic; Charlie had never met one, but he couldn't imagine a talkative vampire, or a werewolf prone to oversharing. Intrigue seemed like part of the gig, and the world was quite intrigued.

But Charlie wasn't—he was completely lost. He didn't have anything against werewolves and vampires, he just knew nothing about them. He'd never met one (that he knew of), and he knew nothing about their lives or relationships, their culture or customs or taboos. He didn't have anything to offer the people writing to him about this viral new topic, and that was the whole point of being an advice columnist: He was supposed to be helpful. Reliable. Wise. These letters about the supernatural made him feel like a fraud.

And the entire strange situation was exacerbated by the fact that the very name *Wise Old Crone* sounded—now—like an advice column *for* the supernatural, possibly even *by* the supernatural. He had to assume he was getting a higher proportion of letters about paranormal topics than his peers, because what had started as a trickle was now a torrential downpour of questions about curses and love spells and yearning across dimensions. It could only be that his readers, at least some of them, assumed that the Wise Old Crone was not merely Charlie's corny joke, but an actual mystical source of wisdom.

In fact, he had an ominous feeling that the new owners of *Midnight* might have even been under the mistaken impression that *Wise Old Crone was* a supernatural advice column. That could certainly be where Ava's pressure on him to "chase the niche" was coming from. Or maybe she was just earnestly looking out for him.

It didn't matter. He'd already tried retooling his column to address the paranormal (he'd seen how much attention *Dear Prudence* got for that wild letter about leprechaun inbreeding)—and he'd failed. He'd decided that before he could write about the supernatural, he had to educate himself, so he'd sought out information. There wasn't a lot to find online, so he'd reached out to a few friends who'd bragged about meeting up with fae guys, and he'd even tried cold-calling any coven or other paranormal group he could find online. But it had all been a bust—no one would talk to him. It seemed mystical creatures weren't eager to have the details of their personal lives splashed about online for public dissection. Which, he supposed, was fair.

But that left Charlie with a bunch of boring letters about humans, a bunch of paranormal letters he had no idea how to respond to, and a career that was circling the drain. In his mind's eye he could see the glowing red rectangle on his calendar for Monday: *COLUMN DUE*. He felt panic crawling up his throat again and took a few deep breaths.

Ava was writing to him. you're going to get through this. your column is awesome and so are you

Yeah, he wrote back. It's so great the click-based model drained my bank account in a few months.

That was the worst part of the buyout and the new owners and the fucking click model: the part where he couldn't even be mad about it.

Because if his column really *was* as popular as it'd been just a few years ago, he wouldn't be in this position.

Somehow, over the last few years, his column had gone . . . stale. He felt like he was always writing about the same problems, giving the same answers, regurgitating the same posts over and over again. No matter how much he tried to spice up his writing, find a new angle, reinvent his point of view, it never seemed to amount to anything. No wonder he was fading away. He'd lost his voice.

This was his fault.

A gust of cold air wafted over him as a customer walked into the shop; it had been balmy during the day, but this late at night it was chilly. Whatever Ava was writing to him, she was wavering on it; her dots popped up and then vanished, popped up and vanished again. Then: is it that bad?

His heart jumped. No, it's fine, he lied.

let me cheer you up, she wrote back. let's get drinks!

He winced. I'm actually not in NYC this weekend, he wrote. Visiting a friend out of town.

oh fun! when you get back then

Yeah, he wrote. When I get back.

He closed his laptop before she could respond. He'd been making excuses for a few weeks, telling people he was visiting friends or couch surfing for a while. Plenty of writers did their work on the road, after all.

It would just be too pathetic to admit the truth.

He stretched some of the stiffness out of his neck and glanced around the twee little coffee shop, which was dim and quiet past eleven p.m. When he was hunched over his laptop, he could forget where he was, the blue-white glow like a portal back to his life in New York. But he hadn't been able to afford rent in New York for a while now. A few weeks ago he'd finally faced reality and sublet his place to a stranger from Craigslist, flagrantly breaking the lease; but it was better than giving the place up entirely. At least this way he could tell himself he'd be back soon. Then he'd packed up his things and moved back home to Brookville.

Most people didn't expect to find a funky little town like Brookville in the middle of rural Virginia, but tourists loved it—the cobblestone streets, eclectic nightlife, and rolling mountains were an appealing package. The coffee shop was classic Brookville: locally owned but with the polish of a chain, rainbow swag already up well in advance of Pride, posters for ukulele lessons and the local DSA on the corkboard. B'ville was the kind of oddball small town most people found charming.

As a local, Charlie had been itching to get out of Brookville his whole life. He hadn't been able to turn down the free tuition that came with being the son of a University of Brookville faculty member, so it had taken him until after college. But he had, eventually, gotten out, for a few sweet years. Brookville was cute, sure, but New York was the center of the universe to an aspiring writer.

And now he was back, because B'ville was dirt cheap compared to New York. He'd rented a tiny, stale-smelling apartment from a grad student who was gone for the summer, and he'd barely bothered unpacking more than his toothbrush and laptop charger. He had no intention of being here long. He was going to get his column on track and move back to the city.

And if he didn't, he'd just have to . . . move in with his father.

Needing to shake off that thought as quickly as possible, he got up and headed to the counter. He got there just as another customer finished his order and moved to the side to wait for it. As Charlie gave his order to the barista, he glanced over at the other customer. He was tall and broad-shouldered, with tousled, touchable black hair and a sharp jawline. A distant part of Charlie's brain, mostly buried under all the panic and stress, went *mmm*.

He finished paying for his drink and moved toward the pickup spot, while the other guy shuffled away from him slightly. He was wearing kind of a lot of clothes for summertime, most prominently a long, well-cut jacket that fell nearly to his ankles, which Charlie had to admit did flatter his frame. He was facing away from him, though, which stymied his efforts to check the guy out fully. He sighed and got out his phone.

There was a nagging text from Ava and nothing else of interest. He slid his phone back into his pocket, and when he looked up, he caught the other customer looking at him, though he whipped his gaze away quickly. This time, with a fuller view of his face, something pinged at Charlie—familiarity.

Did he know this guy?

Just from the quick glance he got, he was able to confirm that, yes, the guy was hot—*very* hot, with rugged, masculine features, though his skin was pale and his eyes a little sunken and red. He was wearing a faded-looking sweatshirt and loose jogging pants beneath the coat; not someone who cared that much about fashion then, but honestly, with his tall, muscled frame, he didn't have to.

It was driving Charlie nuts that he couldn't figure out where he knew this guy from. He didn't think he was someone he'd met in New York, but he didn't remember him from the last time he'd lived in Brookville either.

The guy glanced at Charlie again, his eyes narrowed. It was kind of a . . . glare, almost. A sexy smolder, maybe? Or maybe Charlie was just being optimistic.

Then the barista put a coffee cup on the counter and said, "Lorenzo," and it clicked.

"Lorenzo!" Charlie shouted unhelpfully.

Lorenzo squinted at him some more. "Charles," he said, in a strange, almost formal tone.

"Sorry," Charlie said, embarrassed. "I couldn't, uh. How are you?" It was all coming back to him now: Lorenzo had dated one of his friends, Olivia, for a few months their senior year of college. Charlie and Olivia had been close, but he'd never gotten to know Lorenzo that well—it was more the kind of relationship where Olivia brought him to parties and everyone made stilted small talk with him and mostly just tried to ignore that he was there. Charlie had a vague memory that Lorenzo had been kind of weird and hard to talk to, and Charlie was pretty sure he'd thought Olivia could have done better. He was starting to lose interest in talking to him now.

"I am well," Lorenzo was saying, somewhat stiffly. He had the same faint accent that Charlie remembered now—he must have been an exchange student from . . . somewhere. Europe? "In fact, I am thriving." He picked up a jar labeled *Artisanal Flaked Iron* and tipped some of it into his coffee.

"Uh, great," Charlie said.

"It is great," Lorenzo said. "And I am glad to see you here, so that you can see how well I am doing since your betrayal."

Charlie plowed into the words like a person in front of him who'd just stopped walking. "My—my what?"

"Please," Lorenzo said scathingly. "Your feigned stupidity does not fool me."

"Uh," Charlie said.

"I know what you told Olivia."

"What I told . . ." Charlie said, confused.

"That you told her to leave me," Lorenzo bit out.

"Oh, right," Charlie said distantly. Honestly, he could barely remember much of anything about Olivia and Lorenzo's relationship, because, well, it had been an extremely unimportant part of his life at the time, which was four—no, five years ago now. He did vaguely remember talking to Olivia about Lorenzo right before graduation; she'd been unsure if she should try to make things work with him long-distance after she moved away from Brookville. And she'd come to Charlie for advice about it, because that's the kind of friend he was: the sensible, wise-beyond-his-years one who listened well and stopped his friends from doing stupid shit.

It was why he'd become an advice columnist. He sighed at the memory. It was nice to think about Olivia—he made a mental note to reach out to her, it'd been too long—but all those little moments he'd once viewed as pieces of his calling were tainted now.

Because maybe he'd been wrong.

Anyway, he was pretty sure he'd told Olivia to dump Lorenzo. Lorenzo, who was now standing in front of him, clearly gathering himself up—and wow, he really was tall—to give Charlie some kind of stinging rebuke. "Indeed," he said coldly. "Well, as the Americans say, the best revenge is living well, and I assure you, since your duplicitous actions, I have been living exceptionally well. Or, rather, un-living, but the point is the same. Good day."

"Wait—" Charlie said, taking a step toward him as Lorenzo turned to leave. "Lorenzo, look, I'm sorry about, uh, everything that happened with Olivia, um, back in college, but—well, it was good to see you, and I'm glad you're doing well, and holy shit you're a vampire," he finished, the words and his epiphany happening at the exact same time.

It was like putting on his glasses and having everything suddenly click into a new degree of sharpness. His pale skin. His stiff manner. His *European accent*—oh Christ, he was an idiot.

The guy was getting coffee in the middle of the night. With *iron flakes*.

Charlie's eyes darted up and down Lorenzo's frame, the truth now blindingly obvious.

Lorenzo was nonplussed, though his eyes narrowed after a moment. "Ah, I see," he said. "You told her to break up with me because I am a vampire?"

Now that he was looking for it, the flash of his canines when Lorenzo spoke *did* look extra sharp. Charlie was distracted for one strange, confusing moment wondering exactly how sharp they were. How hard did he have to bite to break human skin?

Then he blinked and found Lorenzo staring at him, unimpressed. "Uh, what?" he said, refocusing. "No. I had no idea you were a vampire. Were you a vampire five years ago?"

Lorenzo rolled his eyes. "Yes," he said, the *you idiot* part clear from his tone. "I have been a vampire since 1809. But you humans are so oblivious, you didn't even notice we exist until we made a big fuss about it."

"Whoa," Charlie said. His friend had dated a vampire. That was weird. He was talking to a vampire, right now. That was weird too.

(Was it bigoted to feel so weird about it? Probably.)

"Yes. Whoa," Lorenzo said scathingly, and turned to leave.

As he reached the door of the coffee shop, Charlie was gripped with another, far more important realization. The letters. The clicks. *COLUMN DUE.* "Wait!" he cried, and Lorenzo turned back to look at him. "Can you help me with something?"

If looks could drain blood, Charlie would have dropped dead. "Unbelievable," Lorenzo pronounced, and stormed out of the shop.

The coffee shop was tucked onto a small, tree-lined street that sloped gently downhill, twinkle lights wrapped around the trees and a large, abstract mural painted onto the brick wall opposite them. Charlie ruined the ambiance by flapping down the street after Lorenzo with no semblance of dignity. "Look, I'm really sorry about all that stuff with Olivia," he said, while Lorenzo kept walking and didn't look at him. "But I'm working on this project right now, and I really really *really* need a vampire to talk to me."

Lorenzo stopped, giving Charlie a chance to catch his breath. "Do you?" he said. "That is wonderful."

"It is?"

"Yes, because now I have the chance to finally wreak my vengeance upon you." He leaned forward. "No. Good day."

"Fuck," Charlie said, running after him as he once again tried to leave. "Listen, I'm trying to learn about, y'know—uh, relationships between vampires and humans—between humans and, and all supernatural beings. You're the perfect person for me to talk to!"

"Yes," Lorenzo said, still walking, "but I have already taken my revenge on you by denying your request."

"Please?" Charlie asked. "I can't get any other vampires to talk to me, and you're . . . I mean, you hate me, but you're still talking to me."

"No, I am ignoring you."

"Look," Charlie said, jumping in front of Lorenzo and planting himself there, which at least got him to stop walking. "I'll do anything."

Lorenzo pinned him with a look of pure disdain. "Please," he said. "Pathetic human. You think I would sleep with you after your betrayal?"

Charlie blinked. "Sleep with me?"

"No," Lorenzo said immediately.

"No!" Charlie shouted, his voice echoing along the quiet street. He glanced around self-consciously and lowered his voice. "I don't want you to sleep with me, I just—I want to ask you questions about your life. About what it's like to be a vampire."

Lorenzo narrowed his eyes. "You said you wanted to learn about the love between vampire and human."

"Yes, but—not by—engaging in it," Charlie sputtered.

"Hm," Lorenzo sniffed. "Well, it is still more gratifying for me to deny you, whatever the nature of your request. Even if you are making it less gratifying every second you continue to bother me."

"Come on, please," Charlie begged. "I really need this. I'll seriously do anything. I—" He broke off. He couldn't afford to pay Lorenzo. What else did he have to offer?

A few steps away was the street corner, where a row of businesses sat quiet and dark—a small clothing store, a diner, and a bank. Charlie smiled as inspiration struck. "I could run errands for you during the daylight!"

Lorenzo frowned, looking taken aback by the idea, and didn't respond right away. The silence drew out as he simply stared at Charlie, maybe considering his offer, or maybe just mulling over the best way to insult him as he declined. He had big brown eyes, long-lashed and bloodshot, sunken and stark against his pale skin. They were such *vampire's* eyes, Charlie couldn't believe he hadn't seen it before.

Finally, Lorenzo's squint curved into a small smile, and he said slowly, "It would amuse me to see you dance to my tune."

"Oh. Yeah!" Charlie said, happy to encourage this motivation. "It'll be . . . super degrading. For me."

"And what do you wish for in exchange?" Lorenzo asked. "What exactly is this project of yours?"

"I just want to interview you," Charlie said. "Ask you about, y'know—vampire stuff."

In an instant, Lorenzo gathered himself up suspiciously. "An interview?" he demanded. "To be published . . . where?"

"Nowhere," Charlie said automatically. There it was again— paranormal creatures were all *so* private. He'd never agree to help him if he knew where the information he gave Charlie would end up; that was how he'd struck out with every other supernatural group he'd tried to contact before.

The answer came to him quickly. "No, no, not published," he continued, doing his best to sound soothing. "It's—I'm writing a thesis. I'm a graduate student here. At the university."

"Oh," Lorenzo said, and the suspicion in his manner drained away. "No one will read that."

"Right," Charlie said, relieved.

Lorenzo was smiling again in that strange, almost manic way. He reached into one of the pockets of his long coat and handed Charlie what looked like an old-fashioned calling card. "Come to this address next nightfall," he said. The card had his name embossed in elaborate script, and beneath that, a Brookville address written in what looked like Bic pen.

Charlie gripped it with both hands. "Thank you," he said. "Thank you!"

"Oh, you will," Lorenzo said, somewhat nonsensically.

And this time when he swept past, Charlie let him go.

Chapter 2

❤

Five Years Ago

"It's just down this alley," Olivia said, skipping ahead of Lorenzo on the rain-soaked pavement.

He hurried to keep up with her. Olivia was small but fearless, and she moved quickly despite the fact that the alleyway was dark and foreboding and her night vision, like all humans', was poor. "This doesn't seem like a safe area of town," he pointed out. "You come here often?"

"Yeah," she said. "They're my best friends. It's fine!" She turned and walked backward for a moment just to grin and waggle her eyebrows at him. "What do you think is going to jump out of the shadows and get me, huh? A monster?"

"Of course not," he said. "Monsters! Hah. Those don't . . . exist." At least, they wouldn't officially exist for a few more years, if the rumors he was hearing were true.

"Uh, yeah," she said, rolling her eyes. "Anyway, I think it's kind of cool that they decided to live off campus this year. It's so, like . . . real. Oh, here it is!"

She stopped at a small bungalow and rang the doorbell, and he stepped up beside her. She was more than a foot shorter than him, her long black hair glossy in the dim light, and she smelled of the perfume he'd watched her dance through as she was getting ready. As a human, Olivia was frail in ways she didn't even understand, but despite that, there was a core of strength in her he found incredibly sexy. She was confident and effervescent. He envied that.

When she looked up at him, she must have seen the trepidation in his face. She smiled reassuringly, squeezing his shoulders, and said, "Don't worry! My friends love you."

It was a common misconception in human stories about vampires that they could always tell when humans were lying. Often this power was said to be related to vampires' heightened senses of scent or hearing; they could supposedly hear a racing heartbeat, or smell the scent of guilt. None of that was true, of course; vampires had no particular advantage over humans when it came to deception.

Olivia, however, was a kind soul who just so happened to be bad at lying in the ordinary way shared by vampires and humans alike. But he didn't want her to worry, so he just smiled and said, "Okay."

The party smelled of drugs and cheap cologne, and the music that was playing wasn't familiar to him, though he tended to be a century or so behind on that sort of thing. The bungalow had a few rooms, with parquet floors and sparse furniture, all of which looked better in the low lighting. Lorenzo wished he could have invited Olivia to his place, but their relationship was still in the bloom of newness; he wasn't ready to tell her the truth about his vampiric nature.

Humans were scattered all around the party, but Olivia bounded straight over to a group standing by a large neon sign that said *FERN*. "Hey, guys!" she said happily, wrapping her arms around one of them. When she pulled back, Lorenzo saw that it was her friend Charles.

He suppressed a grimace.

Charlie laughed as Olivia hugged him, the neon reflecting off his round cheeks. "Hey, babe," he said, while the others waved in greeting.

Olivia turned to Lorenzo, offering her purse. "Hold this, will you? I'm gonna get us some drinks."

She left for the kitchen. Lorenzo smiled and nodded graciously at her friends. "Hello."

They all offered limp greetings in return, some barely more than grunts. Then their eyes collectively slid away from him, as if he had simply vanished from their line of sight, and resumed their conversation. He felt like a wart on their gathering, something unsightly and best ignored.

He tried not to judge her friends too harshly. Olivia was young, and so were her compatriots. Sometimes they behaved with the thoughtlessness of youth, and that was understandable, if irritating.

Charles was definitely the worst one, though. He laughed loudly at a joke one of the others made, his obvious enjoyment of the party only underscoring how ill at ease Lorenzo felt by contrast. Charlie never came across as thoughtless or juvenile, like the others; in fact, he was remarkably self-possessed for someone his age. There was a sharpness to his gaze, a cocky broadness to his smile. He clearly thought he had the whole world figured out. When he ignored Lorenzo, it felt deliberate.

Still, he was determined to win Olivia's friends over—Charles included—so he waited for a pause in their conversation and then jumped in. "Thank you for inviting me into your home," he said. "It is lovely."

The humans stared at him, looking taken aback for some reason. "Uh," one of them said at length. "Thank you?"

"I would love to host a gathering such as this," Lorenzo said, and then trailed off as he realized what a fool he was being. He'd wanted to show off, but instead he'd bragged himself into a corner: he couldn't invite any of these people into his home, even though it was far more spacious and luxurious than this place, which was barely a step up from a dorm room. He smiled nervously as he tried to think of a way to end his sentence other than *but I cannot, because then you might notice that I am a vampire.*

As he stalled, Olivia's friends stared at him blankly. Except for Charlie, who cocked an arrogant eyebrow.

"But . . . my roommates," Lorenzo finished lamely. "They prefer . . . quiet."

"Got it," one of the humans said. An awkward silence fell.

Uncharacteristically, Charlie asked Lorenzo a follow-up question. "I didn't know you had roommates," he said.

There was something insulting in his tone, although Lorenzo couldn't pin down what it was. There was a weight to Charlie's focus that went beyond his simple good looks and teasing amber eyes—every time Charlie looked at him, he felt pinned in place. "Yes, I do," he said cautiously.

"Cool," Charlie said. "Hey, uh, what do you do again?"

"Um," Lorenzo said. He needed a better answer to this question. "You know . . . this and that. The, uh . . . gig economy."

The humans blinked at him, and Charlie frowned. One of the others said, "You're not a student?"

"No," Lorenzo said, to uncomfortable stares from the group. This was going downhill swifter than he had anticipated.

"You're older, right?" Charlie pressed.

Lorenzo grasped for an answer. "I . . . well . . . technically, I am twenty-four."

Charlie's eyes narrowed. "What does that mean? Like, you're about to turn twenty-five?"

Lorenzo paused. "Yes."

The humans stared at him again, and he cursed internally. He was trying to brainstorm the best way to restart the conversation when Charlie leaned casually toward one of the others and muttered, "Oh my god, *where* is Olivia."

A human probably wouldn't have been able to hear him over the music, so Lorenzo kept his smile firmly in place. But he could feel his fangs biting into his lower lip.

Thankfully, Olivia reappeared just then with their drinks. He thanked her when she handed him a beer, and she beamed in response, reaching up on her toes to give him a kiss on the cheek, leaving a smudge of her lip gloss behind. Lorenzo sighed happily, the kiss sending warmth all through him.

He could put up with Olivia's horrible friends, so long as she was by his side.

Present Day

Lorenzo paced by his front door, wearing a hole in the foyer carpet.

A hundred years ago, he probably would have been waiting here to kill Charlie. That would have been the only reason he'd invite Charles to his home—to eat him in a civilized fashion. But Lorenzo had lost his taste for killing long ago.

And he had no desire to taste Charlie.

Charlie was a jerk. He was catty and cruel, and he'd made Lorenzo feel like an idiot every time they'd crossed paths five years ago. He'd never wasted a chance to make him feel out of place and unworthy of Olivia. And in the end, he had destroyed their relationship by counseling her against him.

At least now Lorenzo would have his revenge. Yes, he'd told Charlie he would help him out with his thesis, that he would educate him about the world of the supernatural in exchange for Charlie's help running errands. But that was all a ruse. In reality, he had decided that he would use the situation to get close to Charlie and figure out how best to wreak havoc on him for poisoning his relationship with Olivia. Charlie would never see it coming.

Currently, Lorenzo also could not see it coming, because he hadn't yet figured out just how he would take his revenge. He was confident, however, that he would think of something devious and awful. Nothing violent, of course; vampires were out in the open now, so killing and nonconsensual biting were sort of faux pas. No, his plot against Charlie would be more in the vein of psychological vengeance. Perhaps he would come up with a way to ruin Charlie's thesis, or his entire degree. Yes, he would have to think carefully about just what form his vengeance would take; but whatever it was, it would be *vicious*.

He jumped a little when the doorbell rang. Hesitantly, he cracked open the door, finding Charlie's earnest, irritating face on the other side.

"Oh," he said flatly. "Hello."

"Hi," Charlie said, with a perky smile that faltered after a moment. "You said to come by at nightfall, and it's nightfall . . . I think. I wasn't sure when that was, exactly. But—the sun's not out, so . . . ?"

Lorenzo stifled a sigh and stood aside. "Yes. Come in."

Charlie crossed the threshold, and Lorenzo shut the door behind him. "So I guess that whole thing about vampires is true, then," Charlie said. "That they can't come out during daylight?"

"Have you ever seen a vampire in the daylight?" Lorenzo asked.

"I guess not," he said with a shrug. "You're the first vampire I've ever met. I think."

"How fun for me."

Charlie ignored the sarcasm in favor of craning his neck to look curiously around the house. Lorenzo suppressed a smug smile; his home was a far cry from the dilapidated collection of IKEA furniture where Charlie had hosted him and Olivia all those years ago. This house was only a few decades younger than Lorenzo, if local records were to be believed—large and airy, with wide steel windows facing the busy street below and a garden out back. The tenants on the first floor, a tchotchkes and antiques shop, made very little noise and always paid on time. He and his roommates had the second and third floors—well, the third was all his. He thought he'd done a good job over the decades renovating to keep up with current trends; he hated those vampires who just had to live in darkened castles, as if time and all style must remain fixed in the century in which they'd been turned. He'd redone the kitchen a few years ago, but he'd never gone so far as to strip away the bones of the building. Some of the crown molding in the living room had probably been there for centuries.

Still, as proud as he was of his home, he glanced uncertainly at Charlie to see how he would react. He was gratified to see him looking impressed.

Charlie himself looked almost identical to how Lorenzo remembered him from five years ago—he had recognized him in the coffee shop instantly. He had the same short, round figure, the same square glasses and intelligent eyes, the same boy-next-door features, and the same sharp smile. Looking at him now, though, Lorenzo could spot small differences; he hadn't had this red-brown scruff on his jaw while he was a student, and his clothes had been a little sharper then, more put-together. This Charlie looked a bit worn, like maybe life had not been kind to him since Lorenzo had seen him last. *Good.*

"Wow, this place is incredible," Charlie was saying. "Is it pre-war?" As he chattered, he started pulling a notebook out of his messenger bag.

"What are you doing?" Lorenzo demanded.

Charlie froze. "Uh—"

"We have a deal, you and I," Lorenzo reminded him. "I will only play along with your—thesis . . . thing—once you have fulfilled certain terms."

"Alright then," Charlie said wryly. "So . . . terms. I guess that means—errands? Things you can only do during the daylight?"

"Yes," Lorenzo said imperiously, and then came up short as it dawned on him that he had no idea what errands he could direct Charlie to complete for him. He hadn't put any thought into his supposed reason for agreeing to help Charlie, just the revenge that was his true motive.

"Um," Charlie said, after the silence had stretched. "Do you need anything at the bank? They're never open at night."

"I use online banking."

"Oh," Charlie blinked. He seemed surprised. "That's cool."

Did he think that vampires couldn't use computers? Many humans seemed to believe his kind to be idiot technophobes—or worse. Lorenzo narrowed his eyes at him.

"Uh," Charlie said uncomfortably. "The dry cleaners?"

"I do have a few items that need to be dry-cleaned," he conceded. "And my preferred shop has reduced their hours."

"Okay, great."

"And I need a plumber," Lorenzo added as it occurred to him.

"A plumber?" Charlie asked.

"Yes, there are some repairs I need made in the en suite," Lorenzo said. "I assume most plumbers will only come during the day. You will find me one and make the arrangements."

For a moment, Charlie didn't say anything.

"What?"

"I just—I didn't know vampires, uh. Used the bathroom," Charlie said.

"We don't," Lorenzo said. "I like hot baths."

Charlie's round cheeks tinged with pink. Lorenzo scowled at him. "Okay!" Charlie said, clapping his hands. "So, dry cleaning and a plumber. I'll get those done no problem. And in return . . ."

He pulled out his notebook once more, an ingratiating smile on his face. He probably thought those schoolboy good looks of his were charming. They probably *did* charm most people, though the thought turned Lorenzo's stomach.

"No," he said. "You will do my bidding *first*, and then—*if* your performance is satisfactory—I will deign to answer your questions."

He wouldn't, of course, but this errand-running charade would buy him time.

Charlie sighed. "Okay."

Another silence stretched between them. Finally Charlie said, "So, uh—did you have those clothes you wanted me to get cleaned?"

"I will get them," Lorenzo said severely. "You, stay here."

Of course Charlie immediately ignored his request and followed Lorenzo into the living room. He swore under his breath when he realized that they weren't alone—not one but two of his roommates were in the main room, which had been empty not five minutes ago. He'd checked, in no mood to explain Charlie's presence to others. They must have been lying in wait.

Maggie was the only one openly spying on them—lurking by the couch, chewing on a fingernail. She never seemed to take up much space, even with her seven-foot build and silver-blonde mop of frizzy hair, but her craggy face lit up when she saw them. "Hi!" she said, extending an enormous hand. "I'm Maggie."

"Charlie," he replied, beaming. It all happened so fast that Lorenzo barely had time to intervene. "Are you one of Lorenzo's roommates?"

"Yep!" she answered, bouncing back and forth on her feet in excitement. "Me and Rachel."

Charlie glanced toward the kitchen, where a sizzling sound and the smell of burning meat betrayed Rachel's presence, but all they saw was a hand waving lazily through the cutout. Lorenzo wasn't fooled; she'd planned this.

"How do you know Lorenzo?" Maggie was asking Charlie.

They stared at each other for a frozen moment before Lorenzo recovered. "He is my manservant."

There was a snort from the kitchen. "That's—no," Charlie said, with an embarrassed chuckle. "We're—friends."

Lorenzo glared at him, as this was the furthest thing from the truth. He ground out, "He is to run errands for me during the daylight."

"Hey, man," Maggie said, sounding wounded. "I'd run errands for you during the daylight."

"Yes, but this is not about your kind gesture," Lorenzo explained. "This is about humiliation."

"Oh, it's that kinda thing, huh?" Rachel asked, coming out of the kitchen with burgers on a plate and bottles snagged between her fingers. She looked more outwardly human than Maggie, with her curly red hair and curvy, compact figure, but there was an oil slick quality to her eyes that betrayed her true nature, if one looked closely enough.

Charlie coughed, turning pink again, and fiddled with his glasses. "Hi," he said, waving at Rachel. "Charlie."

"Hmm," she said, settling in to eat her burger and seemingly ignoring them.

"So," Charlie said, after a moment. "Those clothes you wanted me to clean?"

Lorenzo eyed Charlie and his roommates suspiciously, but could come up with no credible reason not to leave them alone. "I will return momentarily," he said, giving them all his best threatening glare, but Charlie just stared back at him blankly, Maggie beamed, and Rachel continued to feign indifference. He sighed.

He jogged up the stairs to his bedroom and slammed the door behind him. Having Charlie in his home was making him doubt the wisdom of having agreed to any of this. Yes, revenge was sweet, but why even go to the trouble of inviting Charlie back into his life at all?

He spotted a wool sweater in the corner of his room and lifted it consideringly. Olivia had liked his clothes—he tried to keep up with fashion just as he kept the house looking modern, but he was often worried about being out-of-date, simply because of how easy it was to become stuck in one's ways at his age. But Olivia had laughed—in a sweet way—at the oversized sweaters he liked to buy, especially the ones with big, silly patterns. (Most vampires, being cold-blooded, preferred dressing warmly.) She'd liked to toy with the drawstrings of his hoodies whenever they sat close together, kissing or talking, or play with his cuff links when they were out at restaurants. She'd been tactile in that way, with a sort of casual possessiveness that made him feel special.

He'd been saddened but not terribly shocked when she broke up with him. Their relationship had been sweet and affectionate, but she had been about to graduate from university, and he'd always known there was a chance that when she left Brookville she would leave him too.

He had not, however, been expecting Charlie to play such a prominent role in their breakup. Seeming unsure of how to explain her own feelings, Olivia had told him that Charlie agreed with her that it was best for them to end things. He had reassured her what a good idea it was to make a clean break. He'd explained that long-distance relationships never worked for anyone. From the way she spoke about him, he could tell that she trusted Charlie implicitly.

Even when she'd told him that she would always remember him, it sounded like Charlie's poisonous words on her breath.

He wondered what else Charlie had said about him to convince her to leave him behind.

He grabbed a few more items of clothing that needed cleaning and marched downstairs, shoving them into a drawstring bag.

He returned to the living room just as Rachel unhinged her jaw, faced the ceiling, and let out an unholy scream, the air around her bubbling and melting like polaroid film on fire. A moment later her head returned to its normal shape and size, and she toyed with the buttons of her flannel while Charlie caught his breath, staring at her wide-eyed.

"How's it going," Lorenzo asked, and Charlie jumped, gaping at him.

"That was rude," Maggie said to Rachel.

"What, um," Charlie managed, his voice sounding wheezy. "What was that?"

Rachel scoffed at him. "Now who's being rude?"

"It's her poltergeist," Maggie explained.

"Hey!" Rachel said, smacking Maggie lightly on the arm. "I told you, I'm not interested in being studied like a bug by some human scientist."

"I'm not a scientist, I'm just a grad student," Charlie said hesitantly. "And—you're a poltergeist?"

"No, I'm Haunted," Rachel corrected him.

"What does that mean?"

She took a precise step toward Charlie, her features darkening. "You really want to know?"

"Actually, y'know what," Charlie said, turning toward Lorenzo a bit desperately, "I need to get Lorenzo's clothes—"

"Oh, I have more," he said, smiling when Charlie's face fell. "I think there are a few more things in the laundry room. I will return."

"Okay," Charlie said. He cleared his throat, and as Lorenzo walked away, he heard Charlie saying, with an admirable attempt at breeziness, "So . . . you're haunted. Aren't we all?"

He'd heard Rachel's speech on the benefits of being Haunted dozens of times before, so he tuned them out as he reached the back of the apartment. He wasn't even sure he had any clothes in the laundry room; he'd only left to prolong Charlie's discomfort. His revenge scheme was off to an excellent start so far. He was enjoying seeing Charlie out of his element.

When they'd known each other before, Charlie had always seemed in his element; always confident and just a touch smarter than everyone else. He hadn't been popular, exactly, at least from what Lorenzo could glean of the university's social dynamics. But he'd been personable, witty, and almost—wise. The kind of person others listened to.

He'd known exactly how to turn Olivia against Lorenzo.

He dawdled one extra moment, hoping that Rachel would scare Charlie properly, and then returned to the living room.

He found Rachel, Maggie, and Charlie huddled together on the sofa, laughing uproariously. His stomach dropped.

"What did you *say*?" Maggie demanded, stifling giggles.

Charlie grinned. "That I don't own a giraffe."

Maggie and Rachel pealed off into laughter again. "What did I miss?" Lorenzo asked tersely.

"Oh, we're doing worst first date stories," Charlie said.

"I thought you were doing research," he said. "For your thesis."

"Well, yeah, but I'm also getting to know your roommates," Charlie said with a big, giddy smile. "Did you know that Maggie can grow her limbs back if they're cut off?"

"Yes," Lorenzo said testily. "She is *my* roommate, and this is a well-known troll power."

"Half-troll," Maggie said reflexively. "And I dunno, full trolls can grow back arms and legs and stuff. I've only ever tried it with fingers. I'm not very brave."

"I think you're amazing," Charlie said fondly. Lorenzo twitched with irritation—he'd met Maggie all of five minutes ago.

"And you," Charlie said, turning to Rachel. "I can't believe I didn't know you could be voluntarily possessed."

"Well, there's not a lot of information out there about it," Rachel said, taking a swig of her drink.

"How did you find out about it?" Charlie asked.

A cool wall fell across Rachel's features. "I don't talk about that."

She stood up from the couch and cleared her dinner things away, as Maggie turned to Charlie. "So, will you publish your thesis? Get the word out there about the supernatural?"

"Oh, no," he said with a quick glance at Lorenzo. "It's just a student thing."

"Okay," Maggie said. "Well, I'd still like to read it."

Charlie smiled at her. "That's really nice." Maggie beamed right back at him, her lower tusks peeking out delicately from her wide smile.

Abruptly, Lorenzo said, "I think it's time for Charlie to be going."

Now he had the gall to look disappointed. "But what about the rest of your clothes?" Charlie asked.

"This is it," Lorenzo said, shoving the drawstring bag at him.

"Okay," Charlie said, and began gathering up his things. "Uh, it was great to meet you all."

"Sure!" Maggie said. "Come over any time."

"No. Don't," Lorenzo said, beckoning Charlie toward the exit. "Only come here when you are invited."

Rachel laughed as she came back into the living room.

"Oh, you know what you should do?" Maggie prattled on, ignoring Lorenzo's warning look. "You should come back when Isolde is here."

Charlie turned around, his face lighting with curiosity. "Isolde?"

Rachel scowled at them. "Seriously, Lorenzo, are you going to trot us all out in front of your human?"

"He is not *my* human, he is *a* human," Lorenzo snapped. "And he is leaving."

"Who's Isolde?" Charlie asked, peeking around Lorenzo's shoulder as he attempted to gently muscle him toward the door.

"Our third roommate," Maggie said, grinning. "She says she's a—"

Before she could finish, a loud thunderclap seemed to split the room, and they all blinked back to find Rachel having thrown a hand up angrily, thick black smoke billowing all around her. "Don't even," she said threateningly, pointing at Maggie.

"I just—"

Rachel rounded on Lorenzo with an evil smile. "You know where you should take him? The wolf thing at Carter's Point tomorrow night."

Lorenzo fixed her with a murderous glare. Charlie said, "The what?"

Rachel was unmoved by Lorenzo's fury. "The werewolf party! Y'know, all the little pups get out and socialize. You should totally go, and talk to people for your thing." With a pointed grin directed straight at him, Rachel said, "Lorenzo's working as security there. He could take you."

At times like these, he was intensely irritated that poltergeists and their hosts were not the natural prey of vampires. Their blood tasted of corruption, which some vampires didn't mind but Lorenzo found to be soapy. Charlie looked giddy. "A werewolf party? Really?"

"No," Lorenzo said firmly.

"Why not?" Maggie asked.

"Charles, our transaction is concluded," Lorenzo said. "Thank you."

He shoved Charlie out the door and slammed it in his face before his roommates could cause any more trouble.

"Rude," Rachel said, walking away with a self-satisfied grin. Maggie, however, followed Lorenzo as he went into the kitchen for a large mug of blood to calm his nerves.

As he busied himself pouring, she said, "He seemed cool."

"He's not," Lorenzo bit out.

"Clearly," Maggie said, leaning against the counter. "How'd you meet this guy again?"

"We met a few years ago," Lorenzo said, staring down into his mug. "He was a friend of Olivia's."

"Oh, okay," Maggie said with faint recognition. "I liked Olivia."

Lorenzo said quietly, "Me too."

There was a faint ache in his chest, the hollow pang of loneliness. He knew it wasn't Olivia he longed for, though. He thought of her from time to time, as he thought of others he had loved and parted ways with. But he knew that she wasn't his soulmate.

It was only that no one was his soulmate. He was 239 years old, and he still didn't have a partner in his undeath. He was a vampire—a powerful and handsome vampire, thank you—but he didn't date that often. It wasn't as easy to meet people as it seemed in all the humans' stories. For one thing, he had no interest in high school students. Where was the vampire version of *When Harry Met Sally*? Why couldn't vampires meet their soulmates on Hinge?

Becoming a vampire had imbued him with many powers, but inherent charisma was not one of them. It wasn't particularly easy to make new friends in your third century; supernatural creatures were all distinct, and some quite prickly, both literally and figuratively. And the older he got, the faster he felt time slipping away from him; the harder it was to keep up with the latest cultural language, the pulse of human camaraderie. He knew himself to be handsome and brooding, but the handsome brooding types spent a lot of time alone, lurking behind things.

He retreated to his room, put the mug of blood on his mantel, and perused his records. He was in the mood to let music do his thinking for him.

He pulled a thin sleeve off the shelf and smiled at the warm wash of yellow. "At Last" was her most famous song, but he preferred Etta's "A Sunday Kind of Love." It was all about getting past the thrill of Saturday night passions and into something like the kind of love he wanted: Predictable. Comfortable. Warm.

He sighed, realizing he'd become the worst kind of cliché—a vampire dreaming of love in the sunlight. How pathetic.

He put Etta back on the shelf carefully. Olivia had smelled of sunlight, somehow—he'd nearly tasted it on her skin when he'd touched her. They may not have been soulmates, but she'd brought warmth to his life. She had been lovely and kind to him.

He would get his revenge on Charlie for ruining their happiness.

Chapter 3

With the hints Rachel dropped, it wasn't hard for Charlie to figure out when and where the werewolf party was likely taking place. His Uber took him out of town and down a poorly paved road with farms on one side and steep mountain cliffs on the other, then wound up and around a small peak a few times before dropping him off in a pebbled parking lot surrounded by forest. A few lanterns illuminated a footpath further up the slope, through the trees.

He was lucky Rachel had clued him in about this event existing at all. *Wise Old Crone* had gotten hundreds of letters about werewolves by this point, almost as many as he'd gotten about vampires, and last night had been a total bust on the latter front. He'd enjoyed getting to know Rachel and Maggie, but he still needed Lorenzo to answer at least *some* questions about vampirism if he was going to have any hope of writing a column people would actually read.

And Ava had been breathing down his neck about the column due tomorrow, which he'd yet to send her. After running into

Lorenzo at the coffee shop, he'd only told her that he *might have something*, a tidbit so tantalizingly vague she'd been blowing up his phone constantly looking for updates. He was ignoring her for now. He didn't want to do anything that might derail his progress, even something so small as express hope to another person.

Maybe he'd actually get enough out of this arrangement with Lorenzo to write something good. Or maybe these were the surreal final days of his dream job; the death rattle of a wizened crone who, it turned out, wasn't very wise at all.

Unhelpfully, his thoughts went to the last time he'd spoken to his father—when he'd opened up about the changes at *Midnight* and the threat to his career, committing the classic mistake of thinking that his dad might be encouraging or even just warm. It was hard enough to convince his rich, boomer father that in this century's economy, anyone could be screwed over at any time, especially when new owners came in——it didn't matter how "indispensable" you made yourself. Insufferable advice aside, Professor George Wever had never respected Charlie's career choice.

It's a blessing in disguise, he'd said. *Go get a PhD.*

I don't want a PhD, Dad, Charlie had replied, for at least the thousandth time. *I don't know anything.*

And yet you're an advice columnist. His dad loved his own sense of humor, regardless of its effect on others. Charlie remembered gripping the phone so hard his palm hurt.

You could go to medical school. People do that late in life, his dad had rambled on. *Hell, go to law school! That's a bit pedestrian, but it's a living.*

I'm making a living, Charlie had told him. *I'm a writer.*

And his dad had said, *You're not making a living at being a writer. That's why you called me.*

Charlie had muttered something about regretting that choice and hung up. And now, here he was, weeks or possibly days away from losing everything. He started climbing the forest footpath faster, trying to outpace his anxiety.

Right as he started to huff from the slope, the footpath emerged from the woods into a large clearing with a small barn on the far end and a dance floor in the middle. Trees decorated with twinkly lights hemmed in most of the clearing, but a small break in the woods opposite him provided a picturesque view of the town below. Off to his right was a table laden with party snacks and a couple of speakers in the process of being set up, and people were beginning to gather on either side of the dance floor, dressed in summer party clothes. He felt a surge of tentative triumph.

And then he got his confirmation that he was in the right place: Lorenzo was standing off to the left, scowling when he spotted him. "What are you doing here?" he hissed.

He walked over to Lorenzo, lifting the cellophane bag he'd been carrying. "I brought you your dry cleaning," he said, knowing he sounded a little smug.

Lorenzo crossed his arms, causing his leather jacket to stretch pleasingly across his biceps. His expression, however, was less encouraging. "I can't believe you came."

"Sure you can," Charlie said happily. "So, what is this? A mixer for all the werewolves in town?"

Before he could answer, a tall man with an air of leashed energy approached them. He was wearing a fantastic blazer embroidered with abstract shapes in dark charcoal thread, and carrying a clear acrylic clipboard with a pen threaded through the mechanism at the top. He had a stiff, polite smile on his face, and didn't seem much like a werewolf. Then again, Charlie had no idea what werewolves seemed like.

"Hi," the man said as he reached them, clicking his pen twice. "Are you with the caterers? Because we've got everything set up—"

"Oh, uh—no. Hi," Charlie said brightly, offering a hand. "I'm Charlie, I'm here with Lorenzo."

The man glanced at his hand and then asked Lorenzo, "Here . . . with . . . ?"

"He's a human who has been . . . following me," Lorenzo said darkly.

"We're working together on a project," Charlie said, turning his outstretched hand into a friendly wave. "Nice to meet you."

"I don't understand," the man said, clicking his pen again twice. "How can I help you?"

"Oh, well, I'm a graduate student," Charlie explained, offering the same cover story he'd told Lorenzo. "And I'm writing a thesis on relationships between humans and supernatural creatures, so I was wondering if I could maybe interview a few folks, or just mingle, or observe."

The man lifted an eyebrow. "You want to observe . . . teenagers?"

"Teenagers?" Charlie echoed. Then he stopped to take in the scene around him in a way he hadn't fully done before.

Most of the people milling around the dance floor did look somewhat . . . pubescent. There were a few ring lights on tripods set up at various points around the clearing, turning them into pre-made selfie spots. And the speakers were pumping out pop songs he didn't recognize.

He looked back at the werewolf, who was clearly in charge

of all this, with a newfound sense of embarrassment and mild horror.

"I—I'm so sorry," Charlie rambled. "I had no idea this was an event for—I won't talk to any of the teenagers, believe me. I just—maybe there are some chaperones I could speak to, or—or maybe you—"

"*I* am busy," the man said, clicking his pen twice more.

Charlie was fairly certain he was about to be booted from the event—or possibly mauled—when Lorenzo jumped in. "I'll keep an eye on him, Gray," he told the man wearily. "I will make sure he does nothing to disturb the event."

The man—Gray—eyed Lorenzo in an *I don't have time for this* sort of way, and then said, "Great," and walked away. As he did, Charlie could see that the shapes on his blazer actually formed an image of a large wolf howling at the moon. He didn't know whether to laugh or shiver.

He did turn to confront Lorenzo, thoroughly appalled. "You could have warned me this was a—a thing for teens!"

"I told you not to come," Lorenzo pointed out.

"That's . . . fair," Charlie sighed. "So, what is this—werewolf prom?"

The werewolves—teens, he now saw quite clearly—were chatting excitedly in small clumps around the dance floor, though no one seemed to have worked up the courage to start dancing yet. A few were taking videos of each other jumping and posing excitedly—for some TikTok trend, maybe? He hadn't felt this old in a while.

"It's not healthy for the packs to only mate among themselves," Lorenzo explained. "So they throw this event every year for the young wolves to meet each other. This way the pack leaders can approve any new alliances. And they hire vampires

THIRSTY   41

as security because we're not allied with any of the packs and are therefore neutral."

Charlie glanced around. "Are there any other vampires here?"

Lorenzo scoffed. "You don't need more than one vampire to control some rowdy wolf pups."

Charlie bit back a grin. Maybe this night wouldn't be a total bust after all. He began rummaging in his bag for his journal and pen.

As Lorenzo spotted him, he said, "You can't be serious. Don't talk to the young wolves, it's creepy."

"I don't want to talk to them, I want to talk to you," Charlie said. "Say more about vampire security, it's fascinating."

"No, it's not," Lorenzo said flatly.

"I brought you your dry cleaning," Charlie pointed out. "So really, you *have* to talk to me. That was our deal."

"What about the plumber?"

"I'll get a plumber."

"And I will answer your questions once you do," Lorenzo said, turning away and clasping his hands behind his back.

"Oh, come on," Charlie said. "Talk to me."

"No."

"Why not?"

Lorenzo thinned his lips and didn't answer.

Charlie sighed and looked back at the dance floor. It looked like the formalities of the event were getting underway; the few adults in attendance, including Lorenzo's friend, seemed to be introducing some of the teens to each other and leading them into a coordinated dance that reminded him of a cotillion. The teens looked notably less excited about this part.

And it was clear that none of these people would agree to an interview with him. The adults were preoccupied, and it *would* be creepy to talk to the kids. The fact was, he was an outsider here. The only person he had any sort of connection to was Lorenzo.

Clearly, then, he'd have to charm him a little if he was going to make anything out of this night.

"Look, can I at least put your dry cleaning somewhere?" he asked Lorenzo, lifting the bag. "I Ubered here, and these look delicate. Are they . . . vintage? Like, from your time?"

Lorenzo gave him a stony look. "They are from ASOS."

"Oh," Charlie said. "Well. Still—I don't want them to . . . wrinkle. So . . . ?"

Lorenzo sighed shortly. "Fine. Come with me."

He followed Lorenzo through the trees back toward the parking lot. Lorenzo walked swiftly, staring at the ground, his shoulders tense. Charlie hurried up next to him and said, "So—*do* you have any clothes from back then? Any, like, waistcoats, or cravats, or whatever?"

"No, I don't have any cravats," Lorenzo said in a long-suffering tone.

"So you're the kind of vampire who likes to stay trendy, huh," he said. "That's cool."

"How long do you think clothes like that last outside a museum?" Lorenzo asked dryly. "How many of your socks have holes?"

"Fair," Charlie said. "But do you miss those kinds of clothes? How long ago did you say you were turned, again—the 1800s?"

Lorenzo stopped walking, bringing Charlie to a sudden halt beside him, and a long silence followed as Lorenzo eyed him in the dim light between the trees. He swallowed uncomfortably, wondering belatedly if it was considered rude to ask a vampire about their age. He was keenly aware that, if he had crossed some kind of line, Lorenzo could very much rip his throat out with his teeth. And not in a horny, stupid *I want him to run me over with his car* sort of way, but like . . . literally.

Finally Lorenzo started walking again, apparently having decided to either murder Charlie elsewhere or simply blow off his questions. Either way, he kicked himself; the whole point of this had been to charm Lorenzo into talking to him.

Before he could strike up another conversation, however, Lorenzo said quietly, "1809."

"Oh—wow," Charlie said, more surprised by Lorenzo talking than by what he'd said. "That's amazing. What was it like back then?"

Lorenzo glanced at him darkly. "What was what like?"

"Uh," Charlie said unimpressively. "Everything?"

Lorenzo glared at him.

"Okay," Charlie conceded. "Well—hey, where were you born?"

"Why do you care?" Lorenzo asked with a surprising amount of acid.

"I'm—just making conversation," Charlie said.

"I thought you wanted to learn about vampires," Lorenzo said. "Why should it matter for your thesis where my human life took place?"

"Maybe I'm just interested."

"Please." Lorenzo scoffed. "You had no interest in me when we met years ago, and your only agenda now is to further your own . . ." He squinted, and finished, uncertainly: ". . . agenda."

"Look, I—hey, wait," Charlie said, grabbing Lorenzo by the arm to make him stop. "Listen, I really am sorry about the whole Olivia thing. I shouldn't have said—whatever it was. I honestly don't even remember what I told her."

He did kind of remember what he'd told her, but that wasn't going to help his cause here. "But clearly, it really hurt you," he continued. "So—I'm sorry. I was wrong."

Lorenzo looked away, his jaw tense, but he didn't argue.

"So . . . will you tell me where you're from?" Charlie said, taking a hesitant step toward the parking lot. "I'm actually interested."

Lorenzo fell into step beside him. After a moment of grudging silence, he said, "Sardinia."

"Sardinia," Charlie said, thinking quickly. "In . . . Greece?"

"Italy!" Lorenzo hissed, then added in a grumble, "More or less."

"Right. That's—okay, Sardinia!" Charlie said. "That's cool. What was that like?"

"It was . . ." Lorenzo started, and Charlie expected him to say something like *fine*, or *normal*, something clipped and conversation-ending, as he seemed wont to do.

So it caught him a little off guard when Lorenzo's eyes softened, and his voice gentled, and he said, "It was beautiful."

Oh, Charlie said, a surprised little exhale. Lorenzo didn't seem to hear. "But no one really had anything," he continued. "Most people there were shepherds, and there were always new conquerors coming in, taking what little we had." He paused. "The sea was lovely, though."

Charlie's head felt a little swimmy, perhaps because he was grappling for the first time with the fact that he was speaking with someone who had lived centuries ago, and could speak simply about what that time had been like. "Wow. So, you were a . . . a shepherd?"

"No," he said. "My family had livestock, but I wasn't interested in that."

"What did you do instead?"

"I set out to enrich our fortunes," Lorenzo said.

"How?"

"By, uh . . ." Lorenzo's voice had gone sheepish. "By taking them from others."

"You were a thief?" Charlie asked, surprised. He couldn't really see Lorenzo as a pickpocket or a cat burglar—he was too tall and broad-shouldered, and he didn't seem particularly stealthy.

"I commanded a small crew," Lorenzo said. "We would sail to nearby villages and strike fast, taking whatever we could get away with. I was much admired among my men," he said proudly. "And Italy was in chaos back then, so there was lots of money to be made."

Charlie blinked, processing this. "So—you were a pirate."

Lorenzo scowled. "No."

"Right," Charlie said, nodding, and then asked, "How were you not a pirate?"

"It wasn't like all that," Lorenzo said, waving. "I was a . . . a businessman. In the . . . business of raiding and pillaging."

Charlie was speechless. *This* he could see—Lorenzo on the prow of a ship, cutlass in hand, a sea breeze in his black hair, wearing that billowy shirt–tight pants combo from *The Witcher*. It was . . . compelling.

He jerked a little when Lorenzo said, sounding irritated, "What?"

"That's so cool!"

Lorenzo rolled his eyes. Finally, they reached the parking lot, and Lorenzo led him over to a small, dark blue compact car. "Place my things in here."

Charlie carefully hung the bag from the hook in the back

seat. It was an aggressively normal car, not piratical in the slightest. Still, that didn't dampen his excitement at all. "You don't think it's cool that you were a pirate?" Charlie asked, as soon as the door was closed.

Lorenzo turned on his heel, heading back toward the party, and Charlie followed him.

"I wasn't a pirate," Lorenzo said. "It was just my life. Just a way to get by."

"Just a way to get by," Charlie echoed scornfully. "With eyeliner. And doubloons. And queer longing."

Lorenzo shot him a quick look. Charlie ignored the flash of heat it set off in his chest. "It wasn't like how they make it out to be now," he said gruffly. "It wasn't as stylish, or fantastical. Or nearly that clean. And my crew had honor." He was glowering at Charlie now, looking almost offended. "We weren't knaves or cheats."

"Okay!" Charlie said. "Well, that . . . sounds cool."

"It wasn't," Lorenzo said shortly. "It was just . . . how things were back then. Boring and brutal."

Charlie narrowed his eyes. This was familiar—Lorenzo was closing off again. "I guess you're right," he said, his voice deliberately casual. "I bet every vampire has some kind of life story just like that—pirates, kings, warlords. All very normal."

Lorenzo glared at him, but didn't take the bait. Charlie said, "Okay, so—how did you become a vampire?"

"You said only questions about my human life," Lorenzo reminded him.

"You were a human when you became a vampire," Charlie said. "Up until the moment of . . . hey, how are vampires made, anyway?"

Lorenzo smiled coldly, but said nothing.

"You know, I'm gonna get you that plumber," Charlie said. "It's not, like, a difficult thing. You might as well talk to me."

"No," Lorenzo said, and with that, they had arrived back at the party.

Things seemed to have deteriorated quickly from the formal, coordinated event that had been unfolding as they'd left; the kids were now completely intermingled into one clump on the dance floor, dancing riotously to loud, bass-heavy house music. The adults on the sidelines looked on haplessly, their elegant affair now thoroughly drowned in hormones. Charlie stifled a laugh.

Lorenzo resumed his position off to the side, arms crossed, every inch the watchful, patient chaperone. Charlie stood next to him and realized, with a bit of surprise, that he was enjoying himself: being outside in the soft moonlight, listening to music, watching silly teenage antics. He felt lighter than he had in weeks. He felt as if he might actually get some writing done tonight, and that it might not be horrible.

Lorenzo said, "Why are you even doing this project?"

Charlie startled. "Hm? Oh, my thesis?" He flailed for a second, not really having put any thought into his cover story, and he felt a flash of guilt at the thought of adding more to the lie. But then he realized that he could simply repurpose the rote answer he always gave when asked why he'd become an advice columnist. "I like listening to people, and hearing about their lives. The stuff that I—uh, the things that my thesis is about—love, family, relationships—they're things that everyone struggles with at some point," he said. "So I figured, maybe by researching those things, I could help people."

He smiled at Lorenzo, but Lorenzo only looked skeptically back at him. Charlie shifted uneasily.

"Why supernatural creatures?" Lorenzo asked.

Charlie blinked. "What?"

"Why are you researching *our* lives and relationships?"

"Oh. Well, uh . . ." This was tricky; he couldn't very well say that supes were trendy, his column needed clicks, and he may have already been mistaken, by a decent portion of the internet, for an ancient witch. "My—my thesis advisor, she seemed to think—uh, that it would help my chances in the job market. It's an emerging area, supernatural studies."

"Mm-hmm," Lorenzo said.

"But mostly, it's about helping people," Charlie said. "Like werewolves, and vampires, and trolls, and the voluntarily haunted." Lorenzo rolled his eyes. "So, really, you should work with me."

Lorenzo seemed a bit mollified, though he was still skeptical. "You think you will help people by writing some dusty tome?"

"Well, you never know," Charlie said. "Someone'll probably read it, at some point."

"Probably not."

"You're right," he sighed. "It's not as cool as being a pirate."

Lorenzo visibly fought back a smile. Charlie beamed at him.

A bubble of laughter and shouts sounded from the dance floor before one of the teens shoved his way out of the group, followed swiftly by some of the adults. He looked like he might be crying—and wow, Charlie did *not* miss high school—but he was also walking strangely, with his hands over his arms and his shoulders hunched, like he was trying to hide his body. One of the grown werewolves was patting his shoulder sympathetically. "What's that about?" Charlie asked.

"Ah," Lorenzo said. "That happens on occasion. One of the

pups gets too excited, and he . . ." He paused, waving his hands in a way that conveyed nothing to Charlie. After seeing his confusion, he added, "Transforms. A little."

Charlie blinked, glancing back to where the teen was being whisked away. "They can do that when it's not a full moon?"

"Well . . . teenagers, you know," Lorenzo said indulgently. "They don't have much control over their bodies, human or wolf."

Charlie sputtered out a laugh. "Poor kid."

Lorenzo smiled back at him. Meanwhile, a club mix of "Howl" by Florence + the Machine came on the sound system, and the baby wolves shrieked their approval. Charlie felt the sweet enthusiasm of the party warming him from the inside out. He was so glad he'd come.

Then a thought occurred to him. "Are there vampire mixers like this?" he asked Lorenzo. "To, you know . . . make alliances?" He wiggled his eyebrows suggestively.

But Lorenzo's face went cold and still. "No," he said, and he didn't elaborate.

From: grose@jmail.com
To: wiseoldcrone@midnight.com
Date: Feb 4, 10:53 AM
Subject: My In-Laws Are Neglecting Our Baby

Dear Crone,

My husband and I are proud parents to the sweetest,
most adorable fur baby—he's half doodle, half pug, and
all heart. There were some tough moments early on with
sleep training and behavior issues, but he's thriving now.
Part of that is the loving relationship he has with our
entire extended family, including my in-laws. They love
seeing photos and videos of him, and they were always
happy to play with him when they came to visit.

That all changed a few months ago, when my husband's
sister got a familiar to help with her witchcraft. Ever since
then our beautiful pup may as well be dead to my in-laws.
They talk our ears off about how my SIL's familiar can
enter the void and levitate toy mice, and how cute it is
when she cleans her whiskers, without ever seeming to
notice that they never ask about our sweet boy anymore.
They haven't even asked to see a picture of him in over a
week!

I'm sick of the favoritism. How do I explain to my in-laws that they can't love one grandchild more than another?

Sincerely,
Furious Fur Mama

From: 44cyan@whomail.com
To: wiseoldcrone@midnight.com
Date: April 23, 1:06 AM
Subject: Didn't Age Well

Dear Crone,

I've been in a relationship with a wonderful woman for the last few months, but I recently learned something about her personal history that horrifies me. We're both physically in our twenties, but she is a vampire who was turned in the early '80s, and recently, when we got to talking about old times, she revealed that she voted for Reagan.

Crone, I'm appalled. We're queer women, and I'm stunned—no, sickened—that she could have voted for Reagan when his policies devastated the queer community (not to mention THE RACISM). I'd been so happy in this relationship up until now, but this feels like a major red flag. Am I asking for too much from a partner? Or am I just going to have to accept the fact that, if I stay in this relationship, I'm effectively dating a baby boomer?

Sincerely,

My GF is Problematic

Wise Old Crone

How Do I Impress a Banshee?

I don't want to blow this for my son.

May 19

Dear Wise Old Crone,

My only son is bringing a girl home next month. We're all very excited because he's quite shy and hasn't dated a lot; but he's been so happy ever since he started this relationship, and we're thrilled for him. Because of all that, their visit feels very high-stakes—we really want his new girlfriend to feel welcome in our home!

But I'm terribly nervous because his girlfriend is a banshee, and I don't know what that means for our hosting her. Do we need to prepare in any particular way? What should I expect? I'm so nervous that I'm going to say the wrong thing or do the wrong thing while she's here, and somehow make her feel un-welcome. The last thing I want is to mess up my son's relation-ship, or, even worse, cause a rift between us! What can I do to prepare and set my mind at ease?

Sincerely,

Harried Hostess

Dear Hostess,

First, breathe—plenty of relationships have weathered awkward first meetings between partner and parents. Even if everything does go comically wrong during this visit, I'm sure your relationship with your son will survive. Bad first impressions are just that—the beginning of something, not the end.

That being said, the Crone understands why you're feeling so nervous. Many supernatural communities are quite insular, and it can be difficult from the outside to determine what's fact and what's rumor, especially when those rumors have been parlayed through thousands of years of Celtic folklore. Why not cut through all that by asking your son if there's anything you can do to prepare for their stay? It doesn't have to be about his girlfriend's mystical roots—you could just check in and see if there are any snacks he'd like you to have on hand, and let him volunteer if any more specific preparations are needed.

Then, during their visit, just try to remember that you're getting to know your son's girlfriend, not a creature of legend. You don't need to be prepared with a list of questions about her connection to the underworld of spirits (indeed, that could make her feel awkward or nervous). Instead, ask her to tell you how she and your son met, and about what interests they share. Remember that supernatural creatures are, well, people—maybe not humans, but people nonetheless, with foibles and quirks and shows they're binging, just like all of us.

The point of this visit is to learn more about the woman who means so much to your son. If you focus on that, this old hag believes you'll avoid any portents of doom.

Sincerely,
Crone

Chapter 4

Lorenzo stumbled downstairs on Sunday night to find Maggie and Rachel on the couch, settled in for their weekly appointment with whatever prestige program had caught their interest of late. The sun had just set and he was still a little groggy, so it took him a few seconds to notice that they weren't alone: Charlie was sitting in the wingback armchair next to the couch.

"Charlie?" he said stupidly, blinking the last remnants of sleep out of his eyes. Charlie turned to glance at him, a grin lighting up his face. Those round, chubby cheeks of his should have made him look cherubic or innocent, but the effect was spoiled by his sharp eyes, slight stubble, and the wicked edge to his smile.

Lorenzo suddenly wished he'd pulled on something nicer than his coffin clothes. "What are you doing here?"

Charlie nodded at his roommates. "Maggie and Rachel invited me over to watch *Shōgun*."

"But . . . why?" Lorenzo asked.

"He's cool," Maggie said, as if this were obvious and not a sign of staggeringly poor taste on her part. "And he wanted to talk more for his thesis thing."

Lorenzo scowled at her. "You shouldn't indulge him."

"Shut up," Rachel said. "It's starting."

Lorenzo grumbled at the lot of them and wandered into the kitchen. In the fridge he found only pig's blood—he needed to do some shopping—but it was all he had, so he took a swig out of the paper cup and grimaced at the stale taste.

When he put it back in the fridge and closed the door, Charlie was standing there. Because Lorenzo was a stealthy creature of the night, he only jumped a little. "Jesus."

"Guess what," Charlie said with a blinding smile.

"No thank you," Lorenzo muttered.

"I got you a plumber!" Charlie said, handing Lorenzo a post-it note with some details scribbled on it. "His Yelp reviews are excellent, and he was very nice on the phone. He'll be here Tuesday night, ten p.m."

"Why did you not check with me before scheduling him?" Lorenzo groused, staring down at the note. "I could be busy Tuesday night."

"Are you?"

He hesitated, then said, "No," and slid the note into his pocket.

"Great," Charlie said, beaming at him like the cat that'd caught the canary. "So. You know what this means . . ."

Lorenzo avoided his teasing smile. "Aren't you here to watch your," he said, waving vaguely, "samurai program?"

"That's one reason," Charlie said, pinning him with a pleased, expectant stare. It was strange being the focus of Charlie's attention, when five years ago he'd barely shown Lorenzo more than dismissive scorn. This Charlie, the one who seemed brimming with enthusiasm to track down and entrap Lorenzo at every turn, was unsettling. The force of his interest made Lorenzo feel like he might fidget out of his skin.

He needed to spend more time brainstorming a plot to wreak his revenge on Charlie, since that was the only reason he'd agreed to help him in the first place. It had seemed like such an obvious idea when he'd first encountered Charlie in that coffee shop, and at the time he'd been sure that the details of the revenge plan would simply come to him with time. After all, he had plenty of long nights to brood on the cruelties of life and all of the discontent that Charlie had brought him; surely something would come of it.

But with each passing day, Charlie seemed to be getting more and more out of their arrangement, while Lorenzo's true agenda was sputtering on air. He needed to seriously rededicate himself to the task. He'd simply have to harness the darkness within.

In the meantime, though, he knew he'd been backed into a corner. Lorenzo sighed. "Fine. I am a creature of my word—I will fulfill my end of the bargain." Before Charlie's smug expression could manifest itself in words, he added: "I will answer one question."

Charlie's jaw dropped satisfyingly. "What? *One* question?"

Lorenzo opened the fridge, took the pig's blood out again, and set it on the counter along with a bowl from the cupboard. "I never said how many questions you would get in exchange for each errand."

By now Charlie had recovered, suppressing a smile as if he were amused by Lorenzo's attempts to stymie him. "Well, I did do more than one errand," he said, leaning against the countertop. "And, technically, if you count each item of dry cleaning separately—"

"Which I won't."

"I think I should get . . . ten questions," Charlie said.

Lorenzo grabbed a block of cream cheese from the fridge and stared Charlie down. After a suitably dramatic pause, he offered: "Three."

"Eight."

Lorenzo unwrapped the cream cheese block, dumped it into the bowl, and poured the blood over it. "Maybe we should forget the whole thing."

"Oh, come on," Charlie said amiably. "You wouldn't do that to me after I ran all over town for you. Not if you're a *creature of your word*." Lorenzo couldn't tell if he was flattered or insulted by the way Charlie had deepened his voice to mimic his.

"You did two things."

Charlie bit his lips. "I'll get Rachel and Maggie in here. They'll beat you up."

"I'm not scared of them," Lorenzo said.

Charlie smiled at him; a small, fond smile, as if he was enjoying their banter no matter where it led. Lorenzo was suddenly seized with the urge to get the entire thing over with as quickly as possible.

"Five questions," he said, stirring his dinner.

"Seven."

Lorenzo rolled his eyes. "Fine."

"Great," Charlie said. He got out a notepad and pen while Lorenzo put his bowl in the microwave and grabbed a bag of tortilla chips from the pantry.

"You really want to do this right now?" Lorenzo asked, grasping for one last excuse. "You won't miss your show?"

"I'll watch it later," Charlie said, clicking his pen with an air of deep satisfaction. He glanced at the microwave as it whirred and said, "So—I guess I don't need to ask, but . . . you can eat human food?"

"Yes."

"That's interesting," he said, scribbling as he wrote. "I thought maybe anything other than blood would be toxic to vampires or something."

Lorenzo shrugged. "It makes my stomach hurt. But sometimes, you know, it's worth it."

Charlie grinned. "I get that." As Lorenzo took the bowl out of the microwave, he added, "Is that . . . human blood?"

"Pig."

"Hmm," Charlie said. He eyed Lorenzo, a hum of excitement beneath his contemplative stare. "But you do . . . also . . ."

He hesitated. Lorenzo waited him out. After a moment, Charlie looked back up at Lorenzo and asked, "You drink people blood?"

Lorenzo's throat prickled uncomfortably. "Not for a while."

"Why not?"

"This way is easier," he said. "You can buy it in a shop, and there's no risk of hurting anyone."

Holding Lorenzo's eye, Charlie asked, "Which one tastes better?"

Lorenzo swallowed a bite of extremely bland pig's blood, and did not look at the fluttering of Charlie's jugular. "I should think," he said, "that would be obvious."

"Hmm," Charlie said. He didn't write anything down, and when Lorenzo looked back after busying himself with his food for a moment, Charlie was still studying him.

"Two questions left," Lorenzo prodded him.

Charlie blinked. "Wait, what? A bunch of those were follow-ups, that doesn't count." He glanced down at his notebook and flipped through the pages, muttering, "We're still on the general topic of food, I have so many more . . ."

Lorenzo shrugged unrepentantly.

"Okay, give me—three more questions," Charlie said.

He sighed. "Fine."

"Thank you," Charlie said, and then paused as he tried to narrow down his ideas. "Um . . . okay, well . . . Okay. When it comes to dating, do you mostly date vampires or humans? Or—werewolves or leprechauns or, y'know"—he gestured, like *yadda yadda yadda*—"whoever."

"Mostly humans. But, most people are human, so."

"So it doesn't matter to you?" Charlie said. "You don't have a supernatural type?"

"What does that mean?"

"I don't know," Charlie said. "You're not looking to date only humans or only vampires? And—these are follow-ups, to be clear, *not* new questions."

"No."

"No, they're not follow-ups?"

"No," Lorenzo said, "it doesn't matter to me what species someone is."

"Really," Charlie said.

"It is as David Rose has said," Lorenzo said. "I enjoy the wine, not the bottle."

Charlie's lips quirked in a small, surprised smile. "You watched *Schitt's Creek*."

"We're not all stuck in the past, you know," Lorenzo said with just a touch of irritation. "I have a television *and* a computer."

Charlie dropped his notebook on the counter as he leaned closer to Lorenzo, looking lost in thought. "Is it so weird having those things—watching streaming video and prestige TV with your roommates—when you grew up with like . . . like

you were saying, shepherds and conquerors and being a literal
pirate?"

"I wasn't a pirate," Lorenzo muttered.

"I mean, sometimes I think about the fact that I used to
watch DVDs when I was a kid and I'm like, whoa, I'm *old*,"
Charlie continued. "But you—I mean, the world must have
changed so much in your lifetime. Is that . . . what is that like?"
He laughed a little. "Can you even explain it to a dumb human
like me?"

"It is . . . odd sometimes," Lorenzo said. "But also . . ."

Charlie leaned toward him, his eyes wide. "What?"

"These new things—TV, streaming, the internet—yes,
they're strange at times. But they're also just machines." He
shook his head. "You humans make so much out of change and
progress and evolution, but really, things are just as they've always been. The world is . . ." He sighed. "You ask me about—
about food, and love, and sex. The same things people always
think about. The things they crave."

A slow grin spread across Charlie's face. "I didn't ask you
about sex," he said. "Yet."

Lorenzo's heart didn't beat anymore, so there was no way it
could thump all the way up in his throat. "But since you mentioned it," Charlie continued.

"Yes?" he asked warily.

Whatever Charlie had been ramping up to, it made him
hesitate. Lorenzo desperately wished he could read Charlie's
question from his face, but he couldn't. Finally, he asked, "Is it
dangerous for a human to have sex with a vampire?"

There was nothing alive in Lorenzo's chest anymore, but
something in there fluttered. "Not really."

"Not really?"

"I chipped a tooth once when a woman headbutted me."

"You know what I mean," Charlie said impatiently.

"No, it's not dangerous," Lorenzo said. His blood didn't pump anymore, so there was no way it could thrum so close to his skin, making him feel flushed and unsteady as he looked down into Charlie's eager eyes. "No more than sex between humans can be dangerous. At least, from what I remember of sex between humans."

"But what about . . ." Charlie pressed.

"What?" Lorenzo asked.

"Do you . . ." he trailed off, and then asked, "Do you feed from humans during sex?"

Lorenzo's mouth went dry. Charlie kept going, his voice low. "I mean, that's part of it, right? . . . Biting?"

Lorenzo pushed away from the counter. "You're out of questions."

Charlie gasped. "Oh, come on."

"No," Lorenzo said, walking away. "We had a deal at seven, and I was more than generous. Good day."

"Wait," Charlie said, following him out into the living room. "Give me more errands to do."

Rachel squawked as they both strode past the TV. "Hey! Lorenzo, get your human out of the way."

"No," Lorenzo said to both of them.

"Please," Charlie said. "This was so helpful, but I need more!"

Lorenzo ignored his entreaties. He needed more time to think, to regroup—he couldn't just send Charlie off on some new lark, knowing that he would return in a day or two with more questions, more jokes, and more curiosity about Lorenzo. He needed a plan.

"Lorenzo," Charlie was calling after him. "Come on, I'll do more of your dry cleaning, or—you can tell me if the plumber doesn't work out, or—"

Lorenzo turned around at the base of the stairs, gripping the rail. "Our business is done," he said firmly.

"But I need more," Charlie said, looking crestfallen.

"You're not gonna help him anymore?" Maggie asked.

Rachel *shh*ed them all. "I can't hear Yabushige-sama!"

"This was a silly idea in the first place," Lorenzo said, trying to buy himself time. "But I have held up my end of the bargain. Now we're done."

"Oh, come on," Charlie said. "There's gotta be more I can do for you. Never being able to go out during the daylight—I mean—that must make things difficult—"

Maggie perked up. "Ooh, what about your driver's license?"

Lorenzo turned his head slowly to glare at her. Rachel stood up, shut off the TV, and stormed away to her room in a huff.

After her door slammed, Charlie asked Maggie, "What was that about his driver's license?"

"The DMV's only open during daylight hours," Maggie explained. "Which I personally think is discriminatory against vampires and other nocturnal-only creatures, but—tell that to Congress."

"And you need a license?" Charlie asked Lorenzo.

"I *have* a driver's license," he said.

"Yeah, but he hasn't gotten it renewed since like the 1970s," Maggie said. To Charlie, she added, "His picture is amazing."

"I'll help you renew your license!" Charlie said eagerly.

"You can't," Lorenzo snapped. "They have rules. You cannot apply for another person, I must go myself. In person. And I cannot."

"I'll find a way," Charlie said.

"No, you won't."

Charlie took a step toward him and tossed his chin back. "If I do—if I can figure out how to get you a new driver's license somehow—then you answer *all* of my questions," he said. "No limits, no weaseling out."

"Weaseling?" Lorenzo demanded, his tone making clear what he thought of Charlie's twenty-first century vocabulary.

"You have to be my full guide to the supernatural," Charlie pressed. "Get me everything I need. For my thesis."

Lorenzo narrowed his eyes at him. He'd needed a stalling tactic, and this would work nicely. Arranging a plumber was one thing, but circumventing byzantine government regulations would take Charlie weeks, if he could manage it at all. "You will never succeed," he said.

"Do we have a deal?" Charlie asked, holding a hand out. "I want your *word*."

His neck wasn't the only place that Lorenzo could see Charlie's pulse; it beat in his wrist too, the skin there so thin and delicate that his veins seemed to be blooming outward, ripe and ready. He stared at Charlie's palm, caught between too many competing desires.

"How about this," he said, when Lorenzo continued to simply stare at him. "If I fail, I'll leave you alone forever."

"Deal," Lorenzo said.

He shook Charlie's hand briefly. Humans' skin always felt searing hot to him, their blood roaring so swiftly just beneath. Lorenzo reminded himself of this when the phantom warmth of Charlie's palm lingered on his fingertips even after he'd turned his back.

Chapter 5

The bartender hadn't said a word to Charlie since he'd sat down. He was drumming his fingers on the wood, and when the bartender glared at him, he realized that his knee was bouncing so hard it was making the whole bar top rattle. He forced himself to stop and smiled apologetically. The bartender was already doing something else.

He hadn't been this nervous since he'd published his very first column. He'd come back from the werewolf prom almost in a trance and filled page after page, staying up until the literal dawn. Writing hadn't felt that good in years—it felt *easy*, as he reflected on everything he'd learned, everything he'd seen and felt, and everything he'd talked about with Lorenzo.

And after that one perfect evening, he'd started to worry that it had all been *too* easy. It was some kind of trick; maybe he hadn't really ever recovered from the writing slump he'd been in, and he just couldn't see that the new stuff was as dull as the old. But when he sent Ava his first full column, she seemed to like it, and then—it actually did decent numbers. It wasn't breaking the internet or anything, but the click gods seemed happy. He had to use the word "engagement" unironically now.

So naturally, he was vibrating out of his skin. First the writing was painless, and now the column was doing well? Something had to be lurking around the corner. It couldn't just be this easy.

No, he was choosing to assess the situation with cold hard dread, and that was why he had to keep going—keep learning more about the supernatural, keep writing more columns leaning into the Crone persona, and get his career up off the mat. He needed this to work so he could get out of Brookville and back to his real life.

He clicked his nails against the soft wood of the bar. He'd lived in this town most of his life, but he'd never been to this particular bar. It was nice inside, dark and cozy, but the exterior was one of those squat, windowless buildings that'd always given him the creeps. He never would've checked this place out if Maggie hadn't texted him the address.

He felt off-kilter living back here in Brookville. He hadn't visited at all since he'd moved to New York, and now that he was back, he'd mostly kept to the same places he knew from college; those were decent memories, at least. Going to the DMV today had been weird. He'd been there just once before, as a teenager, to get his own license—waiting for hours and filling out paperwork just to show his dad that he could do something on his own.

His father had always been vaguely unimpressed by Charlie. That hadn't really mattered much while his mom was still around. Dad may have hovered above the two of them as if having a family were a little beneath him; but Mom was funny and warm and wonderful, and she softened his dad just enough to keep the whole family together.

And then when she was gone, there wasn't anything left between Charlie and his dad to even rebuild. Professor Wever still had his scholarship and the respect of his peers, and Charlie did get out of Brookville, eventually.

For a while.

On paper, the DMV's rules about how to renew your license were indeed very strict, just as Lorenzo had suggested. But DMV employees were human, and it hadn't taken long for Charlie to strike up a conversation with a lovely older gentleman there who'd agreed to trim some of the red tape in exchange for three times the usual processing fee. Plus an extra hundred bucks, because if you weren't going to go all-in on the bribe, what was the point?

That license was all but his. He just needed one thing.

Eventually that one thing walked into the bar, spotted him, and scowled. "How are you—*why* are you here?" Lorenzo demanded.

Despite the aggression, he still took the seat next to Charlie, and Charlie banked a smile. "Maggie told me you like this place."

"Ugh," Lorenzo said. Charlie did feel kind of bad about basically stalking Lorenzo, but he needed it for the column. Sure, Maggie and Rachel were happy enough to talk to him, but by far the most frequent questions he got in his inbox were about vampires. And last night with Lorenzo had helped, but he needed more—a *lot* more—and he wasn't afraid to dog Lorenzo to get it.

Besides, he'd all but invited this with his whole *you will never succeed* bit. He looked great sitting at the bar, even if he was trying to exude a threatening, grumpy air. It couldn't be true that all vampires were this attractive—that had to be a myth—but Christ, his hair, the rugged line of his jaw, those full lips. There was something about the set of his features and the shadow on his jaw that made Charlie want to touch him, to tilt Lorenzo's face toward his until he could stare into those big brown eyes at close range.

There was something vampiric about his eyes too, though not in the way he'd seen in movies—those marble-like eyes that were beautiful like abstract glass. No, Lorenzo's eyes were almost human, sunken and deep and bloodshot; except that there was something molten about them, tectonic, like Charlie would start to slip and fray if he stared into them too long.

Charlie realized he *was* staring at Lorenzo, and cleared his throat. "So, this is a supe bar, right?"

"A what?"

"Y'know. A bar for supernatural creatures."

"It's a normal human bar."

The bartender put something brown and expensive-looking in front of Lorenzo without being asked, and then said, "Did you say this is a human bar? I'll slap you right across the face."

Charlie grinned. "I knew it. This is a supe bar, right?"

The bartender stared at him. "You have money?"

"Yes," Charlie said. The bartender stared some more, so he fished a twenty out of his wallet and put it on the table.

"Welcome human," the man said, palming the cash. "What do you want?"

Charlie ordered a beer. After the guy left, he leaned closer to Lorenzo and asked quietly, "So, uh—what's he?"

"What are you doing here?" Lorenzo asked him.

"Oh right," he said. "I need a picture of you, for your license."

Lorenzo glanced at him sidelong, making a dismissive noise. "You are bluffing."

"And I need to see the old one," he added. "I need your license number."

"I don't believe you."

Charlie waited a moment. When Lorenzo didn't budge, he said, "Okay, but if you don't give me what I need, I'll interpret that as you defaulting on our deal, and—" He paused dramatically. "—your vampire honor will be lost."

Lorenzo said nothing.

"Your . . . Sardinian honor?" Charlie tried.

Lorenzo said nothing, but his eye twitched.

"Your pirate honor."

Lorenzo hissed at him, then pulled his wallet out of his pocket and threw his license at Charlie. It was definitely old, the paper inside yellowed and the plastic edges cracking. And—

"Oh my god," Charlie breathed. "This is *amazing*."

It was Lorenzo all right, looking just about as '70s deep-fried as could be. His hair was huge and poufed around his face, there were some *very* sharp collar points on either side of his neck, and he was giving the camera a huge, delighted, open-mouthed smile.

It was remarkably at odds with every other expression Charlie had ever seen on his face, including the one he was wearing now. "Shut up," he said weakly.

"Never," Charlie said, taking a picture of the license. He slid it back to Lorenzo. "There you go. Honestly, I don't know why you'd even want to replace that. It's perfect." When Lorenzo didn't answer, he continued, "How are you even driving around, anyway? You just never get pulled over?"

Lorenzo shrugged. Charlie wondered if he had mind control powers—a classic vampire thing—before deciding that, no, he definitely would have used them to drive Charlie away by now. He seemed annoyed enough.

The bartender walked back toward them, wiping the bar with a dingy towel. "You're bringing humans to my bar now?" he asked Lorenzo conversationally.

"Sal, please," Lorenzo said, scrubbing a hand down his face.

"Sal," Charlie said, turning to him with a hundred-watt smile. "Loving this place, and this vibe. It's like one of those diners where the waitresses are rude to you."

Sal raised one bushy, offended eyebrow and said, "Rude?" And then his leather-beaten face—flickered, briefly, the illusion of it spacing out just enough to give Charlie the sense that Sal wasn't made of flesh at all, but some sort of billowing, chalky smoke, trapped inside a thin candy shell that just so happened to look like a middle-aged bartender. It was pulsing and wet and deeply terrifying.

Charlie flinched, he knew he did, but then he shook his head, put on a poker face, and said, "You think you're the first creature to manifest in front of me this week?"

Sal snorted. "What're you, a groupie?" He glanced at Lorenzo, unimpressed. "Checking your vampire box?"

"What?" Charlie asked. "No, I—"

"You should know better, Lorenzo," Sal said, flicking one last resentful look at Charlie. "You can't trust them."

Charlie felt a twist of something uneasy in his gut as Sal walked away, and swallowed. "Um . . ." he said quietly to Lorenzo. "Should I leave?"

Lorenzo frowned, seeming distracted. "No, he's just in a mood." It took him a second, and then he scowled at Charlie. "I mean, yes. Leave. Please."

Charlie smiled wryly as Lorenzo retreated back behind his grumpy facade. "Look—I know you, like, pretty much still hate me from when we knew each other before," he said, watching

Lorenzo's shoulders tense up even as he started. "But—I'm gonna get this license for you. And when I do, you're going to have to guide me around town as my supernatural Sherpa, and show me everything I need to know for my thesis, just like we agreed."

Lorenzo said nothing, so Charlie continued on. "And since that's the case, we're going to be spending a lot of time together. So, y'know," he said, tentative and open. "Would it be the worst thing in the world if we started over, and maybe even tried to become . . . friends?"

"I have plenty of friends," Lorenzo grumbled.

"Hmm," Charlie said. He idly checked his phone and saw a text from Ava that set his heart pounding. the numbers just spiked again!!! we need another COLUMN COLUMN COLUMNNNN. when??

He put the phone away, trying to ignore the band of anxiety tightening around his shoulders. "Okay, not friends then," Charlie said. "Just—professional colleagues."

"We're not colleagues," Lorenzo said flatly. "We're not anything."

"I told you, I'm going to get you this license," Charlie said. "You might as well answer my questions now."

Sal dropped off Charlie's next beer and said, "He'll leave if you answer some questions?"

"Or," Charlie said, "if you're interested in talking about your life or your relationships—"

Smoke seemed to be pouring out of Sal's ears—literally. Charlie shivered. "Handle this," Sal said to Lorenzo with finality, giving them both a threatening look before walking away.

Charlie grinned at Lorenzo.

"Five minutes," he growled.

"Okay, great," Charlie said. "So—you mentioned that a lot of the people you date are human."

Lorenzo rolled his eyes and sighed. "Yes, all my many conquests."

"Is that hard?" Charlie asked. "Dating humans?"

"What do you mean?"

"Well, y'know," Charlie said. "There must be—differences between vampires and humans that could be hard to bridge. The day and night thing, for one."

Lorenzo shrugged.

"Religious issues . . . ?" Charlie tried.

Lorenzo glanced at him stonily.

"I can see the age thing being a problem too," Charlie mused. "I mean, you could simultaneously be too old and too young for someone. Has that ever been an issue?"

"No."

"Hm," Charlie said, taking a few notes down on his phone. He thought for a minute, and then said, "And then I guess there's the whole blood drinking thing." He looked Lorenzo up and down consideringly. "Has anyone ever been too scared to date you because you're a vampire?"

"Not really."

Charlie sighed. "Are you going to expand on any of these answers?" Lorenzo's shoulders just crept another inch up toward his ears, and Charlie gave him a playful shove. "C'mon, I want to know what it's like to be the vampire lothario."

Lorenzo's eyes had a pinched look to them. "I'm not a—*lothario*, or whatever you say. And no, no one has been afraid to date me," he said. "I am not a violent person."

"Oh, no, of course not," Charlie said quickly. "I didn't mean that. Just . . . I mean, before vampires were even, y'know, *out*—well, that must have been really hard. Trying to forge a relationship with someone when you have to keep a part of yourself secret."

Lorenzo stared at the row of bottles across the bar. "Yes," he said quietly.

"And at the same time, you're gonna outlive any human partner you'd ever have," he added, as it occurred to him. "That must be tough."

Lorenzo said nothing, looking as lost in thought as Charlie was becoming. "You've probably loved and lost a lot over the years, right?" he said, thinking about what a fertile area this must be for his readers. "I mean, before everyone knew about vampires, you must've had to leave people behind to avoid getting found out."

Charlie jotted down some notes on his phone as the many dimensions of potential vampire relationship drama unfolded before him. "Some heartbreak in your past, I bet," he mused, as Lorenzo continued to sit in silence beside him.

When the silence had stretched on for another beat, Charlie looked back up at Lorenzo. He'd craned his head to stare at Charlie, his eyes narrowed, expression unreadable.

Before Charlie could ask what was on his mind, Sal broke down into tears.

"Hey—hey man," Charlie said, concerned. He was standing closer than he'd realized, obviously listening to their conversation, and now he was dabbing his face with increasingly damp cocktail napkins. Charlie reached across the bar toward him. "Are you okay?"

"'S nothing," he said wetly, his voice wavering. Lorenzo was speechless.

"What's going on?" Charlie asked.

"I'm sorry," Sal said heavily. "Just—those things you were saying about—about how hard it can be to find someone when you're . . . living in secret . . ."

Charlie gasped. "Yeah?"

And as Sal launched into a story about a cosmic chasm opening in his demonic home realm, which had thrown him and a few of his compatriots into the human dimension, forever separating them from their home and loved ones, Charlie almost entirely forgot that Lorenzo was still sitting there next to him.

"I do care about her," Sal said a while later. "But there are so few of us left in this realm, I feel like I'm betraying our cause by loving a human. I mean technically she's a faerie, but, y'know, to our people you're all the same."

"Sure," Charlie said, nodding deeply. "But it sounds like, from what you've told me, she's not making room for your life and your culture. She's not putting in the time to learn about your demonic rites. If she can't do that, what kind of life are you going to have together long-term?"

Sal sat silently for a moment, his brow furrowed. "You think . . . I should leave her?"

"I think you deserve someone who cares about the things that are important to you," Charlie said.

Lorenzo's barstool scraped loudly as he pushed away from the bar. Charlie jumped at the sound, belatedly realizing how long he'd been consoling Sal—and ignoring Lorenzo. "Hey," he said, as Lorenzo threw some money down on the bar. "You're going?"

He pulled his coat on, not looking at Charlie, and didn't answer. Charlie wondered if he'd annoyed him by getting so distracted. "Hey wait, before you go," he said, getting his phone out of his pocket. "I still need a new picture of you for your license."

Lorenzo looked up at him, his features twisted into a glare. Charlie raised his eyebrows, surprised, but snapped a picture of Lorenzo anyway.

"Great," he said uncertainly, glancing down at it. He'd have to wash out the background to make it suitable for the license, but it was a great pic of Lorenzo, despite his thunderous expression.

When he looked back up, Lorenzo was gone.

Chapter 6

Lorenzo slammed his bedroom door behind him.

Fucking Charlie Wever.

Ever since he'd returned to Lorenzo's life, something had been off. His inopportune entreaties, his budding friendships with Maggie and Rachel, the reminders of their past—all of it had been grating on Lorenzo's nerves.

But tonight had been a step too far. To appear at one of Lorenzo's haunts expressly to badger him, and to ask the things he did—with such lightheartedness! Charlie had asked him about his heartbreaks and his regrets, about losing people to secrecy, time, and pure awful chance; and he'd posed each question like it meant nothing to him, as if Lorenzo were simply a fascinating butterfly Charlie was pinning to a page, whistling while he worked.

His questions had stirred up something ugly inside, several lifetimes of loneliness and loss scrubbed right to the surface—and all of it, apparently, beneath Charlie's notice. And then, just as Lorenzo had perhaps been poised to make some reply, he'd shifted right into taking over Sal's life. Not that Lorenzo begrudged his friend any comfort in a difficult time—but he couldn't help but notice that Charlie's prescription had been the same thing he'd told Olivia: End it. Cut ties. Move on.

Charlie claimed such an interest in the sensitivities of Lorenzo's heart, and in the lives of all supernatural creatures, when he was, in fact, nothing more than an overly meddlesome human who left nothing but emotional debris in his wake. Someone careless and cruel.

Some heartbreak in your past, I bet. Lorenzo took a deep breath, a leftover human impulse that had no real effect but still felt calming, as he tried to ignore the sound of waves in his ears.

He hadn't known that the last time he ever saw his home under the sunlight would be the last time. He could remember the moment he'd last seen the blue sky—just before it was washed away by a merciless wave that smelled of blood and musket grit. But he couldn't remember the final time he'd seen the sun's light on his cottage, or on his wife's hair.

He'd gone back to see them only once afterward, from a distance, hidden in the tree line; but the cottage didn't look the same at night. The crash of waves was there, but the shriek of laughter was gone, and the warmth that clung to the stones so briefly after sunset.

Lorenzo looked exactly the same now as he had that night. The same as he always would, the same as he'd look in that picture Charlie had taken of him at the bar, so that he could get what *he* wanted from their arrangement. So he could move on.

With a sick twist in his gut, Lorenzo realized that it'd been days since he'd even bothered trying to come up with a plan to get his revenge on Charlie. In all the chaos he'd been causing, appearing randomly and trying to flirt his way into Lorenzo's good graces, he'd actually *forgotten*.

Charlie thought it was so fun to meddle in others' lives, to pry open their hearts and see what lay within. Lorenzo would see how he liked it.

He hadn't turned on the lights in his bedroom, but that was fine; this would be easier in the dark. He lay on his bed, shaking out his limbs and trying to release any lingering tension in his body. He hadn't done this in a long time, and he needed to focus.

It wouldn't be as easy with Charlie as it would have been with a random human. Charlie was studying the supernatural, had a vested interest in them, and had shown up time and again seeking information about them. Clearly, he wasn't as spooked by the paranormal as many humans were. But Lorenzo was willing to bet Charlie still had a healthy fear of the unknown lurking somewhere deep within. He could use that.

He would need a bit of luck too. A vampire could only enter a human's home when they'd been invited, and the same was true for their minds; he could only walk into a human's dream if the human would have dreamt of him anyway. But he had a feeling Charlie would be thinking of him.

Closing his eyes, he sought to center himself and clear his mind. Then he turned his focus to his own body—or more accurately, his corpse. He focused on the desiccated blood in his veins, the piercing hunger in the core of his fangs, the dirt under his fingernails. He felt the call of moonlight, the whistle of the wind, and felt his presence slip from his body and the physical world into someplace else. Into the ether.

He began to hunt.

He prowled, not in any place he could see or describe. He

was a sightless, senseless animal following a trail more primal than scent, and he moved through the ether until he found something that felt familiar. Something that felt like Charlie.

He touched it, pushing against it, until it gave way.

Blinking, he realized he was in a dark alleyway. The colors were a crisp duotone of black and red, and the pavestones looked wide, like they'd been distorted by a fish-eye lens. Fog clung to the corners of the street, and something buzzed in the distance—an insect drone, too high-pitched to be soothing.

Yes, he was in the right place. This was Charlie's dream.

Now he just needed to find his prey.

The alley stretched on endlessly as he walked; it had no real dimensions, of course, but he knew it would deliver him to Charlie eventually. Dreams felt endless to dreamers, but Lorenzo had done this once or twice before, and he knew that they were more like conveyor belts, pulling the dreamer through surreality and sensation to whatever they were supposed to see. Charlie was here somewhere.

He stopped when he heard the sharp scream of metal. A door appeared in the wall of the alley and then opened, party music and lights spilling out of it. Charlie giggled as he stumbled out of the door and into the dream's red evening, heaving a delighted breath into the frigid dark. Lorenzo waited, letting the shadows cloak him from Charlie's awareness. He'd take his time. He wanted to do this right.

After a moment, Charlie turned and walked away from him, humming a drunken tune, his hands in his pockets. Lorenzo waited until he'd almost lost the sound of Charlie's footsteps, then began to follow.

It'd been a long time since he'd hunted like this. The dream helped him, wrapping fog around Charlie's ankles, twisting what little light there was in the alley until it all seemed to pierce the eye, illuminating nothing. The ambient noise around them dropped away, until the only sounds were Charlie's breathing, the rustle of his clothes, and then—one of Lorenzo's footsteps.

Charlie shivered and stopped short.

He looked over his shoulder, uncertainty in his eyes. Lorenzo waited, statue-still, concealed in the shadows. He could hear Charlie's heart beating faster, his breath coming sharper.

When he turned back, he hurried down the alleyway, but Lorenzo kept pace easily. He let out a low, menacing growl, and Charlie jumped, his frame tightening. Lorenzo could almost feel the gooseflesh of his skin. This time, Charlie didn't bother looking for the danger—he broke into a run.

Lorenzo descended upon him. He grabbed Charlie's jacket and threw him against the wall face-first, keeping him pinned there with only a fist in his back. Charlie screamed, fighting uselessly against him. His lips didn't move—dream paralysis, most likely—but Lorenzo could tell he was trying to beg for his life.

He snarled, baring his fangs, and fisted his other hand in Charlie's hair. He yanked his head to the side and leaned close, ready to take a deep, painful bite—one that would surely jolt Charlie awake, and with a deep, abiding fear of vampires.

And then he realized—he didn't just want Charlie scared of vampires. He wanted him scared of *him*.

He needed Charlie to leave him alone.

So before he bit, he spun Charlie around to face him and shoved him back against the wall.

A gasp broke out of Charlie's throat when he saw who'd been hunting him. His eyes were wide with fear. Lorenzo's fangs were still out, his lips curled in a menacing snarl, and he knew his eyes were burning red. He growled a low, deadly warning, and pushed closer to Charlie, trapping him in place. He buried his hand in Charlie's hair and yanked, baring his neck, licked his teeth, and leaned in.

Charlie shivered and pressed closer to him.

Lorenzo froze. But Charlie didn't stop—he ran his hands up Lorenzo's arms and dug his nails into his shoulders and the curve of his back. Charlie's heart was still beating a mile a minute, his blood pumping hot under his skin; but where before he'd been stiff with fear, straining to get away, now he pressed into Lorenzo, pushing back, away from the wall, chasing every place they could be crushed together. His eyes had fluttered closed, and his breaths were fevered, frantic—each one rushing past Lorenzo's ear as a hot, hungry sound.

And Lorenzo realized too late that the rest of the dream had shifted too—the air was boiling, the angles of the world seeming to liquefy around them so that they were pitched even closer together. There was music, bass-heavy and drugging, and blood-red flowers bloomed all over the walls around them, lichen and soft, springy moss.

The dream swayed, and Lorenzo pressed more firmly against Charlie, seeking his footing. Charlie pulled him close. *Yes*, he breathed out.

Lorenzo *felt* it, his low, hot whisper, and swallowed back a coarse reply. He didn't need to breathe here—he didn't need to breathe at all—but he was gasping anyway, for sanity, for mercy. Charlie's jugular was fluttering, the skin there slick and hot, and it wasn't even why he'd come here, and—the scent of Charlie's sweat was making him delirious. Confused, overwhelmed, he leaned his forehead against Charlie's.

Charlie opened his eyes and looked up at him. His gaze

dropped to Lorenzo's lips, to his fangs, and his pupils dilated. He wrapped a hand around the back of Lorenzo's neck.

Lorenzo surged awake in his own bed, out of the ether and Charlie's mind, covered in sweat.

He was still panting.

From: lvstrom@jmail.com
To: wiseoldcrone@midnight.com
Date: March 3, 9:52 PM
Subject: Ghost in the Slack

Dear Wise Old Crone,

I think my workplace Slack is haunted. No one in the
company has died recently, but for the last few months
this weird, unclaimed profile has been showing up in our
channels, sending all-caps messages and then vanishing.
Sometimes the messages are just nonsense or warmed-
over dril tweets, but sometimes they make the screen
flash brightly, causing us to fall unconscious and wake
up covered in blood or . . . worse. Also, the ghost profile
seems to have access to our private DMs, because sometimes he'll show up during all-team meetings and start
spreading gossip that he couldn't possibly know otherwise. But lately he's been talking a lot about pay dispari-
ties, and I think he's trying to unionize everyone. How can
we stop corporate from exorcising him?

Sincerely,
Don't Salt and Burn

From: pbailey@jmail.com
To: wiseoldcrone@midnight.com
Date: April 30, 10:03 AM
Subject: "Faked" Allergy

Dear Crone,

My girlfriend "Alex" is a faerie, and as you may know, faeries are allergic to honey. (Apparently this dates back to some kind of long-standing feud between faeries and bees, but honestly I kind of zone out anytime Alex starts talking about her ancestral backstory.) My mom does not believe that Alex is actually allergic to honey. She keeps slipping it into everything she cooks for us when we come to visit, I guess in an attempt to "prove" that Alex is just making up her allergy, for attention or whatever? So far this hasn't caused any harm, because Alex can smell it before she eats anything, so she just puts down whatever my mom's been expectantly waiting for her to eat, and the worst that's happened is some awkwardness at the dinner table and a fight on the drive home. But a few weeks ago I learned that my family on my mother's side is descended from this ancient druidic cult that worshipped bees, and when I told Alex about this, her fangs emerged and her skin turned hard and brittle, like one of those beaches made of rocks instead of sand. What can I do to mediate this conflict?

Sincerely,
Honey for my Honey

Wise Old Crone

Should I Cross Dimensions for a Fling?

My friends think I'm crazy (or possessed).

May 26

Dear Crone,

Years ago I hooked up with this demon at a festival. Time of my life, etc., but the guy was literally between dimensions and we figured we'd never see each other again.

Well we randomly became twitter mutuals lol. We started DMing, and now it's been over a year of us flirting and—I think—falling back in love, but all over text! We're never in the same dimension so we've never had a chance to meet up, but the other day he said he wants to. Actually, he said he wants to perform the ritual that allows humans to vibrate on the demonic dimensional frequency, because he asked me to come traveling with him.

Crone, this guy wants me to leave my whole life behind for him, and I'm . . . kind of into it? Am I crazy to want to leave the human world behind and travel with him through the void? I'm finally at a good place in my career, and my friends and family all think I'm crazy for even considering it—but it sounds fun.

Sincerely,
Portal Hopping

Dear Hopper,

Go for it.

—Crone

Chapter 7

♥

Low lights and loud music greeted Charlie when he arrived at Lorenzo's apartment. The place was filled with people, and the mindless party atmosphere immediately loosened a little of the tension in his shoulders.

Maggie spotted him and swayed over. "Hey, you came!" she shouted over the music.

"Thanks for inviting me," Charlie shouted back. Maggie smiled a little drunkenly, her dainty tusks on display, and Charlie felt a rush of affection.

It did not completely dim his nerves about being here. When Maggie had texted him about the party, he'd felt as if he couldn't say no—she'd mentioned that other supes would be here, and it was too good an opportunity to pass up. Plus, the party sounded fun, and he was psyched at the chance to hang out with Maggie and Rachel more. He wasn't going to pass on any of that just because of a dream.

And who didn't have weird sex dreams from time to time? The only reason for the awkward, prickling tension he was feeling right now was the fact that this dream had been about someone he knew. Someone who was here at this party somewhere, and who he'd eventually have to face.

And because the dream had been, well—upsettingly hot. The dark alleyway, the pulse-pounding fear that'd bled instantly into blistering need, the feeling of being crushed between a brick wall and Lorenzo's thick, unyielding body . . .

And then there'd been the whole bite of it all. Some of the details were fuzzy, but he knew he'd dreamt of Lorenzo either attacking him or stalking him, and he'd woken up just before getting fangs in his throat. Something that, in the dream, he had badly, badly wanted. Either way, it'd been piercingly, achingly intense. And no fun to wake up from.

But so what? He'd survived as a fat, gay kid in the South; he could handle an awkward sex dream about an acquaintance. It didn't mean anything. It didn't mean he actually wanted Lorenzo to grab him by the neck with one hand and squeeze.

He shook his head bracingly and tried to ask in a casual tone of voice, "Is Lorenzo here?"

Maggie couldn't hear him over the music, so he had to ask again. "Yeah," she shouted, "I think he's—"

He turned in the direction she was pointing and found himself face-to-face with Lorenzo, who, upon seeing Charlie, jerked violently, dropping several of the beers he was holding and the contents of a red solo cup.

As the puddle of foamy red blood spread at Lorenzo's feet, he gaped at Charlie, then glared, and then tried to yell at him over the music. His rant was barely audible, though, so after a few seconds, and as Charlie watched with mounting amusement, Lorenzo scowled, gave up, and stomped away, presumably to clean up.

Charlie heaved a relieved sigh. So he'd had a sex dream about Lorenzo, but that was just his subconscious; real-life Lorenzo was still a big, goofy dweeb. He had nothing to worry about. "What's up with him?" he asked Maggie.

"He gets nervous at parties," she said.

"Why?"

Maggie shook her head sadly, like she'd explained this many times before. "He just does."

Charlie wanted to ask what she meant, but he was distracted when another woman walked across the room. He could tell immediately she was supernatural—she seemed to be lit from within, putting off light as if she were a pool of water, soft and rippling. She was tall and willowy, with pin-straight pale blue hair, and walked past them into the kitchen with an unnaturally smooth, otherworldly gait.

"Who is *that*?" he breathed.

"Our third roommate," Maggie said. "Isolde."

"What is she?"

Maggie waggled her eyebrows, drawing out the suspense for a moment, and then said: "A unicorn."

"No," Charlie gasped. Maggie just nodded, very satisfied to have delivered the news. "But she's—"

"Decided to take on human form for a while," Maggie said. "I don't know all the details."

A glimmer in the corner of his eye caught his attention, and he realized that there was a faint trail of what looked like dust along the floor where Isolde had passed by—dust that was glowing like something under a black light. He bent down to rub some of it between his fingers. "Holy shit, she emits glitter?" he said, standing up to observe it more closely. "That's amazing. Is this biodegradable? Wait, what am I touching right now."

Maggie grinned. "Want me to introduce you?"

They went into the kitchen, where Isolde was standing in front of the sink, staring at the faucet as water poured out. Rachel was standing next to her, holding a mug and tapping her foot impatiently.

"Isolde?" Maggie said. "This is my friend Charlie. He wanted to meet you."

Isolde craned her neck to stare at him. She was unbelievably beautiful—not colloquially unbelievable, but in a way that truly seemed beyond belief. Her skin was moonlight blue and impossibly smooth. She had huge eyes, long eyelashes, and delicate features, and her eyebrows and lower lip were pierced with something that looked like bone. She seemed to move less than a human would, even down to the speed with which she blinked. Staring at her, he felt caught between elation and pure terror.

"Hello," she said. Her voice was soft, raspy, and deep.

"Hi," he managed. "Nice to meet you."

Rachel shook her head, seeming exasperated. "Wait for it."

Isolde said, "You are unchaste."

He hesitated. "Un . . . unchaste?"

"Impure," she said. "Sullied by your earthly hungers."

Rachel leaned past Isolde and clarified: "She means you're not a virgin."

"Oh!" Charlie said. "Wow, so the whole thing about unicorns and virgins is not a myth, huh?"

"No," Isolde said, then turned back to stare at the water pouring out of the faucet.

"Is something wrong with the water?" Charlie asked tentatively.

"No," Isolde said softly, craning her neck just a bit. "And yes."

"Wow," Rachel said. "That's profound."

"All water is pure," Isolde said. "And it is all impure. Just like all of you," she finished, turning to look at Rachel.

Rachel flushed and glared at everyone in the room before stalking off, her mug forgotten. Isolde turned back to the water and then shut off the tap before also leaving. The sound of her footsteps was deeply unsettling for reasons Charlie couldn't put his finger on at first, before he realized: there was nothing organic about her at all. The sounds of her footfalls and her clothes rustling as she passed by weren't soft but crystalline and brittle, like a machine made of finespun glass.

"Wow," Charlie said to Maggie. "That was—wow. Thanks for the introduction."

Maggie smiled at him. "You're fun."

He stayed for a few minutes to chat with Maggie, but just as they started to head back to the party, Lorenzo came into the room. Once again he stopped short when he saw Charlie, looking uncomfortable. "Hey," Charlie said.

"Charlie," Lorenzo said shortly. His pinched expression was swiftly devolving into a glare.

Charlie sighed. He supposed he did owe Lorenzo some sort of apology for hounding him so much over the last few days. "Look, about last night," he said lowly, as Maggie sidled past them back to the party. "I'm sorry if I offended you. I realize I was asking a lot of questions, and—I don't know. Maybe I was out of line."

"Uh-huh," Lorenzo said. His glare softened, but he still looked like he'd rather be anywhere else.

Charlie was hit with a grim pang of genuine guilt. "Look, if I touched a nerve or something—I'm sorry," he offered. "Really."

"Hm," Lorenzo said, his dark eyes darting up and then away; but some of the tension left his shoulders.

He still looked like he was itching to get away. Just then, Charlie remembered. "Oh, I almost forgot."

He dug around in his pocket and pulled out Lorenzo's new driver's license. "Here you go."

Lorenzo just stared at it, shocked. "You didn't."

"I did," Charlie said, trying not to sound smug.

"But—how?" Lorenzo asked. "The rules—"

He shrugged. "I bribed a DMV employee."

Lorenzo looked thunderstruck. "What?"

"Don't worry, it's still a real license," Charlie said. "*I* could go to jail, maybe. But I doubt it."

Lorenzo seemed to be having trouble processing. Charlie glanced at the license. "Good picture of you, though."

After he just stood there for another moment, Charlie held the license out. "So," he said, "a deal's a deal." As Lorenzo finally reached out to take it from him, he added, "Looks like you're stuck with me."

Lorenzo's fingers brushed Charlie's as he took the license, and the rough drag of it sent a shiver down Charlie's spine. He met Lorenzo's eye, and suddenly he was right back in that dark, narrow alley, caught in Lorenzo's arms and the lee of his body; inside the almost painful desire to have Lorenzo's hands on him, his fangs breaking his skin, his hot mouth dragging down Charlie's neck.

Lorenzo was staring at him, looking strangely open and lost. And for some reason that reminded Charlie of the dream too.

Lorenzo yanked his hand from Charlie's and stuffed the license into his back pocket. "Yes," he muttered, and bolted out of the kitchen.

Charlie swallowed thickly.

Chapter 8

Sometimes Lorenzo's supernaturally heightened senses felt like a curse. Usually he didn't notice them; he'd been a vampire for over two hundred years, so he was used to the sharp eyesight and sensitive hearing by now. He remembered being overwhelmed by it back when he'd first turned—on a ship, of all places, suddenly feeling the pitch of the boat and hearing the boiling spray of the ocean to such a heightened degree that it felt like torture.

Now, of course, it was better. Enhanced eyesight helped when you could only ever go out at night, and the sharp hearing was useful. The heightened sense of smell was the strangest part, though. Humans ran the gamut—many smelled awful, like body odor or vape smoke; but sometimes he could smell a person's blood so clearly that he could almost taste it on his tongue. Most of the time he tried to just shut it out, though it was hard to do so entirely. Rachel smelled like pears and rotting eggs; Maggie smelled like pebbles and rainstorms; Isolde smelled like something primally terrifying that he couldn't put his finger on, and a little like horse.

Here, in his car, as he drove down a dark, winding road with Charlie in his passenger seat, it was very, very hard to shut out his scent.

He smelled nice—soapy and clean, the faint call of blood under a much stronger layer of warm human familiarity. He'd gotten a whiff of Charlie's scent before, but it was stronger here, in the small car. He was starting to notice all its delicate layers—the floral and artificial scents that must have been his laundry detergent, fabric softener, maybe cologne; the city scents that clung to him, as they did all humans, going largely unnoticed—soot and dust.

And beneath all that, the sweat of his skin, tangy and tempting. And something more; a scent that seemed to seep into Lorenzo's very bones; something just of Charlie's, like a color only he could see. It drifted around him, maddening.

And it was impossibly distracting, knowing what Lorenzo knew now.

He hadn't been able to smell, touch, or taste Charlie in the dream, because he hadn't actually been there—it had all been in Charlie's mind. But Charlie's mind had still pulled him close, unafraid and clinging. Charlie had turned the dream into something hot and inescapable.

Charlie wanted him.

It was only a dream. There was no way to say for sure what it meant or what it portended. It was just that here, now, with Charlie right next to him and his delicious scent bottling up in the car, he couldn't help but wonder what Charlie would be like—what he would taste or smell like—if Lorenzo touched him like that for real.

He cracked his window and cool air rushed in, dissipating the scent. He breathed a small sigh of relief. Charlie glanced at him. "You okay?"

"I'm fine," Lorenzo said levelly.

Why oh why had he told Charlie that he was a creature of his word? Luring Charlie in with his false promises at first had been no great sin, but to outright refuse to help him now, when they'd made a deal? One that had been struck after spending more time with Charlie, getting reacquainted with him, even letting him meet his friends?

No, he couldn't deny him. He'd lost their bet. There was no sense in losing his honor too.

He was stuck with Charlie—for now, at least.

He'd just have to ignore how tempting he smelled.

"Alright," Charlie said. "So, druids! I'm excited."

"Really?" Lorenzo asked. "Why?"

"Because I didn't even know there was a kind of supernatural creature called druids before last night? And now I'm about to meet some?" He grinned triumphantly. "Good thing I won our bet."

Lorenzo clenched his jaw and said nothing. "So, how do you know these druids?" Charlie asked.

"I've worked with them in the past."

"Like when you were security for the werewolves?"

"Yes," Lorenzo said. "Like that."

"Hm. Well, until we get there," Charlie said, getting out his phone to take notes, "I still have a lot of questions for you about vampires."

"Ugh," Lorenzo said.

"Where to start," Charlie said, tapping a finger against his lips. "Oh—is any of that religious stuff true? Like, do crosses and holy water burn you?"

"I don't think so."

"You don't think so?"

"I don't go around touching crosses," Lorenzo said.

"Fair enough," Charlie said. "But as far as you know . . . ?"

Lorenzo shook his head. "Okay," Charlie said, tapping on his phone. "And, clearly the mirror thing is fake."

"Yes," Lorenzo said, glancing in the rearview.

"But you can't go out in daylight?" Charlie asked.

"Yes, that's true."

"What happens if you do?"

Lorenzo raised an eyebrow at him. "I've never tried it."

"So you just don't know?"

Lorenzo sighed. "It is said we burst into flame. Or disintegrate into ash. Possibly both."

"That . . . sucks," Charlie said, sounding surprisingly upset. Lorenzo glanced at him. "I mean, you said you grew up by the ocean. You must . . . miss the sun."

Lorenzo gripped the steering wheel, feeling a phantom warmth on his arms, the grit of hot, wet sand between his fingers. He hadn't lost just one thing when he'd lost the sun: he'd lost long summer afternoons and colors you could only find in a sunset, the special laziness that comes from loafing around first thing in the morning, the look of joy on a loved one's face as they squint up into a burst of starlight after a long winter.

"Sometimes," he said quietly.

It took him a moment to realize that Charlie hadn't responded. "What?"

"I can just keep asking questions, y'know," Charlie said. "You answer in monosyllables and I'll just keep asking more and more questions until I get what I want."

"*Sometimes* is a duosyllable."

Charlie bit his lip, but it didn't hold back his pleased smile.

His eyes were dark and sharp, like he was pinning Lorenzo in place just by looking at him.

Or maybe he was remembering the dream.

Lorenzo cleared his throat, noticing the turn he had to take just in time. "A clinic?" Charlie asked, sounding surprised. "Is this the right spot?"

Lorenzo parked next to some scrubby bushes and didn't bother to respond.

Inside, the clinic was as dreary as these things usually are— there was a door that led to private rooms, a screen to one side setting off a section of the room for shots, and an old TV in the corner playing *Bluey*. Luckily, though, they were the only patrons aside from a woman up front who was speaking with Dylan, Lorenzo's druid friend.

"Now, heat-quenching potions are kinda unreliable," Dylan was explaining as he handed her a small prescription bottle. "And your insurance is only going to cover some of them."

"Which ones?" the woman asked, peering at the runes on her prescription label.

Dylan grabbed a sheet from under the desk and handed it to her. "Call this number, and then this number, and they'll send you some forms. Once you submit those, a shaman will perform a ritual that will indicate whether the insurer will cover it. But sometimes they change their coverage, and even the shamans can't predict it, so." Dylan shrugged, looking sympathetic. "Best be prepared to pay out of pocket."

The patient thanked him and left, and Dylan grinned when he realized Lorenzo was waiting. "Hey man, haven't seen you in a beat." He was one of the younger druids, beefy and hand-some in a grungy kind of way. Dylan was a bit more of a free thinker than the rest of his family—he'd left town after high school and only come back a few years ago.

"Dylan," Lorenzo said. "This is . . . Charlie."

If Charlie noticed that he'd given up trying to define their relationship, he did nothing other than flick Lorenzo a quick look. "Hi!" he said. "Nice to meet you."

"Same," Dylan said. Turning back to Lorenzo, he asked, "So, you need some potions, or are you selling again?"

"Selling?" Charlie asked him.

"Neither," Lorenzo said, hoping that would dispel Charlie's questions. "Charlie . . . has some questions for you. He is a student."

Dylan looked intrigued, and Charlie leaned forward against the counter, his smile widening. "Well, I have a lot of questions," he said. "About you, and this clinic. But first, and most importantly . . ." He turned to look at Lorenzo. "What does he sell you?"

Lorenzo stifled a groan. "Vamps, man?" Dylan said. "Oh, we buy everything—hair, teeth, nails. Blood, obviously. It's all great in healing spells." He clapped Lorenzo on the shoulder. "But this guy's usually only good for the little things."

Because Lorenzo's blood could be used for magicks far more dangerous than mere healing spells. But he declined to mention that; he could only imagine how insatiable Charlie would be with that knowledge.

"The little things," Charlie was echoing. "So—you sell him . . ."

"Locks of hair," Lorenzo grunted. "On occasion."

"Wow," Charlie said. "What does that get you?"

Lorenzo refused to dignify that with anything more than flinty silence, so Charlie turned to Dylan. "I mean, generally, what would you . . ."

"Depends on the day," Dylan said, dragging a small scale from the side of the counter closer to them. "We got some vamp hair the other day, actually, where was it . . ."

He fished a small plastic baggie with a few locks of reddish-blonde hair out from under the counter and put it on the scale. Rather than displaying the weight, the scale glowed faintly bluish-purple for a moment before displaying some glyphs on the readout. "This was thirty-five bucks. Damn, that's rough."

"Hang on," Charlie said, leaning in closer. "Is that . . . surge pricing?"

"Yep," Dylan said, putting the scale away and crossing his thick arms. "That's the coven for you."

"Wow. So—you're not affiliated with them?" Charlie asked. "The coven?"

"Oh, no. I'm a druid, not a witch," Dylan explained. "I just work for them."

Charlie leaned forward, a smile on his face like a set of cocktails was about to materialize between them. "Tell me more."

Lorenzo zoned out as Dylan droned on about the history of the druids. He was more interested—more fixated, really—on Charlie. He was so incredibly at ease here; meeting someone new, asking all about them, joking around and fitting in. Charlie was every bit as smart and catty as Lorenzo remembered him being— well, maybe a bit less catty—but he was also as sharply insightful as Lorenzo remembered. And wasn't that the real problem?

What was so wanting in Lorenzo that Charlie had spotted and disdained all those years ago? And why couldn't Lorenzo find his same comfort and ease?

"Well, thanks," Charlie said at length, flicking a glance over at him. "This has been so useful. So far, Lorenzo hasn't taken me to meet a single witch."

"Of course not," Dylan said. "They hate vampires."

"Not druids, though?"

"Oh, no," Dylan said. "I get a ton of side gigs for the vamps."

Other vampires, he meant. Lorenzo swallowed back his discomfort as Charlie flicked a curious glance at him.

"Side gigs?" Charlie asked.

"Mm-hmm," he said. "I work vamp parties, mostly."

"Parties? Doing what?"

"Well like, druids are nature mages," Dylan explained. "So I can enchant human blood so it tastes like—anything."

"Wow," Charlie said. "Like what?"

"I can't get into that," Dylan said, leaning back. "Client confidentiality, you understand."

Charlie contemplated that for a minute, and then turned to Lorenzo. "What would you want a human's blood to taste like?"

Lorenzo felt his lips part.

He had no idea what to say.

Before he could embarrass himself, Dylan said, "Oh, Lorenzo's never at those parties. He's a stand-up guy."

Lorenzo winced. "Oh yeah?" Charlie asked, his gaze lingering on Lorenzo as he fought a wave of prickling heat.

"Yeah. Those things can get pretty wild, when you've got a whole nest of vamps together," Dylan said. "Dark stuff. But Lorenzo's cool. More of a lone wolf. Or a lone . . . corpse."

"Thanks, Dylan," Lorenzo said quietly.

Charlie narrowed his eyes, glancing back and forth between them as a small smile grew on his face. "Tell me more about Lorenzo."

"I think we're done here," Lorenzo said swiftly.

Dylan laughed good-naturedly. "I see how it is. Listen," he

told Charlie, "Let me know if you ever want to come meet more of the circle. My cousin Jude does these crazy rituals, you could come see."

"I would love that!" Charlie said warmly, offering his hand again. "It was so nice to meet you."

Back in Lorenzo's car, Charlie said, "So, about those parties . . ."

"I am not taking you to a vampire party," Lorenzo said with finality. That was impossible for any number of reasons.

"I don't want you to," Charlie said defensively. "I just want to know." He stared at Lorenzo for another moment, seeming to weigh his words, and then said: "What flavor blood would you pick?"

Lorenzo scoffed and didn't answer, while Charlie wheedled him, smiling that ingratiating, silly smile that made Lorenzo want to do many, many things that he shouldn't.

Charlie *was* insightful, uncomfortably so—that much was true. But unlike the last time they'd known each other, this time Charlie was noticing him. Focused on him. He seemed to be waiting Lorenzo out at times, curious about him. This Charlie was almost . . . gentle with him.

No. That was a dangerous line of thought.

"Come on," Charlie was saying. "If life were a giant Coca-Cola custom drink machine at a druid-assisted vampire party, you'd pick—"

"Nothing," Lorenzo snapped. "I'd want—"

He glanced over at Charlie, and then couldn't help but hold his eyes as he said, "I would want to taste your blood just as it is." He swallowed. "If it were me."

"Okay," Charlie breathed.

Chapter 9

Saturday night Charlie was once again trekking with Lorenzo through the woods. There was a path, but it was faint, narrow, and entirely absent in spots, and it was treacherous whenever it turned steeply downhill. "If we keep meeting people like this," Charlie said, huffing slightly, "I'm gonna need some DEET."

Per usual, Lorenzo ignored him.

"Y'know, bug spray?" he said.

"Bugs do not bite me," Lorenzo said. In the darkness under the trees, Charlie could barely make out his expression. "My flesh is cold and repellent to them. One of the perks of being undead."

"Hmm," Charlie said, brushing aside more branches and trying his best to get a glimpse of Lorenzo's skin. Judging from the letters he kept getting from humans who were sleeping with vampires, he doubted *repellent* was an accurate word. Cool, maybe. He wouldn't know.

"You know, you don't usually talk about the perks of being a vampire," he told Lorenzo.

Silence again. "Hm," Charlie said. "I'll take it from your brooding silence that you really resent being incredibly strong and impervious to injury and disease."

"But not to being badgered by questions from graduate students," Lorenzo said.

Charlie beamed at him, and this time he could see that Lorenzo was smiling a little in return. Not for the first time, he thought about how strange it was that he'd barely remembered Lorenzo when they ran into each other at the coffee shop—that his memory of him from five years ago was so dim. All he could recall of that time was Lorenzo, Olivia's kind of strange, off-putting boyfriend.

But this Lorenzo could be nudged into smiling if Charlie told the right joke. He handed out tiny morsels of information about being a vampire like each one was precious, but he wasn't too stuffy to make fun of himself. He'd been standoffish at first, sure, but even though he put up a good front at being dragged along into Charlie's world, he was well aware that Lorenzo could have just blown him off after the whole driver's license thing—or even after they'd first reconnected. But he hadn't. He was holding up his end of the deal.

Not that it'd been easy to get him to agree to this particular mission. Werewolves were by far the most prolific supernatural creatures, and the Crone got hundreds of letters about them. Readers were curious about complicated pack dynamics, safety around the full moon, and, of course, the ever-present question of what counted as bestiality.

And he needed to learn more, because the column was—amazingly—still doing well. Somehow all of his supernatural-themed posts had been putting up great numbers. He wasn't sure whether to be grateful, excited, or fearful that it would all get snatched away. Ava was smug as hell, thinking they'd finally cracked the secret code—that focusing on the paranormal had been the key to the Crone's success all along.

Charlie wasn't so sure. Meeting all of these people had definitely been interesting, but he thought it was more than that. He'd just been feeling . . . inspired, lately.

Lorenzo brushed a branch out of his way, muttering something irritated under his breath. He seemed most at ease when he could complain about something; when Charlie had asked him for a proper introduction to a werewolf pack, he'd turned him down flat, claiming they were touchy and insular, and that Charlie hadn't done himself any favors by crashing the werewolf prom (which he wasn't supposed to call werewolf prom).

But Charlie had begged and wheedled, and joked and pestered and flirted, and eventually Lorenzo had arranged this outing. He hadn't let Charlie down yet.

He had been a little vague on who exactly they'd be meeting. Charlie snuck a quick glance up at the moon, but it was barely more than half-full. He shook off any nerves and plowed ahead behind Lorenzo as they scaled a particularly steep crag.

Finally they emerged from the woods and spotted a cabin with what looked like camping equipment spread out around it—firepits, tents, and more. But no one else was there. "So—where are your friends?" Charlie asked.

"I told them we were coming tonight," Lorenzo said mildly. "And they're nearby."

"How can you tell?"

"I can hear them," Lorenzo said. "And smell them."

"You can *smell* them?" Charlie asked.

That was when he heard a twig snap. "Hey," Charlie said. "About that thing you said, about the wolves being mad at me—"

A growl sounded from across the clearing, and he grabbed Lorenzo's sleeve, entirely too spooked to be able to appreciate the firm bicep underneath. Then a wolf appeared between the trees, with another just behind. So much for the half-full moon.

Two more wolves emerged to his left as Charlie tried not to panic. "Uh," he said, inching closer to Lorenzo.

That was when the wolf at the head of the pack shifted back into human form seamlessly, revealing a fully naked, elderly man who beamed at the both of them. "Lorenzo!" he said cheerfully. "You came."

"Hello, Kenny," Lorenzo said. They shook hands as the rest of the wolves transformed back into humans, all of them naked, all well past retirement age. Charlie tried not to gape.

Kenny, who seemed like the leader of this particular group, had thick gray hair on his head and all over. "This must be your friend," he said, turning to Charlie.

"Uh, nice to meet you," he said, shaking his hand gingerly.

"Welcome to our community!" Kenny said, clapping his hands together in satisfaction. The others had gotten to work lighting fires and setting up the campsite, not seeming to let their nakedness interfere with their work. "Sorry to be late meeting you, we were just going for a midnight run."

"I . . ." Charlie was lost for words, which was rare.

He caught Lorenzo's eye, and realized that he was smirking. A blush rose to Charlie's cheeks.

Twenty minutes later they were sitting around a campfire with the werewolves, most of whom, to his gratitude, had finally pulled on clothes. A woman across from him was assembling s'mores and passing them around the circle, while a guy to his left lit a joint. "So—the full moon thing—" Charlie asked.

"Eh, that's a young wolf's game," Kenny said, waving a

relaxed arm. "Once the pelt starts growing in a bit grayer, all that stuff gets easier. You can shift on the full moon, on the half moon, during the day. Whenever you want, really."

"Wow," Charlie said. "So you just—do you all live here?"

"Here, around," Kenny said. "Wherever the beast calls us."

"The beast?"

"The beast within," he said, waggling his coarse silver eyebrows. "We run for miles sometimes, making the mountains our home."

"Wow," Charlie said again. As he grasped for a more cogent response, he glanced at Lorenzo, and saw him gazing back smugly again. Like he'd engineered all this to put Charlie off his game.

Sitting up a little straighter, he said, "Y'know, you all are the first werewolves I've had the chance to talk to in depth. I'd love to ask you some more questions—is that okay?"

"Sure," Kenny said easily. "There's nothing wrong with ignorance, only incuriosity."

"Thanks," Charlie said. "So—do all, um, senior werewolves live like this? Nomadic, more in touch with nature?"

"Some do," Kenny said. "Some stay tethered to their human-passing lives."

The woman making s'mores scoffed at him. "Human-passing? You still go down the mountain once a week to check in on your accounting firm."

"I want to make sure it's in good shape for when Niall takes it over! My youngest," he said to Charlie. He added pointedly, to the woman who had laughed at him, "And we don't judge here."

There were nods around the fire. Across the clearing, two of the werewolves had wandered over to a small stream and started splashing each other, quickly shifting into wolf form so they could grapple and snap at each other playfully. Charlie sighed. "You seem so . . . happy."

"We are," Kenny said. "We don't concern ourselves with the things that defined us when we were younger. The rat race, the struggle for material goods, the duality of man and beast. We're at peace here."

"Sounds nice," he said.

"It is," Kenny said. "Say, speaking of the rat race—did you say your name was Wever?"

"Uh—yes," Charlie said hesitantly.

Kenny sat forward. "Any relation to Professor George Wever, over at the university?"

"Oh," Charlie said. "Yes. That's my father."

Lorenzo glanced over at him, but Charlie didn't look. "Fascinating," Kenny was saying. "I must say, I disagree with just about every one of his theories on economic stimulus, but you can't deny he's made quite a contribution to the university's scholarship."

His father's scholarship was the beginning and end of his priorities. Charlie honestly couldn't even be sure if his dad would be upset to learn that he'd been back in Brookville for weeks without reaching out, or if he'd just be . . .

Well. It wasn't like Charlie being here or not had any effect on his dad's career, so he dismissed his guilt and decided that none of this made for good conversation. "I'll tell him you said that," he said politely.

Kenny looked as if he was about to launch into another question about Charlie's dad, so he jumped in. "Speaking of family—what about your children? You all must have younger werewolf relatives here in town, right?"

"Yes, we do," Kenny said.

"Do you stay in touch with them?" he asked. "Are you, uh—affiliated? Is that the right word?"

"In a manner of speaking," Kenny said. "We still have our pack ties, but there are multiple different packs represented here in our group. It's just—not something that matters to us as much anymore."

"Hm," Charlie said. "And is that how you met Lorenzo?"

Lorenzo jerked a little, as if startled to be mentioned, but Kenny beamed at the question. "Yes, Lorenzo! He was a great help to us back in—what was it, '92? That was a bad year between the packs, there was lots of tension. It's always good to have a vampire around to sort us hotheads out."

"Yes, well," Lorenzo mumbled, looking embarrassed.

"'92, huh?" Charlie said, as Lorenzo glared at him. "What was he like back then?"

"Oh, wonderful!" Kenny said. "So helpful and polite. Just as handsome then as he is now—he hasn't withered away like the rest of us. But y'know, if I recall correctly, back then, he had that great '90s hair—the swoopy bangs and all," he said, pantomiming with his fingers draped over his forehead.

Lorenzo rolled his eyes as Charlie put a hand over his mouth to stifle a giggle. "Wow. '90s hair, '70s hair . . . there's so much to unpack with you," he murmured.

Lorenzo shot him a look, but it did nothing to quell Charlie's curiosity. If anything, the dark, quiet humor in Lorenzo's eyes made Charlie feel like they were alone in the woods, with nothing but the crackle of the fire to interrupt them. "Do you have daguerreotypes of yourself? Wearing 1800s clothes?" he teased. "I'd love to see those."

"No," Lorenzo said flatly, but there was a reluctant, amused slant to his scowl.

"Hmm," Charlie said. "I bet you're one of the founders of Brookville. Actually." He frowned a little, realizing something. "How *did* you find yourself in rural Virginia? It's a long way from Italy."

This time it was Lorenzo who stared at the fire, letting the slow disappearance of all good humor from his face be Charlie's answer. The fire crackled, and thankfully they weren't alone in the woods—one of the elderly wolves got distracted wanting to tell stories of their own youth in B'ville, and soon enough the slight pause was forgotten by everyone.

Almost everyone.

By around 2:30 a.m. they decided to call it a night, when Charlie was starting to flag and the werewolves looked ready to pack it in. He'd known Lorenzo would be wide awake, but he was a little surprised to be getting tired faster than the elderly wolves. "Don't you know? You need less sleep as you get older," Kenny told him. "Plus, we like to nap during the day."

Charlie laughed in Lorenzo's car, thinking of the group of elderly wolves napping in a sunny clearing in the middle of the afternoon. "What?" Lorenzo asked.

"I loved them," Charlie said. "I want to go visit them once a week."

"Ugh," Lorenzo said, though his annoyance seemed tinged with amusement.

"You know, you really were the perfect person for me to run into for my project," Charlie told him. "You've worked all these odd jobs for other supernatural creatures, so you know everyone."

The smile he thought he'd seen vanished from Lorenzo's face. Somehow, he'd hit a sore spot again. He was starting to think that Lorenzo had a lot of those. It'd probably be best to let the rest of the drive pass in silence.

But this wasn't the Lorenzo he'd known five years ago. He wasn't trying to get out of some awkward small talk at a party—he was actually interested in why Lorenzo might be upset. Trying to sound casual, Charlie said, "I'm surprised you have to do these sorts of jobs for cash. I thought vampires were all, y'know."

"Rich?" Lorenzo asked.

"I—I dunno," Charlie said. "Isn't there a thing with like . . . compound interest?"

"You should stop making assumptions like that."

"You're right," Charlie said after a moment. "I'm sorry. I really am learning a lot from you."

Lorenzo seemed mollified by that. "So," Charlie said, "Do you do these jobs for the cash, or is it something else?"

"Like what?"

"I don't know." He shrugged. "A sense of community?"

"Community?" Lorenzo asked, as his face darkened.

"Yeah, the—the supernatural community," Charlie said uncertainly.

"It's not a community," Lorenzo said flatly. "Werewolves, vampires, fae—we don't have anything in common. Even vampires barely have anything in common with each other. I do these jobs because—" He stopped abruptly.

"Why?" Charlie asked.

"For the cash," Lorenzo said gruffly. "As you said."

That was clearly bullshit, but Charlie said nothing. This wasn't the Lorenzo of five years ago; this was his Lorenzo, and Charlie didn't want any of those sore spots to become a bruise.

Chapter 10

Tensions always ran high in Lorenzo's apartment on game nights. Rachel organized them and brought a rotating group of her friends, most of whom took the whole thing far too seriously. As a vampire, Lorenzo was naturally skilled at games of wit against humans and other lesser beings, so he enjoyed the gatherings. He was less pleased when Charlie showed up to the latest one.

"It's about betrayal," Rachel's friend was explaining as Charlie listened raptly. He was wearing a pair of dark blue glasses that made his skin glow, and he looked like he'd shaved just before coming over, like his skin would be damp and just the slightest bit rough. "We're all loyal knights, but one of us is lying—he's betraying the group."

"Got it," Charlie said, eyeing the cards and tokens.

"Why did you even invite him?" Lorenzo asked the room at large. Rachel was deep in strategy talks with a friend and didn't respond; Maggie, who was counting out everyone's game pieces, said, "Hush."

He supposed he couldn't complain—he was the one who'd subjected them all to Charlie in the first place. He was also the one who'd cemented the unfortunate situation by losing that foolish bet. For now, he was stuck; he'd have to set aside his grand plans for vengeance until he'd fulfilled the terms of their agreement. No matter how grating it was.

Predictably, Charlie had already won everyone over, carousing with Rachel's friends as if he'd known them for years. "Stop pretending you hate this," Charlie told Lorenzo amiably. "I know you can't wait to somehow murder me in this game."

"Only if you're the traitor," Lorenzo said equanimously.

"No mercy," Charlie said with a small, private grin. Lorenzo wanted to slap him. He wanted to lick his neck. Maybe grab him by the throat and watch his pulse flutter.

He caught Maggie looking at him, her rugged features pulled into a small smile. He glowered at her. She bit down on both lips.

"Let's get started," she said to the group. "Everyone put their tokens in for the first vote."

Things went decently with the game—in a satisfying turn of events, Charlie was a terrible player—until Isolde came home. She didn't make much noise or greet any of them, but every head still turned in her direction as she crossed by. Except Rachel, who scowled at the rest of them.

One of Rachel's friends—an orc who Lorenzo thought was named Kevin—called out to her, ignoring Rachel's forbidding glare. "Hi!"

"Hello," Isolde said placidly. She gazed at the table where the game was laid out and said, "What are you doing?"

"Playing a game," Kevin said. "Want to play with us?"

Isolde paused for a moment, then narrowed her eyes at him.

"Why are you propositioning me if you're in a relationship with her?"

She was referring to the orc's girlfriend, a very pretty young wraith sitting next to him, whose jaw dropped at Isolde's matter-of-fact pronouncement. Kevin sputtered by way of reply. "I'm—I'm not propositioning you!"

"Your lust is obvious," Isolde said quite calmly.

The orc looked frantically at his girlfriend, whose pitch-black eyes were rapidly filling with hurt. "Um, I really wasn't—"

"You'll have to excuse Isolde," Rachel jumped in. "She's **not** house-trained."

Isolde turned on Rachel icily. "Are you comparing me to a dog?"

"I was comparing you to a horse," Rachel said with a cocky smile, though it faltered after a moment. "A . . . pet horse that's . . . house-trained."

"I—I wasn't hitting on you!" Kevin insisted. "I just thought you might like to play with us."

"I can see it within you. This human form I have taken on is, for some reason, incredibly appealing. You lust after it, as do you, you, and you. Not you," Isolde said, indicating each of Rachel's friends one by one. "And you," she added, nodding at a man across the table whose head was on fire. "Though you feel incredibly conflicted about it because up until now you've only experienced attraction to men." She shook her head, seeming almost disgusted. "Humans are so bizarre."

"Okay, you can't do this shit." Rachel stood, making her chair scrape loudly. Her friends were shifting uncomfortably, exchanging anxious looks.

"Do what?"

"Read people!"

"Hey!" Kevin objected, indignantly.

"Say creepy things," Rachel corrected herself, her voice steely.

"I—okay, her human form is—whatever," Kevin admitted, pleading mostly to his girlfriend. "But I wasn't hitting on her!"

The wraith let out a wounded sob and ran out of the room crying. Kevin followed swiftly after her. Isolde watched them go and then said, curiously, "Huh."

"Huh?" Rachel demanded. "You caused that, and all you've got is *huh*?"

"I caused nothing," Isolde said.

"You really don't see what an unbelievably self-righteous—"

Before Rachel could land on a noun, Charlie jumped in. "Hey, why don't we all cool down for a second?"

"Cool down?" Rachel seethed. "She's being creepy. She needs to back the hell off."

"I am not creepy," Isolde said. "I know who is pure and who is not. It is my very essence."

"Fucking—stipulated," Rachel said. "But—"

Isolde had already turned to address Lorenzo. "You are a vampire and thus by your very nature you are carnally deviant. Also, you were unchaste even before you became a vampire, and you continued your sensual depravity once turned. Were I in my true form, you would never be able to detect me."

A long pause followed. Rachel was the first to recover. "What the hell is your problem?"

"It is true," Lorenzo added.

"Rachel," one of her remaining friends was saying in a pained tone of voice, "it's fine."

"No, it's not fine," Rachel started, but Isolde cut her off once more.

"You have indulged in human sin," she told Maggie, "but it has been so long since then that, by the standards of my people, you would be considered pure once more."

"Alright!" Maggie said, pumping her fist happily.

"Stop it," Rachel snapped, her dark gaze fixed on Isolde. "You can't say things like that."

"I came here to live among other supernatural creatures so I would not have to conceal my true nature," Isolde said.

"Maybe you should conceal it."

"Whoa whoa whoa, let's all take a second, okay?" Charlie said. Lorenzo watched in surprise as he stood from the table, walking toward Rachel and Isolde with his arms outstretched. "Whatever your . . . true natures, you are roommates, so—let's all calm down and talk this out."

"I do not wish to talk," Isolde spat, as Rachel yelled something similar over her.

"Well I don't know if you've heard, but I'm actually writing a thesis on supernatural relationships," Charlie said, "so I'm kind of an expert here. Please, just try."

After an uneasy pause, Rachel and Isolde both backed away from each other and waited grudgingly for him to continue. "So," Charlie started, "it sounds like what we need here is a compromise about topics we can agree to discuss and what's off-limits."

"I don't wish to compromise," Isolde said.

"Me neither," Rachel said. "Because I'm right."

"Well, everyone *thinks* they're right," Charlie said with a chuckle.

Rachel glared at him. "Who do you think is right?"

Charlie gaped for a moment. "Well, I—"

"She has to respect everyone else who lives here," Rachel spat.

"You have no respect for me or my kind," Isolde shot back.

"What if," Charlie said, "we agreed that—Isolde is new to human society, so we could cut her a bit of slack when it comes to social graces—"

Rachel started to object, while Isolde spoke over her. "I don't want or need your slack," she said sharply.

"Great," Rachel said, baring her teeth at Isolde *and* Charlie. "Then here's your first lesson on *social graces*: no one wants to talk about their purity, ever! Human or otherwise."

"You," Isolde intoned, staring her down. "*You* have voluntarily chosen to give yourself over to a malevolent poltergeist, a creature of pure filth from which I can detect a distinctly violent energy."

Rachel crossed her arms. "I thought you could only detect sex things."

"Its violent urges are carnal in nature. You crave bondage and brutality and blood," Isolde said, unblinking. "But they are not the only impurities staining your soul."

Rachel went white, her jaw clenching.

"Hey, uh, maybe we should just head out," one of her friends said in a desperate sort of way.

"No, *she* should leave," Rachel spat back. "She's the one upsetting everyone. You can't talk to people like that."

"I am not a person," Isolde replied, her own flinty composure starting to crack. If he wasn't mistaken, Lorenzo thought he could see two spots of faint blue rising in her cheeks.

"That," Rachel bit out, "is obvious."

"Y'know, Rachel," Maggie said, "you're the one who voted for Isolde. I wanted that gremlin guy to move in."

Isolde stared at Maggie coldly, as a dawning look of horror covered Maggie's face. "I—no—I *love* that you're here," she said. "I'm just saying, Rachel, y'know, that she—that you—"

Rachel looked from Maggie to Charlie back to Isolde, her face darkening; then she took a step back from the table and roared up at the ceiling—a painful burst of noise that made everyone flinch and rattled the game pieces. In the next moment she shook her shoulders and shed what looked like a full-body suit—a sort of mystical snakeskin—shimmering, translucent purple ephemera that fell off her like thick, gelatinous dust.

When she was done, she stormed off to her room. Isolde glided away to hers, as Maggie ran after her, shouting, "Isolde!"

There was a near-simultaneous slamming of doors, followed by a long, quiet moment. "Wow," Charlie said, sitting down slowly. "I made that situation a hundred percent worse."

He looked crestfallen. And it occurred to Lorenzo, for the first time, that when Charlie meddled in other people's lives like this, he was actually trying to help.

It was enough to prompt him to be kind. "No," Lorenzo told him. "Fifty percent, at most."

Charlie peered at the floor where the purple cloud Rachel had left behind was still hovering, glinting in the light. "What's this stuff Rachel . . . shed?"

"Ectoplasm," Lorenzo said. "Don't touch it."

Charlie shrunk back. "Is it toxic?"

"Probably."

"Probably?"

"Magic works off intent," Lorenzo said. "And Rachel was very upset. I wouldn't touch it."

"Well," Charlie said, sighing. "I guess we can't have a two-person game night."

"I suppose not," Lorenzo said.

It wasn't until they'd said it aloud that it seemed to strike both of them that everyone else in the room had gone. Their eyes met for a loaded moment.

"Okay, well—" Charlie said, as Lorenzo chimed in with "Yes, goodnight." They both stood, and Lorenzo busied himself with cleaning up the game so he didn't have to watch Charlie leave.

He turned back just before he'd reached the door. "Oh, hey—are we still on for that thing tomorrow night? You finally found me some witches?"

Lorenzo had almost forgotten. He was seeing a lot of Charlie these days, and it was starting to feel natural in a way he didn't want to examine. "Yes," he said. "We are."

"Great," Charlie said with a wide smile. Lorenzo's lifeless stomach fluttered. "Can't wait."

He smiled again as he left. Lorenzo only relaxed when he was gone, and realized when he opened his hand that he was still holding a rumpled card that said *LIAR*.

From: fliparip@microsoft.net
To: wiseoldcrone@midnight.com
Date: Feb 26, 9:08 AM
Subject: [Anon Please] House-Flipping

Dear Crone,

I own a house-flipping company: I mostly handle the
financials and sales aspects, and my business partner han-
dles the construction and is also a medium who can speak
with the dead. Lately business has been booming—we've
been on this amazing streak of getting properties at
rock-bottom prices. But when I mentioned this run of
luck to my partner, he reacted oddly—almost like he felt
guilty about it. I later heard from one of the parties we
purchased a home from that the only reason it went for so
little was that every time tours came through, there was
moaning in the walls and dismembered arms trying to
crawl out of the toilet in the powder room. I didn't notice
anything strange on our walk-through, but now I'm wondering if my partner might have been using his abilities to
direct ghosts to these houses and get them for us for a
bargain. Should I confront him with my suspicions?

Sincerely,
Ghost Flipper

From: rseamus92@jmail.com
To: wiseoldcrone@midnight.com
Date: April 5, 1:13 PM
Subject: Leprechaun Litmus

Dear Wise Old Crone,

This is probably a stupid question, but—how can you
tell if you're *really* a mystical creature? I know it's technically all about bloodlines, and my mom's family are
leprechauns (my dad's are human), but I have barely any
magic, and I do "pass" as human. I still think of myself
as half-leprechaun though—except that when I say that
around my mom's family, they get really offended. I know
leprechauns have to deal with a ton of prejudice and
bullshit that I've never had to. But I don't want to just call
myself a human when I know that's not true. But maybe
it is, in every way that counts? How do you know if you're
paranormal "enough"?

Sincerely,
Hearts, Stars, and Questions

Wise Old Crone

How Do I Know My Own Feelings?
My friend is marrying into a great pack, but I want her to howl at me.

June 2

Dear Crone,

My best friend "Xara" and I have been BFFs our whole lives—we literally grew up across the street from each other, and our parents' photo albums are full of pictures of us both as toddlers running around playing together. We went to high school together, made the same fashion mistakes, went through all the millennial traumas together, and still hang out almost every night to this day.

A few months ago Xara got engaged to a great guy who I totally get along with. Her family's really excited about it because he's a werewolf just like she is, so I guess that's great for the pack or whatever. But ever since Xara got engaged, I see so much less of her than I'm used to, and it's really bugging me. I get that wedding planning is a lot of work (especially when you're dealing with moon phases and blood feuds between packs). But it's like she's never emotionally available anymore—all our hangouts are quick catch-ups, not the all-night deep talks we used to have. It feels like the Xara I have now is just a pale imitation of the woman I used to have in my life.

And all this emotion that's being stirred up has me wondering if maybe my feelings for Xara are stronger than friendship. The thought of her moving in with her fiancé and starting a family with him makes me sick. I can't stop thinking about her. All I want to do is spend the rest of my life with Xara, just the way we've always been. Does it sound like my feelings are romantic, or is this normal for friendship? And if it is love, what do I do? Beg her to leave her fiancé? Tell her that I want to be the one she chases through the woods under the moonlight? I just don't know.

Sincerely,
Wife or Longing Friend?

Dear WOLF,

If you're asking the Crone, then yes, your feelings sound romantic—you're thinking about running away with Xara, whether you've admitted that to yourself or not. You obviously care about her deeply, and that's why I'm going to say: I think you should swallow your feelings, and not tell her.

I can understand what you're going through. Sometimes our feelings change slowly, but sometimes it takes a major shock, like an engagement, to wake us up to what was there all along. You may have felt this way about Xara since your childhood together, and it took her meeting this wolf to make you see what was right in front of you.

But you can't be careless with this. You didn't mention in your letter how Xara feels about all of this. Have you talked to her about it? Is she happy in her relationship? How is she feeling about your sense of loss?

Xara could be in a good place right now, and if you're not absolutely sure that she returns your feelings, you shouldn't cause trouble. If this is only happening on your end, it would be selfish to risk destabilizing what should be a happy time for her. No matter what she is to you, you're still her best friend.

I know it hurts to want what you shouldn't have. Be strong.

Sincerely,
Crone

Chapter 11

I thought we were going to meet some witches," Charlie said.

"She is a witch," Lorenzo replied. "More or less."

Charlie looked skeptically at the house Lorenzo had brought him to—a little white bungalow that had seen better days, with a neon pink palm reader sign in the window. "So—fortune tellers are witches?" he asked.

"In a manner of speaking."

"What does that mean?"

Lorenzo led him to the front door, looming over him the entire time. He'd started doing that lately, at these supernatural outings—moving around Charlie like his bodyguard, always close and connected. "Shh," he said, ringing the doorbell. "Don't be rude."

Charlie bit back a smile.

He tried to ignore the swell of guilt that accompanied it. He loved going on these outings with Lorenzo and learning about all these new communities—aside from being fun, it was extraordinarily helpful. He couldn't quite believe it, but *Wise Old*

Crone was still doing well; in fact, she'd been doing so well for so long now that he was actually starting to believe that he might have saved his job. Last week's column had even been popular enough that he'd gotten a congratulatory note from the new owners, with all the warmth and wit of something written by ChatGPT. Ava had sent him a separate message saying that he should come into the office to meet with them, to pump up their enthusiasm, maybe even try to persuade them to invest more in the column. He'd brushed her off.

As far as he was concerned, if the column was doing well, he should just keep doing what he'd been doing: touring Brookville's supernatural scene with Lorenzo and annoying the crap out of him the entire time. He had a sneaking suspicion that it wasn't just everything he was learning that was contributing to the column's success; it's that he was enjoying himself.

He just had to deal with the nagging guilt of his enormous lie. It wasn't even that enormous; it was a small lie, really. A minor detail about his . . . true life and intentions. But a small lie, nonetheless.

He had a feeling Lorenzo wouldn't see it that way.

He snuck a glance at Lorenzo as they waited at the door. He seemed as brooding as ever, but lately, Charlie had been wondering if that was all that was going on with him. He was so attentive on these outings, so ready to joust with Charlie. Maybe to flirt with him.

He didn't need to go there. He didn't even know if Lorenzo was into men.

Still, as they lingered on the doorstep, he couldn't help but eye him, wondering if the vibe he'd been getting was only on his end.

His thoughts were interrupted when the door opened,

revealing a small, stooped woman with an enormous cloud of curly black hair. She wore plain, comfy-looking black clothes, huge, colorful jewelry at her wrists and neck, and a face full of tropical-colored makeup. She could have been fifty or a hundred and fifty. "Lorenzo!" she cried in a husky, ravaged voice that immediately made Charlie like her. "Thank Satan you're here."

"Thank Satan?" Charlie asked Lorenzo pointedly.

Lorenzo had a look of weary resignation. "Hello, Roberta."

"And this is the human companion you mentioned? Charmed," she said, holding a hand out to Charlie. Her long acrylic nails had Ouija symbols inked onto them.

"Nice to meet you," he said. "Thank you for having us over."

"Thank me? Hah!" She beckoned them inside. "Your pal here's the one doing me a favor."

"Is he?" Charlie asked, staring at Lorenzo. He made a mental note to ask about the phrase *human companion* later.

They followed Roberta through her home to the dim, black-curtained room where she conducted her business. She offered them each a seat at a circular table with a crystal ball in the center. The room was decorated in the occult-glam style he would've expected—jewels and macabre artifacts, talismans and feathers and glitter. On the mantelpiece, in a place of pride, was a very old, very well-loved troll doll.

"I was thrilled when you called," Roberta was saying to Lorenzo. "This is going to tide me over nicely. We should make it a regular thing!"

"I told you," Lorenzo said firmly. "Just this once. And you have to answer Charlie's questions." In a faux aside, he added, "He can be quite annoying."

"Oh shush," Charlie told him. Turning to Roberta, he said, "So, uh, how do you two know each other?"

Roberta beat Lorenzo to the punch. "We go way back, Lorenzo and me! Of course I shouldn't say that about a vampire, I'll date myself." She laughed throatily at her own joke. "And I guess I have you to thank for Lorenzo's help tonight."

"Help? With what?"

"Oh, vampires are fantastic conduits."

"Conduits?"

"It's like a—a pulley and a lever," she explained. "I don't know shit about physics, but I know you rig up one of those contraptions and you can lift double, triple the weight, right?" Charlie nodded, unsure, and she continued: "Vampires are like that for those of us with the gift. They enhance," she said, with a meaningful waggle of her entire slight frame.

"Does it—does it hurt?" he asked. "Is it dangerous?" Lorenzo glanced at him, looking surprised and maybe even—touched?

"Not at all!" Roberta said. "It's like, ah—when you shine light through a prism and it becomes a rainbow. Don't hurt the prism. But you and me, we get all those gorgeous colors."

Lorenzo was glaring at her. "Okay," Charlie said slowly. He still felt like he was missing something—namely, why Lorenzo seemed so reluctant to help this woman. "And what—I mean—what is he going to enhance, exactly?"

"Her ability to scam people," Lorenzo said flatly.

"Hey, whoa, hey, oh!" Roberta protested, throwing both hands in the air. "I don't scam. I provide a service."

"She's a hustler."

"Excuse you," she snapped back. "I am a bona fide medium. I speak to the dead."

"I'm confused," Charlie said. "Are you—do you have magic?"

"In spades, doll," Roberta said with a toothy smile.

"She is a very weak medium," Lorenzo retorted. Roberta

gasped, but he continued on: "And rather than use what little gift she has to make legitimate readings and communications with the dead, she—"

"I make it work," Roberta cut him off. "Look, you think that every time someone comes in here wanting to talk to their great-aunt Patsy, she's actually in the room with us? What kind of luck would that be? Most of the dead, they've moved on, they're at peace. So I—"

"You lie," Lorenzo said flatly. Charlie shifted, uncomfortable.

"I tell people that their beloved friends, their lovers, their pets—that they all knew in the end that they were loved," Roberta said. "That all their arguments were settled and all their grudges gone, and that they're at peace. That they can move on."

"You make things up," Lorenzo said, unimpressed.

"Not anymore." She held her hand out to Lorenzo, but still he hesitated. To Charlie, Roberta said, "One night with this one, and with my powers enhanced, I actually *can* reach all of my regulars' loved ones. I can get them real answers."

"And you'll use that to keep them on the hook for more appointments and more fees," Lorenzo said, shaking his head. "More scams."

She sat forward, quirking an eyebrow. "You want me to answer the kid's questions or what?"

Suddenly understanding, Charlie said, "You couldn't find any other witches for us to talk to."

"Oh, of course not," Roberta answered for him. "Most witches hate vampires. They're predators, after all, and witches think they're the most human humans."

"You're not a fan?"

She shrugged, making a noncommittal hand gesture. "Eh.

Technically, I am a witch. Which means our deal's still on," she added, threateningly, to Lorenzo.

"What does that mean, technically?" Charlie asked.

"People have all different kinds of magic," she said. "Some are your more traditional types. Some, like me, can do something else."

"So—can all witches communicate with the, um—beyond?" he asked.

"No," she said. "Some might have a bit of the Sight, but most can't do it at all."

"Can you do other magic?"

"Some."

"Can I see?"

"Ah ah ah!" she tutted at him, offering her hand once again to Lorenzo. A wicked smile curved her lips. "Time to pay the piper."

Lorenzo sighed and put his hand in hers. They both closed their eyes.

In the middle of the table, the crystal ball started thrumming. Charlie looked at it, expecting it to maybe start glowing or flashing visions of the dead, but then it—it expanded. It was as if the whole room became subsumed by the crystal, flinging them into a warped surreality, with the black cloth walls of the room becoming an endless starry night.

Across from him, Roberta and Lorenzo seemed to be sitting still, but Charlie could suddenly hear Roberta's voice. "Oh, fabulous!" she shouted. There was a scratching noise, like a pen on a piece of paper, but as far as Charlie could see, her lips and hands were still. "Lemme get this down. One at a time, dolls, one at a time."

Charlie tried to breathe normally, not sure if he couldn't

move or just didn't want to. He felt a bit like he'd taken a Klonopin—like he was freaking out somewhere deep down, but it'd all been dampened. It was kind of like being on a lazy river in space.

And when he looked at Lorenzo, he found Lorenzo looking back at him. He felt any remaining traces of his panic melt away. Lorenzo was right there.

He wasn't sure if Lorenzo was affected by the spell too—if being the conduit for it exempted him somehow—but he had a feeling that he was. He seemed as diffuse and disarmed as Charlie, staring back at him steadily without trying to hide or play it off. Like he'd forgotten to pretend to be grumpy.

His soft brown eyes anchored Charlie in the strange, crystalline dream. It made his chest unlatch, let air rush into his lungs. Lorenzo was here.

"Hang on, hang on," Roberta was saying. "You'll all get your turn. Oh sweet Satan, this is not gonna work—oh *shit*—"

A cloudy pressure seemed to fill the room, and then there was a horrible shrieking noise. Charlie flinched back as something—the crystal ball, he realized a moment later—exploded.

He came back to reality with his heart pounding and small but sharp pains all over his face and arms. The warped world of the crystal ball was gone, and Roberta was muttering as she poked through a heap of glass shards on the table, as if she were looking for something.

Lorenzo, though, leapt to his feet and was at Charlie's side instantly. "Are you alright?" he demanded, pulling Charlie's arms back from his face gently.

Lorenzo's face was covered in small cuts and abrasions, but as Charlie watched, they started to knit back together seamlessly. "Um," he said.

"You have injured Charlie," Lorenzo shouted at Roberta. "How dare you!"

Charlie touched his face, which felt painfully raw, and found blood on his fingertips. And now that he was looking more closely, he could see small, shallow cuts all over his arms and the back of his hands.

"Oh don't worry, you big lump," Roberta said, though she was wearing a worried frown that belied her breezy tone. "Actually, y'know what, this is perfect—a great chance for me to show you my witchy woo. And vampires are great conduits for healing spells."

She held a hand out to Lorenzo, who glared at her for a moment. Roberta's eyebrows flew upward. "You want me to heal him or not?"

With a violent scowl, Lorenzo threw himself back into his chair and grabbed Roberta's hand. She gestured with their clasped hands at Charlie. "You gotta touch him," she said. "Right there, where he's hurt."

For the first time, it occurred to Charlie that he was bleeding in front of a vampire. But Lorenzo didn't look crazed or blood-hungry—his eyes, when he looked at Charlie, were tentative; his touch, when he took Charlie's tender, abraded hand in his, was gentle.

Charlie swallowed and closed his eyes.

At first he felt nothing. Then slowly a thick, pleasant heaviness settled over him, not unlike the sensation of drifting right before falling asleep. He assumed this must be what magic felt like.

After a moment, though, the feeling prickled and became more specific—became, somehow, an intangible impression of . . . Lorenzo. It was as if, even with his eyes closed, even with the very real sensation of Lorenzo's palm clasping his own steadily, he could also feel some shadow version of Lorenzo moving his hand, drifting his fingers over the gash on Charlie's knuckles. He felt a whisper of heat where this shadow Lorenzo touched him, and then a coarse, verdant sensation that felt like healing.

He shivered.

The dream Lorenzo ran his hands over Charlie's forearms, the backs of his hands, and a small cut on his jaw, leaving heat and perfection in his wake. Charlie struggled to keep his breathing steady. "Put your hand there—near his forehead," he dimly heard Roberta say.

Lorenzo's fingers brushed lightly over Charlie's temples, and in his trancelike, enchanted state, Charlie felt that warmth again, that luscious rightness. He opened his eyes and looked at Lorenzo, the pain on his face drifting away like steam. Lorenzo was still cradling his head in his palm. Charlie licked his lips and put a hand on Lorenzo's chest.

And then Charlie blinked his eyes open for real. Lorenzo was sitting across from him, their only contact his fingertips lightly touching Charlie's forehead. The rest had been—a dream? A vision?

He had no idea, but Lorenzo didn't meet his eye as he struggled to understand.

"There, see?" Roberta said, crossing her arms as she sat back in satisfaction. "Told you I was a real witch."

Chapter 12

Lorenzo was making a cocktail when Charlie accosted him in the kitchen, blurting without any preamble: "So I—I heard about something."

Lorenzo sighed. He hadn't actually been aware that Charlie was here at his apartment, but Maggie and Rachel invited him over so often now that he couldn't really be surprised. "Heard about what?"

Charlie bit his lip and stared at him for a moment. "What?" Lorenzo asked, his trepidation rising.

Charlie said, "Remember when Dylan was telling us about those vampire parties he's worked?"

Lorenzo bent under the counter and found a miniature bottle of gin. He cracked it open and dumped the entire thing into his tumbler of blood. "Yes," he said.

Charlie was watching him carefully. "You knew about those? About—the other vampires living here, in Brookville?"

Lorenzo shrugged, stirring his cocktail.

THIRSTY 133

"Okay, well—" Charlie continued, "There's apparently this, like, big deal vampire . . ." He paused to read the name off his phone. "Sebastian St. Tour de Sang."

Lorenzo stifled an annoyed noise in the back of his throat. "Oh, him."

"You know him?" Charlie said. "How come you never said anything?"

Lorenzo shrugged again.

"Well," Charlie said, "I found out that he's having this big party tomorrow night, and—I think we should go."

"It's not a good idea."

"I knew you were going to say that," Charlie said, wheedling. "But really. We've gone to werewolf prom, we've gone to the free clinic, we survived an explosion of crystal ball energy— how bad could this be?"

"Bad."

"How bad?"

Lorenzo searched for the right words for a few moments, before deciding that the unvarnished truth would have to do. "They are dicks."

Charlie blinked. "They're . . . okay," he said slowly. "But—so what?"

"So I don't think they'll answer your questions," Lorenzo said, sipping his drink. "Most vampires are very private."

"You answer my questions," Charlie said with a small grin.

"You entrapped me," Lorenzo said as Charlie's grin widened. "Besides," he added, trying not to sound too personally invested in the question, "why do you need to talk to other vampires for your thesis when you have me?"

Charlie cocked his head to the side, his expression softening.

"I can't base my whole project on information from just one vampire—however helpful he's been. I need to talk to lots of different people to get a good cross section, including other vampires."

Charlie's unfortunately sound reasoning aside, Lorenzo had no desire to see Sebastian or anyone who'd be at his party. And the thought of Charlie hanging around him like some eager, easily impressed puppy made him almost sick to his stomach.

Charlie read all that on his face. "Fine," he said, "I'll go on my own."

"No," Lorenzo said quickly, "don't do that."

"Why not?"

"I told you, they're . . . it could be dangerous."

Charlie rolled his eyes. "Vampires are out in the open now," he said. "They can't just murder anyone who comes to talk to them."

"Yes, because humans never murder each other," Lorenzo said.

Charlie sighed. "Then come with me," he said. "Be my vampire bodyguard."

"No," Lorenzo said. "And you shouldn't go either. Hey," he said, as Charlie started to turn away, and before thinking about it, he got a hold of Charlie's hand—just a few of his fingers, really—to keep him there.

Charlie looked back at him, eyes wide, and Lorenzo dropped his hand just as quickly. At least he had his attention now. "It's dangerous," he said again, his voice low. "I'll answer any vampire questions you could have, just—don't go to that party."

Charlie chewed on his lip, his amber eyes dark. "Okay," he told Lorenzo.

Lorenzo didn't buy it for a second.

And so the next night he headed up to Brookville's tiny, uber-wealthy neighborhood, where Sebastian had renovated what must've been a ten-million-dollar town house. Parking was of course a nightmare. He waited across the street, listening in irritation to the music dimly filtering out from the mansion's many windows. And sure enough, just past midnight, Charlie showed up.

Lorenzo stepped out of the shadows as he approached, pleased with the look of shock on Charlie's face. "Lorenzo?" Charlie said, sounding breathless. "What—have you been following me?"

"No, I waited for you here," Lorenzo said. He glanced meaningfully at the town house. "At the place where you said you wouldn't go."

"Oh," Charlie said, deflating slightly.

"Luckily for you, you are a terrible liar," Lorenzo added. Charlie blushed, looking away. "Let's go."

"Wait," Charlie said.

As he took a step back toward the house, three more men approached from the other direction, stumbling over each other with the kind of giddy incoherence of a party already in progress. When he realized who they were, Lorenzo stiffened.

By then, of course, it was too late. "Hey man," one of them called, laughter in his voice, as they drew close enough to recognize him. "Aren't you, like . . . a vampire?"

Lorenzo grit his teeth and turned to face them. It was a clique of Sebastian's flunkies—younger vampires he'd seen in town occasionally and spoken to once or twice. They had that dirty boyish vibe a lot of rich white vampires had—unbothered and well financed; all wellness and no showers.

The one who'd recognized him threw his hair out of his face to get a closer look, while one of the others protested drunkenly. "*He* is? No way."

"No, he is, he really is," the first one said, amusing himself. "He lives here. You live here, right? In Brookville?"

He'd encountered this same pack outside a supermarket a few months ago. "Yes," Lorenzo said stiffly. "We've run into each other."

"Oh, I'm so sorry," the vampire said, mock apologetic and formal, as the others giggled. "Good to see you again, sir."

Charlie whispered, "You know these guys?"

Still laughing, the vampire added, "Don't you, like, live with a leprechaun or something?"

The other vampires snorted. Charlie cocked his head and blinked at them. "Yeah, and I heard you run with the werewolves," the vampire said, grinning broadly. "No, wait, you live with a troll. A she-troll! That's fun."

The vampires were hiccupping with laughter now. Before Lorenzo could think of something to say, Charlie surged forward at his side and offered his hand enthusiastically. "Hi!"

The giggles died away as the vampires took in Charlie with withering apathy. "This is your human?"

"We"—*were about to leave*, had been what Lorenzo was going to say, but Charlie jumped in again.

"Actually, I'm a grad student," he said. He'd drawn himself up, polished and charming, though the vampires still stared at him with open contempt. "I'm studying supernatural creatures, and I heard Mr. St. Tour de Sang was throwing a party, so I thought it might be a good chance to introduce myself and ask him some questions."

One of the vampires snorted in disdain. "He's not here."

"He's not?" Charlie asked.

"It's Cannes," said the first one, as if it were sort of embarrassing that they'd forgotten. "Where do you think he is?"

"He has houses all over the world," another added. "He doesn't actually *live* in Brookville."

"That would be pathetic," said the third, as they all stared at Lorenzo.

"Do *you* guys live here?" Charlie asked.

"We're just lair-sitting," the first one said. "And, y'know, drinking people, and taking some meetings about start-up ideas."

"Could I talk to you for my paper?" Charlie asked, polite and undeterred. "Or, maybe set up a time that I could meet with Mr. St. Tour de Sang when he's back?"

"Um, no," the first one said.

"I'll pass," said another.

"Lorenzo, your human is annoying," the last one said. "You should take care of that."

Lorenzo didn't like the look in their eyes as they stared at Charlie—not hungry, just frighteningly bored. "We were just going," he said, hustling Charlie backward with an arm around his waist. "Goodbye."

Cruel laughter followed them down a small alley alongside Sebastian's house. As soon as he was confident they were out of the vampires' earshot, Lorenzo whipped Charlie around to face him. "What was that?"

Charlie seemed entirely unbothered by the encounter,

straightening his shirt where Lorenzo had mussed it. "Well, those guys were dicks," he said, "but I figured I could still get something out of it, or try to."

"You're lucky your throat is still connected to the rest of your neck," Lorenzo hissed.

"So those are the vampire cool kids, huh?" Charlie mused. "Y'know what's pathetic? Being however many centuries old they are and still acting like you're in high school."

Lorenzo felt some of his churning unease melt away. "I suppose."

"Hey, look at that," Charlie said, gesturing to the side of the house. It was mostly covered in ivy, and the alley was dark, but just where Charlie was pointing, he could make out a sliver of light and a strain of music.

"It looks like a back entrance," Charlie said, stepping closer. "A kitchen or something."

"So what?"

"So, let's sneak in!" Charlie said, grinning excitedly.

"What?" Lorenzo demanded.

"It's a big party, they won't notice us!" he said. "We can drink their booze, and, I don't know—sneak into Sebastian's room and, like, rub garlic on his sheets or something."

"That's . . . we're not actually allergic to garlic," Lorenzo said.

"Then we can steal something. Or break something. C'mon," Charlie said, taking a step closer to Lorenzo and looking up at him with laughter and challenge in his eyes. "Those guys want to act like high schoolers—fine. Let's prank them!"

This was the wonderful inverse of what Lorenzo often thought of as Charlie's Mean Girl tendencies; he may have been sly and cutting, but Lorenzo did not mind having Charlie's ruthlessness at his disposal.

Lorenzo stared back down at Charlie. He was intoxicating like this, fizzing over with warmth and excitement. The way their eyes met felt just like a hand slipping into his, conspiratorial and warm. He wondered what would happen if they actually touched.

Lorenzo wasn't sure how to keep him at bay.

"Five minutes," he said fervently.

Charlie made an excited sort of *yip*, and they crept toward the door.

Inside, the music was painfully loud, and Lorenzo frankly found most music from this millennium to be grating at best. The house was stately and moneyed, but the party was cheap—colored lights splashed along the walls, cups and cigarettes littering every surface, and vampires feeding out in the open. Thankfully, it at least appeared to be consensual.

"Wow," Charlie shouted at him over the music as they explored a few different rooms. "It's so . . ."

"What?"

They passed a hallway where a vampire was feeding on a topless woman as she chugged a bottle of champagne. "So . . . cliché," Charlie said.

Lorenzo laughed. "Really?"

"Yeah," Charlie said. They stumbled out of the path of a drunk man who was barreling toward them, and found a place to sit at the foot of an enormous staircase. "Your and Maggie and Rachel's parties are way cooler than this."

That was a ridiculous thing to say, but pleasantly so. Charlie found an unopened seltzer on the floor and cracked it open, taking a sip as they took in the atmosphere of the party.

"So are all these people going to become vampires?" he asked, gesturing to the humans around them in various states of being fed on. Most of them were cradling their vampire's heads in their hands, or urging them on in low voices. Lorenzo looked carefully for any humans who seemed as if they might be struggling or incapacitated, but he didn't spot any.

"Probably not," Lorenzo said.

"Probably?"

He shifted a little, not sure if he wanted to be looking at Charlie while he explained this. "A new vampire is made when a human and a vampire drink each other's blood," he said slowly. "But only when both the vampire and the human *want* them to be turned."

Charlie seemed to be drinking him up with his stare. "Right," he breathed. "Because, um . . . magic is intent, right?"

Lorenzo nodded.

"So if that's not the intent, the bite could just be to feed," Charlie mused, looking out over the party. "Or for fun," he added, turning back to Lorenzo.

He didn't think he was imagining the glint in Charlie's eyes. "Right?"

Lorenzo grunted. Charlie smiled and stood up, finishing his drink. Once he had, he cracked his back and took a look around the party. "Hmm," he said, before turning behind them to the rest of the staircase. "Why don't we go up there?"

A few steps up, a velvet rope hung with a sign reading *PRIVATE*. Lorenzo pointed at it.

"So what?" Charlie said, waggling his eyebrows. "That's why we're here, right?"

It was such a bad idea. "Two minutes," he stressed. They crept under the velvet rope and climbed the stairs.

The second level was as large as the first, but quiet and empty. They took a wild guess that Sebastian's suite was the one behind the massive, elaborately gilded doors at the end of the hallway. Lorenzo had Charlie wait while he listened inside, using his sharper hearing to make sure that no one else was there, but the room was silent. They ventured inside hesitantly.

Charlie snorted out a laugh as soon as they made it past the threshold. The room was quite . . . bold, decorated in shiny black wood, red velvet, and neon. There was a collection of artwork leaning against one wall, ornate paintings in gold frames next to unframed modern art. And there were bloodstains on almost every surface.

"Oh my god," Charlie wheezed. "This is so stupid."

Lorenzo examined a dresser that had several objets d'art displayed on top, including a katana and what looked like a pair of engraved metal fang tips. "You think so?"

"It's so cringe!" Charlie said, laughing as he picked up a black and white photograph of a naked woman covered in blood. "It's like a set from *Riverdale*. It's not even worth trashing."

Lorenzo was about to respond when he heard a sound in the hallway. He gestured to Charlie, who looked confused and then panicked, as a gruff voice from outside called, "Is someone in there?"

Charlie's eyes widened, and Lorenzo ran to him, pushing him back against the far wall. "This area is off-limits!" the voice called, getting closer.

He'd reach the door in a moment. They weren't even supposed to be in this house, much less this room. And Lorenzo did not want Charlie getting in trouble at a party filled with vampires. Especially these vampires.

Footsteps approached, and Lorenzo turned around, ready to shield Charlie from whatever was coming their way.

Then he felt a hand on his shoulder—Charlie turning him back around, pulling him closer. "Quick," he said urgently. "Pretend we're—"

He didn't get a chance to finish before the door swung open. Instead, Charlie just pulled Lorenzo roughly against him, hands fisted in Lorenzo's shirt, and threw his head to the side, baring his neck. Lorenzo's hands came to cradle his head and the small of his back instinctively, and with Lorenzo crowding him back against the wall, his head buried in Charlie's neck, he knew exactly what they looked like: a vampire and a human locked in a passionate bite.

He did not actually bite Charlie. He brought his mouth down to Charlie's neck, burrowed his face into the crook of Charlie's throat, and kept his lips about an inch away from his skin. But with the way they were pressed together, their bodies entwined and wracked with tension, no one would be able to tell the difference.

Charlie was panting out into the room, his pulse pounding wildly in his throat. His scent, so thick and close now, was rapidly fogging up Lorenzo's ability to focus. Charlie had gasped and arched into him when Lorenzo grabbed him, wrapping his arms around Lorenzo's shoulders and digging his nails in. That would help sell it, as would the way Lorenzo growled and ground himself against Charlie.

But it wasn't real. That's what Lorenzo had to hold on to, as he tried to ignore the sweet warmth of Charlie's thin, delectable skin just a hair's breadth away from his lips. His pulse was right there, beat beat beating away, a delicious bass note to the sound of Charlie's frantic breath. And he could feel, in the way Charlie's muscles jumped under his hands, and the way Charlie clutched at him back, that he wanted it.

"*Guys*," someone said, with the irritated tone of having said it more than once.

Lorenzo pulled back and wiped his face, hiding the fact that there was no blood there. Charlie hastily grabbed his own neck, covering the nonexistent bite. "Yes?"

"This is an off-limits area," the guard explained wearily. He'd probably chased people out of here dozens of times before. "You want to get your bite on, do it downstairs."

"Oh, uh—very well," Lorenzo said shakily. "Come, human."

They made their way unsteadily down the grand staircase and back to the party.

Chapter 13

Charlie had been staying up so late with Lorenzo, he'd taken to sleeping in until one or two in the afternoon. So when his phone rang and rang and rang at 9:48 a.m. on the Sunday after the vampire party, he was jolted out of an otherwise deep sleep.

He picked up his phone and saw his dad's unamused face filling the screen, bobbing slightly as he paced around their family living room.

Panicking, Charlie hit ignore. But even as he dove back under the covers, he could tell it was too late; he was up, and after ten minutes of grumpy denial, he decided that he might as well have an early morning.

There were fewer emails waiting for him to get through— that was nice. He decided to go for a walk to take in the sunshine, mentally plotting a path to his favorite Mexican place for breakfast.

It was unsettling, as he walked, to realize how strange it all seemed—the sight of Brookville under the daylight. This was his hometown, and these were street corners he'd walked past hundreds of times; but they looked different now, crisp and warm and bright. It all looked different since he'd started spending so many of his hours with Lorenzo, under the moonlight.

If he lived a thousand years, he would never forget Lorenzo taking him into his arms last night, even if that was, unfortunately, the only way in which Charlie had been taken. The moment he'd realized that Lorenzo was going to go along with his ridiculous plan, the air had been knocked out of his lungs; and then Lorenzo had touched him, molded their bodies together, brought his fangs oh so close to Charlie's throat—and it was like a damn *Bridgerton* cover started playing. He would never forget the drag of Lorenzo's hands against his back, pulling him closer; the heat of Lorenzo's mouth; the dampness of his breath against his throat. He felt branded there. It was the worst kind of ache—the tendons of his shoulder felt tense and raw, the skin of his neck tender. Like he couldn't stop bracing himself for something that would never come.

He couldn't stop replaying it in his head, tormenting himself—the almost-bite. The bite that nearly was.

And he couldn't stop wondering—what would have come next, if it had been real?

He got an outdoor seat at El Varadero, and waited until the waiter had left after putting in his order before he succumbed to his shameful curiosity. Charlie pulled his phone out and searched—

Fuck. What was he supposed to search?

Dying with embarrassment, he tried vampire bite real :reddit

The first result read: My (M, 29) girlfriend (F, 351) won't bite me bc she hates the taste of aspartame, but I can't give up diet coke, I just can't

He sighed, and clicked to the next result.

HELLLLP!! I've been betrothed to the dark prince of the under-world against my will, what are my legal remedies ???

Vampires real or conspiracy theory

Oomfs said Hozier is a vamp, can anyone confirm?

Vampires sun real

Vampire bite kill?

What it vampire bite feels like?

That one at least seemed promising. He opened the replies.

go get bitten gurl! find out

Painful, I'd imagine.

Many predators secrete a chemical that makes their bites pain-less, or numbs their victim's flesh. I can only assume that vampires would have something similar, as evolutionarily . . .

He sighed, before his eye caught on a random reply that had only a handful of likes.

blissful

Suddenly the air was punched from his lungs, and he flipped his phone screen-down onto the table.

He had to get a grip on himself. He pulled his laptop out and started trying to get some work done. A Mexican restaurant in Brookville was a long way from a Manhattan coffee shop, but he should have been able to get some decent writing done here. The cobblestone streets were picturesque, the air soft and almost meditative. Charlie had always wondered how Brookville had become one of *those* small towns, the kind that had such a dis-tinctive life of its own. He may have resented its dreary familiar-ity just because it happened to be the place of his birth, but just like how New Yorkers could always tell when a TV show had actually been filmed in the city or when it was Vancouver, he felt like he'd always be able to recognize a street corner in Brookville.

And Lorenzo had been in this small town long before Charlie was even born, despite the fact that he'd always felt as if he was the local in their relationship. But he wasn't, not really. And Lorenzo hadn't reacted well the one time Charlie had tried to ask how he'd come to live here.

But that had been a while ago. Surely things were different now. Maybe he could ask again.

He was desperate to know.

He was startled out of his guilty lust haze by Ava DMing him. theres my rockstar!!! she said by way of greeting. burning up the charts! breaking the internet!!

Ava, he typed. I love the sentiment, but I hate every word you just said.

She sent him a tongue-out emoji and shared some files. here's your latest column back. love it!!! that letter was NUTS— and I want to see this hot guy hahaha

He rolled his eyes. Well, think of a horny headline.

She got back to him right away. let's brainstorm!

He sighed. I'm actually trying to get some work done on a new column.

boo! she wrote back to him. you re not allowed to be this crabby when youre almost literally rising phoenix-like from the ashes??!?! WOC is a hit!

Her dots were still going. He was about to put down his phone when she added: btw—when are you coming in to capitalize on it??

Coming in? he wrote back, his heart thumping.

to brag to the owners about what a fucking champ you are!! Ava wrote, as if this were obvious.

She was all sunshine and encouragement, but Charlie felt as if a coarse knot was forming in his chest.

She was right—*Wise Old Crone* was a hit. And as that reality started to sink in, so too did his guilt, which was becoming harder and harder to ignore.

Crone was a hit because of what he was doing with Lorenzo. What he was learning from Lorenzo. What he was taking from him, if one wanted to be uncharitable.

And why did he deserve charity? He was lying to Lorenzo. Scheming to profit from their relationship. Their friendship, whatever.

I'll find some time to come in, he wrote vaguely.

He slammed his computer shut as soon as he saw Ava drafting dots in reply. He didn't want to hear it.

He'd started to think about when he was going to come clean to Lorenzo. He had to eventually, right? If nothing else, the column's increasing popularity would make the secret harder to maintain. Oh, no one knew who the Crone was in real life, but every time his phone pinged with some sort of notification, he could feel the truth creeping in.

The sun started to smart on his neck as it crept further and further into the sky. He'd find a time to tell Lorenzo the truth, he thought—when he could tell him without making it all sound so terrible. Until then, he'd stick to the darkness.

From: pbarrone@jmail.com
To: wiseoldcrone@midnight.com
Date: May 3, 1:12 AM
Subject: Summer Wedding in Hell

Dear Crone,

Am I the only one who cannot follow wedding dress codes anymore? I've been invited to a commitment ceremony between two Litches of the Eastern Frozen Gate, and the dress code is Tortured Casual. What the hell does that mean?

Sincerely,
Die, Wedding Wear

From: lafftaff@ipmail.com
To: wiseoldcrone@midnight.com
Date: May 12, 4:16 PM
Subject: AITA?

Dear Wise Old Crone,

I'm sick of people choosing my stepsister over me just because she's undead. Like yes, I support reanimated

people of all mystic origins, but she literally STOLE my
boyfriend while she was alive, murdered him, killed
herself, and then arranged for them to be reanimated
together so they could run off as immortal corpses. (And
now they're engaged.)

Like, what the fuck??? All my friends think it's "so
romantic," they're even posting photos from the grave-
side shower and the reanimation party and just—I
just want to go NC with both of them and maybe
even a few friends over this. I'm not wrong to be mad,
right?????

Sincerely,
The Best Revenge is Living, Period

Wise Old Crone

How Exactly Does One Fuck a . . .
Point me to the encyclopedia of monsterfucking, please!

June 9

Dear Wise Old Crone,

This is so embarrassing. I don't even know if you can help me.
But here goes: there's this guy I work with, and . . . we're not really
supposed to hook up with coworkers, but ever since this guy got
transferred into my group, there's been a spark between us. More
than a spark, really—a blaze, a fireball, an all-consuming veil of

flame. Because, in addition to our wild sexual tension, this guy is literally a dragon.

And Crone, he's so hot; we made out after a work happy hour last week, and he keeps texting me. I feel like it's only a matter of time before I invite him over, but—he's a dragon! What the fuck does that mean? How does he look (and feel) like a human right now? And what does that mean for his . . .

I don't even know what I want to know about fucking a dragon. And I have no idea where to find out more! I don't want to feel like some awkward stuttering virgin when we get to-gether (so not my scene), but how can I avoid that when there's no INFO out there about what to expect?

Tl;dr—I want to ride the dragon dick, but I'm fluttery and scared. What do you advise?

Sincerely,
Wannabe Monsterfucker

Dear Wannabe,

Take to your fainting couch and assail yourself of smelling salts. Anyone hoping to seduce a creature of the paranormal, mythic, occult, or bestial persuasion needs to be made of stern stuff—especially if they are human. Such affairs are not to be taken lightly.

I wish I could answer your questions, delicately phrased as they are, but I don't have a manual or compendium on fuck-ing dragons-in-human-form (I guess I'd tentatively come out as against fucking him in full-on dragon form, but I'd need more details). And why would I? Instructions on sex between humans can be maddeningly hard to come by. For the most part, we all learn the same way: curious whispers and awkward talks with parental figures, lewd rumors and startling diagrams, lurid flashing screens and fumbling, sweaty attempts.

In other words, I think you should take this guy home and *talk to him*. I get not being into the shrinking virgin thing, so don't be one. Invent a new virgin trope: the virgin . . . archaeologist? Workshop this.

My point is, if you can be bold enough to imagine inviting a creature of the night into your bed, you should be bold enough to imagine talking to him about it. Imagine taking it slow; being open to things that may be new and unfamiliar; supporting each other; listening to each other; figuring out what you like and what works for the both of you, together.

That's the best I can offer for now. Circling back, though, we should definitely start working on that compendium of monster-fucking. I couldn't agree more that necessary lore on slamming the supernatural is sorely lacking.

Sincerely,
Crone

Chapter 14

Lorenzo arose at the crack of sunset, which was new for him; left to his own devices, he often didn't get out of bed before midnight. But these trips he was arranging for Charlie tended to be in the early part of the evening, so he'd been adjusting his schedule.

Waking more abruptly than he was used to had a tendency to remind him more of his dreams. They weren't really dreams, of course. Vampires could enter others' dreams, but they had no dreams of their own. Their sleep was more like death—a minor death triggered any time the sun was overhead, to be precise—so Lorenzo's mind couldn't invent colorful new worlds in his sleep the way Charlie's could.

But his dead neurons weren't all the way dead, and they kept on firing during the day just enough to transmit memories, albeit slowly. Necrotic brain tissue working at a fraction of its normal capacity produced hazy flashes of memory that could be savored at a tenth their usual speed, even if sound or color or faces were usually lacking or absent.

So when he slept, Lorenzo could relive the night of Sebastian's party. Specifically, the reason he'd nearly gotten thrown out of Sebastian's party in such frankly spectacular fashion.

His dead flesh didn't dream, it simply remembered, with sluggish devotion, the feeling of pulling Charlie close to him and playacting at what he hadn't even let himself think about. His synapses sparked stubbornly along, dampened under the sunlight, and brought him brief watercolor handfuls of memories.

The heat of Charlie's skin washing against the inside of his mouth like the worst kind of torture.

The press of Charlie's body calling to him, clawing against him.

The little noises he'd made.

He could savor those details while he was dead and his brain blissfully slablike. They felt enough like dreams, and Lorenzo clung to them as he woke up, as he brushed his teeth, even as he picked up Charlie for their latest excursion, this one courtesy of the druids. Dylan had invited them to witness some formal druidic rituals, and of course Charlie had jumped at the invitation.

"Hi," Charlie said, hopping familiarly into the passenger seat. His bag had its own resting spot by now, just against the gear shift on Charlie's side.

Lorenzo swallowed. "Hi."

Charlie was staring at him, smiling in that open way that always left Lorenzo briefly but fully disarmed. He needed to figure out a better way to diffuse these silences that were cropping up between them—moments that made him want to reach out and touch.

Then he remembered what he'd told Charlie. "Did you bring it?"

"Oh! Yes," Charlie said, rummaging around in his bag. "I gave it a ton of thought. An *offering to nature.* So you said it should be something like food, fruit—something fresh?"

He offered Lorenzo a cup of pomegranate seeds. Lorenzo shrugged and took it from him, cracking open the plastic sealing just as Charlie started to ask, "Do you think they'll . . . like it?"

The seeds were tart and delicious. This had been a good idea. Charlie's face was darkening as he realized the depth of Lorenzo's deception. "There's no such thing as an offering required to witness the druids' ceremony, is there?"

Lorenzo smirked at him. Charlie ground his teeth, but the challenging spark in his eye still seemed like an invitation.

Maybe this hadn't been a good idea. Death-dreaming of the almost-bite was one thing, but toying with Charlie over something truly inconsequential could only lead to disaster. Lorenzo looked away, trying to gather himself.

Charlie glanced at the half-empty cup in Lorenzo's hands. "That good, huh?"

"Can't bring outside food in," Lorenzo answered, polishing off the rest of the seeds.

"In?" Charlie asked. "In where?"

When they pulled up to the ticket booth, Charlie seemed confused; it was almost impossible to see among the thick foliage on either side. The ticket-taker appeared at Lorenzo's window before he could voice a question. "Which screen?"

"Actually, we're here to see Jude," Lorenzo told him.

"Oh, sure," the teen said. "Just take that path there, it'll bring you straight to the diner."

"The diner?" Charlie asked. Lorenzo rolled up his window and turned the car onto a small, bumpy dirt road.

And he didn't bother to answer Charlie, because in the next moment, as the trees to the side thinned out, he realized where they were. "A drive-in theater?" Charlie said, aghast with delight. Two huge screens stood to their left, on either side of a wide grass lawn that had been divided into neat rows with narrow driving paths. There were a good number of cars in front of each screen, one of which looked to be showing the latest superhero movie, the other a classic Miyazaki.

"This is amazing," Charlie said, leaning far over the center console to peer out Lorenzo's window. Lorenzo stiffened and pulled back as much as he could, trying to concentrate on the road. "How have I never been here before?"

His pulse was beating inches from Lorenzo's face. "Don't know," he managed, his voice husky.

Eventually they reached the low, squat building where the kitchen and bathrooms were. Charlie was still craning his head around, fascinated, as they entered the diner, which was really more a cross between a greasy spoon and a concession stand.

A long line of customers were waiting for their candy and fried goods, but Dylan was working the counter, and he spotted Lorenzo and Charlie after only a moment, waving them through. "Hey man, you came!" he greeted them, wrapping Lorenzo in a quick hug.

"Thanks for inviting us!" Charlie said happily. Lorenzo glared at him a bit, in suspicion—Dylan looked much more fetching in his apron and the constant sheen of sweat from the ovens than in his scrubs from the clinic—but Charlie didn't seem to be checking him out. Lorenzo felt himself relax a smidge.

"So," he asked, "is tonight still a good time to . . ."

Dylan grinned, like he wished he could join them. "Yeah, they're back there doing their thing." He waved his hand, and on the wall behind him, a narrow door creaked open. Charlie's eyes widened.

"Tell them to hurry up, wouldja? We got a full house," Dylan said, though he winked at Charlie. Then there was a loud clang and the sound of sizzling oil. "Shit, gotta go."

"So they're . . . druids," Charlie asked Lorenzo lowly, as they made their way to the door. "But they run a . . . drive-in?"

"They have many businesses," Lorenzo said. The diner was packed, and he allowed himself a brief touch to the small of Charlie's back to steer him. Charlie glanced up at him, and he dropped his hand quickly, clearing his throat. "It's more profitable for them than, well—"

"Nature magic?"

"Hm."

They walked through the door Dylan had shown them, and as they passed through, a small rock that had been holding it open skittered back around to the other side and pushed it shut behind them. "Whoa," Charlie said.

The door led to a small gravel yard behind the diner, hemmed in by trees. From around the corner they could still hear the distant sound of the movies filtered through a few dozen car radios, and the chatter and laughter of people walking around. Floodlights on the diner roof and the reflected flicker of the screens illuminated the space, and the whole yard smelled thickly of grease.

Standing in the clearing was Dylan's cousin Jude and three young druids. Lorenzo had known their family for a few decades, and Jude had always been a bit more . . . spiritually inclined than his cousin, or anyone else in their family for that matter. He had a feeling the rest of them wished that Jude would pitch in a bit more with the human business side of things, but Jude marched to the beat of his own drum.

The young druids with him, all about high school age, were wearing their best approximation of formal initiate robes; one of them looked like a nightgown. Jude's robes were ornately sewn, and he wore a eucalyptus crown on his head as well as ivy wrapped around his forearms and the backs of his hands. "Lorenzo!" he said when he saw them. "You came."

"Thank you for letting us observe," he said. "Jude, this is Charlie."

"Nice to meet you," he said to Jude. "And—just to make sure—I don't have to make any kind of . . . offering, do I?"

Jude blinked at him, while Lorenzo stifled laughter. "A donation, hon? We take Venmo, but truly, your presence here is enough."

Charlie glared at Lorenzo again, who simply stared at the ground, trying to will the smile off his face.

"Um, can I ask—what is all this?" Charlie asked Jude. "If you don't mind."

"Not at all! It is an initiation for our eldest pupils as they become full members of our sacred druidic circle. And of course, as with all of our ceremonies, it is a celebration of nature," Jude said solemnly. In the distance, there was some kind of explosion from the superhero film.

"Wow," Charlie said. "I can't wait to see."

"Of course. Initiates!" Jude cried, and the kids did their best to stand at attention. "We have guests for this evening's ceremony. So please, let's give them a show."

Charlie and Lorenzo took a respectful step back as the ceremony started. It began with Jude rattling off some formal opening remarks, and then the kids started performing small feats of nature magic on his prompts: pushing and pulling small rocks as Dylan had done, coaxing leaves and vines to spring up from the earth before them, summoning small gusts of snow. Charlie reached out a hand to catch a few of the snowflakes before they faded back out of reality. "This is amazing," he whispered to Lorenzo.

"Nnh," Lorenzo grunted, keeping his eyes fixed on the druids.

As the ceremony wore on, it became more and more uncomfortably clear that there was a divide in the class—two of the initiates seemed fairly competent in their nature magic, while the third failed at almost everything Jude set out for him. "Poor kid," Charlie muttered.

"And for our last endeavor," Jude said, his arms held aloft, "I am a salmon in the pool."

The initiates repeated the phrase, and then set about their magic, intense looks of concentration on their faces. After a moment, a crow fluttered down from the sky and landed on one young druid's arm.

"Did he . . ." Charlie asked. The crow flapped its wings a few times as it settled down, its black eyes sharp.

A moment later, a doe walked hesitantly out of the forest and came to stand by another of the initiates. "Very nice," Jude said. The third initiate—the one who hadn't successfully done any of the tasks—was still chanting quietly to himself, eyes closed.

Charlie gazed at the doe in awe, as it took a few more coltish steps forward. "Are they . . . creating them?" he whispered. "Calling them?"

"I'm not sure," Lorenzo said. The doe nuzzled at the young druid who had summoned her, innocent and beautiful.

He was so distracted by its beauty that it took him a moment to notice the earth rumbling at the feet of the third initiate. He was still chanting in a low, muttered voice, standing with hands fixed over the ground as if he were trying to get greenery to bloom, as the others had. But nothing had yet emerged from the soil at his feet.

Charlie spotted it after a moment too. "What is he . . ."

The ground in front of the initiate churned and then broke, a small mound of earth being pushed up and out of the way. And something was emerging from the soil—not greenery at all, but something that looked like it was tunneling or crawling upward in rough, jerky movements.

"Okay, that's enough," Jude said, grabbing the initiate's arm. It broke his concentration, and he complained as Jude dragged him off to the side. The broken soil at his feet had stopped moving.

"Uh," said Charlie.

"I . . . don't know," said Lorenzo, but he felt unaccountably relieved.

Jude was scolding the third initiate, who had his arms crossed in a huff. A moment later the kid went back inside through the diner, and Jude returned to the group.

"Well done," he said to the remaining two initiates. "I am proud to say that you are now full members of our order. Congratulations."

The kids broke into relieved smiles. "So, um," one said, "does this mean we can watch the movie?"

Jude sighed. "Come with me."

They walked around the diner until they were within sight of the screen showing *Kiki's Delivery Service*. Jude stopped on a patch of grass that looked too lush and full to be a regular parking spot, and waved his arm widely.

As they watched, an enormous tangle of flowers, branches, vines, and roots emerged from the ground, and after a moment, fixed into the shape of a vintage car. The detail was impressive— sheets of interwoven wildflowers formed the sinuous curves of the car's body, thick roots snaked under and around the car as the ducts and spoilers, and panes of whisper-thin ice served as windows. The doors opened just like real car doors as the teens squeaked and climbed gleefully inside, and after a moment, Lorenzo could hear the movie coming through on whatever served as the car's radio.

Next to him, Charlie was agape. "Lorenzo, thank you for coming," Jude was saying formally. "And Charlie, it was our honor to host you here tonight."

"Oh, uh, thank you," Charlie said. "This was great."

Jude noticed his eyes straying back to the flower car. "Please, allow me," he said.

With a wave of his hand, another earth-woven car sprouted up beside Lorenzo and Charlie. Charlie emitted something between a gasp and a giggle. "Enjoy the film," Jude said, inclining his head and then walking back into the woods.

Charlie spared a moment to give Lorenzo an amazed, irrepressibly excited look before he hopped into the car. For a brief, ridiculous moment, Lorenzo thought of Dorothy, of all people. She would have liked nonsense like this—cars made of flowers and vines.

And she would have liked Charlie.

Lorenzo sighed and followed him. The car was just as impressive inside as it had seemed from the outside: their seats were soft, gnarled tree trunks, the bark hollowed out into the perfect shape for reclining, and at Charlie's feet were several squat mushroom pedals. The honeycomb center console was softly glowing, and the flower doors snapped behind them just as precisely as a metal car's.

"This is incredible," Charlie whispered. "I can't believe he made one for us too."

"And we didn't have to do any magic," Lorenzo said.

"Well. You *are* magic," Charlie replied, flicking a teasing look at him.

Lorenzo bit his lip. "I feel bad for that one kid," Charlie added, looking pensive as he played delicately with a thin, almost translucent blue petal.

Lorenzo grunted. "It can be difficult," he said. "With some of these older orders, when you're not . . ."

Charlie frowned. "Not what?"

They were entirely too appealing, his eyes, and the earnestness of his focus. "Nothing," Lorenzo muttered.

Charlie pursed his lips a little, but contented himself to study the flower car in wonder, running his fingers over the delicate petals of the roof. Then he spotted the log dashboard. "Do you think it's in park?" he asked Lorenzo.

He looked for a gear shift but couldn't find one. "Don't know. Why?"

Charlie pointed at a dandelion sprouting from the dashboard about where the odometer would be. Then he gingerly pressed on the mushroom pedal to his right.

Individual stamens on the dandelion began to float away, one at a time.

Charlie looked at Lorenzo, giddy with wonder and delight, like the joy of it was a secret they were sharing. *Can you believe this?*

It caught in Lorenzo's throat like honey, behind his eyelids like the afterimage of sunlight. Charlie went back to exploring the car, but Lorenzo sat stone-still as it washed over him in waves; the unsteady feeling that he was too late, in too deep, and had no way of swimming back to shore.

"Look, look," Charlie said, having realized that if he gently brushed the honeycomb with his fingers, the soundtrack of the movie started playing in the car; a wash of gentle music as Kiki took flight on her broom.

"This is—this is amazing," he said, smiling warmly at Lorenzo. "Thank you for taking me."

"You're welcome," Lorenzo whispered.

Chapter 15

Next Saturday, Lorenzo took Charlie to a wedding.

The bride and groom were both werewolves, but so far Charlie had found the affair to be indistinguishable from a human wedding—a very expensive one. They were back in the same clearing where the werewolf prom had been, but it was almost unrecognizable, save for the identical, breathtaking view of the town spread out below them. Where the prom had been decorated like a low-budget music video with twinkling lights and streamers, the wedding was pure opulence: panel-glass floors covered the grass and earth, enormous stage lights had been affixed to trees all around the clearing, and in the center of it all, a circular black marble podium was dressed for the ceremony, surrounded by hundreds of delicate, spindly white chairs. It felt elegant and muscular.

And it all glowed under the light of an extremely full moon. Lorenzo had assured him—multiple times—that they would leave well before the moon reached its zenith. Apparently all inter-pack weddings ended with a communal run through the woods. It was unnerving to realize that almost everyone he could see here now, dressed in their formal best, would transform in a few short hours. But he desperately needed more werewolf content for his column, so it had been an easy choice to come.

So far, the many highly scripted preceremony rituals were more tedious than pulse-pounding. Just in front of the marble podium, the fathers of the bride and groom were toasting each other as the rest of the guests listened respectfully. Charlie got the impression that their remarks were less about the couple than a subtle contest to imply which one of them had paid for more of the wedding.

Charlie and Lorenzo were toward the edge of the clearing, standing with Lorenzo's friend Gray—the pack's formal event planner, who had almost kicked Charlie out of the prom. "Have you slept at all in the last three months?" Lorenzo asked him quietly. Gray was clutching his usual clipboard and wearing a ridiculously well-cut suit with fur detail at the cuffs and lapels.

"It doesn't matter," Gray said, tossing his head back to cover a nervous twitch in his neck. "Because this toast was the last of it. Everything from here on out is, y'know, whatever."

"You mean like . . . the wedding?" Lorenzo said, shooting a small, private grin at Charlie.

Charlie flushed and looked away. Lorenzo looked so good; Charlie couldn't believe how hard a time he was having acting normally around him, when all he was doing was standing there in his crisp black tux and smiling. It was so stupid. Nothing had happened between them.

Nothing but all of his stupid fantasies come to life.

He didn't know what had come over him. He had never, ever been into *biting* before. Playful pain was one thing, but being bitten? So that someone could drink his blood? It had never held any appeal.

That was before. Since reconnecting with Lorenzo, he'd started to fantasize about it: Lorenzo slamming him against a wall, pushing him around, grinding their bodies together, and leaning in for a painful bite at the soft, vulnerable juncture of his neck—piercing, achy, and sweet.

In reality, it hadn't been nearly so dramatic. Lorenzo had made it look like he was manhandling Charlie, but he'd only guided him into place with his big, careful hands. He was cool to the touch, but not unpleasantly so—being wrapped in his arms felt like sinking into cool sheets after a long day. And even though his skin was cool, touching it had made Charlie flush with heat that he could still feel creeping up his spine. He couldn't stop hearing Lorenzo's low almost-growl when he'd grabbed him; couldn't stop feeling the phantom touch of Lorenzo's lips just barely grazing his skin.

He wanted Lorenzo to bite him. He had no idea what lay beyond what they'd done at the vampire party, but he didn't care.

He needed it.

It occurred to him that he hadn't dreamt of Lorenzo once since that first, startlingly hot dream. He missed it. Maybe in a dream he could have found some relief from this aching preoccupation with getting bit. All he had now were daydreams, daydreams that were . . .

Leading him to stare at Lorenzo shamelessly. His small smile widened a bit as he noticed Charlie's attention. "Like the tux?"

"Mm-hmm," Charlie said, strangled. He prayed that was all Lorenzo thought it was—the intoxicating effects of formal wear.

Not the desire for Lorenzo to touch him, pierce him—drink him down.

He cleared his throat, focusing on Gray. "So, um, the actual—wedding part's not important?"

Gray turned to stare at him slowly. "No, it is," he said, dripping scorn. "We're all just here to witness true love."

He wandered off to glad-hand some of the pack luminaries. "Ouch," Charlie said. "So he's not a romantic, huh?"

Lorenzo sighed, though he was still smiling. "Well, you can't blame him. This is all a bit . . . staged."

"Aren't all weddings?"

Lorenzo shook his head. "This isn't really a wedding. It's a . . . an Instagram backdrop. An ad for the packs." He tossed back a flute of champagne from a passing tray, and Charlie tried not to stare at the bob of his throat. "It's a big, expensive party to celebrate the merger. A few months ago these two packs were on the verge of ripping each other apart. Now they're . . ."

"Making peace?" Charlie said.

Lorenzo shrugged. "I was going to say horizontally integrating."

Charlie chuckled. "Are werewolf packs subject to antitrust law?" He blinked. "Wait, are they?"

Light music started playing, and the guests quieted as it became clear that the ceremony was about to begin.

An elaborately gilded officiant made his way down the aisle, followed by a dozen groomsmen, all walking to a Vitamin String Quartet cover of something Charlie couldn't place. "Why is it always so many people in the wedding party?" he muttered to Lorenzo, as another of the nearly identical groomsmen passed by.

"VIPs from each pack," Lorenzo answered. When the

groomsmen were finished, the groom walked down the aisle and took his place on the marble podium.

Next came a dozen bridesmaids, all in the same diaphanous shade of blush pink. Once they were in place, the music swelled, and all eyes turned back to the edge of the clearing. After a moment, a woman came walking down the aisle wearing a knee-length black dress. She had dark circles under her eyes, and she looked nervous. "Huh," Charlie said.

Before Lorenzo could respond, the woman reached the podium and whispered hurriedly to the groom as the officiant watched on in astonishment. Whatever she said, the groom reacted badly, turning his back on her and speaking swiftly to his groomsmen. "What . . ." Charlie started.

"I don't know," Lorenzo muttered.

Finally, the woman turned to the mic that had been set up for the ceremony, and said in a smooth, corporate voice, "I'm so sorry, everyone. A quick announcement, um, the wedding has been slightly . . . delayed."

Furious murmurs swept through the crowd, and an older woman in a very expensive pantsuit stood up. "Where is she?"

"She's—um," the woman at the mic stammered, while seeming to gesture to someone across the clearing. "She'll be—she'll be right here."

The groom's voice was starting to become audible even without the mic. Turning from his groomsmen back to the corporate flunky, he shouted loudly enough for the whole wedding to hear, "Is she with Emily?"

Shouts and chaos broke out among the audience. "Uh," Charlie said. "What does that . . ."

Audience members were starting to argue with each other.

What had been a serene, almost boring ceremony a few minutes ago was swiftly starting to feel bruised and ugly. "I think perhaps," Lorenzo said, sounding distracted, "the bride has run off with . . ."

Charlie was starting to hear things like *liar!* and *betrayal!* in the rising din. "A wolf from another pack . . ." Lorenzo added, as they watched the dawning mayhem.

The arguments were rapidly getting physical. The groomsmen were starting to brawl, and the bridesmaids were putting distance between themselves, two distinct sides giving each other forbidding looks. The very air seemed to darken.

"What—uh—what do you do?" Charlie stammered. Lorenzo had been invited to the wedding for the same reason he'd been at the prom, to serve as security. "You said vampires can, um—can handle werewolves?"

"Yeah," Lorenzo said faintly. As they watched from the edge of the clearing, two hundred wedding guests—two hundred werewolves—were shouting, shoving each other, and starting to grapple.

Then a wash of bright moonlight hit the clearing as a cloud passed by overhead, and the human noises in the fray began to lose their grip, becoming low, loose, animalistic rage.

"We're getting out of here," Lorenzo said, and grabbed Charlie's hand as they fled into the woods.

They weren't the only ones running—human guests maybe, or werewolves who just had no interest in fighting, joined them as they fled—and soon the darkening woods were filled with the sounds of twigs snapping and desperate panting. Charlie's shoulder and arm were screaming with how fast Lorenzo was tugging him along, forgoing the path in favor of darting as quickly as they could between the trees, but he didn't mind—he just ran.

He knew they were being chased. Something about the sight or scent of skittering prey must have caught the interest of the wolves back at the wedding, because he could hear snarls behind them, almost smell the scent of blood. The air seemed to get colder and colder as it whipped by, and then a scream ripped through the air, followed swiftly by another.

Then Lorenzo stopped short, Charlie collided into him, and he realized it was because a wolf was in their path.

She was still human—mostly—but her beautiful gown was streaked with mud, and her eyes glowed red. She let out an inhuman snarl as her face collapsed in on itself, taking on a canine shape, and her lips pulled back to reveal jagged yellow teeth.

Charlie's feet left the ground.

The world tilted, he thought he might puke, and then he realized that Lorenzo had picked him up as if it were nothing and vaulted *over* the werewolf, then crashed back through the woods, down the hill, away from the carnage.

Charlie held on tight and tried not to scream. Lorenzo was running so fast they were in the trees half the time, covering ground with a desperate efficiency that was somewhere between running and falling. The further they ran, the more steeply the ground started to roll downhill, and the sounds of mayhem from the party faded away.

He heard the crashing of foliage, felt it whipping by on his hands and face. Then there was a snap of teeth by his ear, startlingly crisp; Lorenzo yelped, and there was a jolt as they both slammed suddenly to the side. Lorenzo roared something Charlie couldn't make out, and they ran—leapt—for another few heartbeats. Then there was a final horrible jolt, and he realized that he and Lorenzo were falling, like they'd been shot out of a cannon.

And then they landed.

The first thing he registered was dissonance. The crash had been so loud, and the impact had jarred him down to his bones. He hurt all over, and as he regained his senses, one of the first to return was a harsh, horrible smell—like rended metal and leaking gasoline.

But he was resting on something nice. Something supple and soft, whose gentle hands were roving over him. *"Charlie?"*

"What," he whispered, as more sound filtered in around him, like waves passing overhead.

"Are you okay?" Lorenzo asked. Charlie blinked, and his face came into focus slowly—covered in tiny cuts that were rapidly healing. Charlie's own skin felt raw and abraded, and his heart was pounding.

"What happened," he said again. There were trees around them, silver in the moonlight, and asphalt, and—cars. Other cars.

It started coming back to him—the carnage at the wedding, the flight into the woods. The fall.

He and Lorenzo were lying in some kind of twisted glass and metal wreckage that was groaning and popping as it buckled. Part of it was on fire, hissing and crackling.

They'd landed on Lorenzo's car. They'd punched a crater into it.

He was probably only alive because Lorenzo had taken the impact. Taken it as if it were nothing—he didn't seem injured or in pain at all, just slightly frantic. He was cupping Charlie's head in one hand, looking at him like he was worried Charlie had a concussion. There were blunt shards of glass digging into Charlie's palms and the backs of his elbows, he still ached from the fall, and his eyes stung. But he could breathe; he could feel the ground beneath them, somewhere. The wolves were gone, and the night was quiet. They were safe.

He blinked at Lorenzo, his focus still sharpening. He was sweating, and there were streaks of blood on his face. But his brown eyes were soft with concern in the firelight.

You saved my life.

That's what Charlie tried to say, but instead he surged forward and kissed Lorenzo clumsily.

Lorenzo gasped and Charlie climbed on top of him, clutching them together as Lorenzo's hands found his hips and he canted his head to kiss Charlie deeper. The car screamed and groaned around them as they shifted to find their balance, Charlie's knees bracing Lorenzo's hips as Lorenzo slid a hand onto his neck. Lorenzo was—god, he was cool to the touch, just like Charlie remembered, which was actually kind of perfect with the flames catching nearby, and he felt incredible, his soft tongue and his hard chest and his clever hands fumbling at Charlie's belt.

They managed to get a few clothes off but kept getting distracted, because there wasn't so much a goal as a shared, frenzied need to keep going. Finally Charlie got clearheaded enough to pop the button on Lorenzo's waistband. Lorenzo pulled back, looking dazed, and shook his head a little. "Charlie," he said, in a tone that sounded like reason was beginning to seep back in.

Charlie kissed him, a hand firm on the back of his neck, while his other hand pulled down Lorenzo's zipper. "Charlie," he gasped. Nearby, something glass screamed and then shattered.

Charlie touched him, and shivered with a rush of jagged need. Here, at last, something was alive and pulsing beneath Lorenzo's dead flesh; the rest of him may have been cool to the touch, but he was searing hot in Charlie's hand, hard and sweaty and demanding. He squeezed gently, and what felt like every muscle in Lorenzo's body rippled. "Charlie," he panted.

Lorenzo's eyes darkened when Charlie licked his palm, and he groaned, shuddering backward, while around them the ruin of the car buckled and popped menacingly. Everything was on fire—the night and Charlie's skin and the frantic pace of his arm, the way he was panting into and biting Lorenzo's throat. He knew he was going too fast, being too rough, but he couldn't help it—he felt blinded with need, starving, touching him like he could pull his own pleasure out of Lorenzo's skin.

Lorenzo didn't seem to mind the brutal pace, hanging on to Charlie for dear life and slurring something unsteady and desperate in what sounded like Italian. Charlie sucked on Lorenzo's neck and scratched his stomach, and when his hand went dry he moved down and took Lorenzo into his mouth, sucking him steadily until Lorenzo came down his throat, his fingertips scraping against the back of Charlie's neck. That hurt too but it felt good; it was all so good.

They sat together for a moment, silent but for their panting breaths and the groaning of twisted metal. Everything hurt a little and tingled a little. Charlie briefly wondered if the car was going to explode.

He almost didn't notice when Lorenzo started touching him again—long slow passes of his hands over Charlie's body, lingering in achy places that were just starting to wake up. He realized he was panting again, and Lorenzo kissed him, molding him more aggressively now, lifting him back onto his lap, shaping him how he wanted him, hands trailing up his thighs.

"Oh," Charlie gasped into Lorenzo's mouth. He was kissing him in the strangest way—so calm and completely single-minded, as if he hadn't just come in his mouth, as if they hadn't been chased through the woods, as if the world wasn't ending. Even as his hands roamed over Charlie's body, making him shudder, it was as if he wasn't distracted at all, kissing him slow and intoxicating as he stroked Charlie, as he drove him wild. It was too gentle, too maddening, too delicate to feel so good, but it did.

And when he wasn't kissing Charlie's mouth or throat or shoulder, Lorenzo kept whispering low, soft encouragement into his ear as he touched him, like he was amazed to even be here, to even have the chance to watch Charlie like this. "Charlie . . ." he said over and over again, his voice hoarse. "Charlie."

Lorenzo kissed him, and Charlie clung tight to him as he came apart.

Chapter 16

Lorenzo spent the early evening filling out paperwork that had been brought over by a few of the packs' lawyers. Werewolves could be beasts under the full moon, but they were nimble after a crisis, and quick to ensure that all parties affected by any sort of incident were incentivized not to cause trouble. He'd signed a few of these before.

This time, he was distracted as he initialed page after page by thoughts of Charlie. Charlie, so smart and funny and sharp around the edges, turned out to be . . . touchable.

Very touchable.

Nothing like Charlie's dream, which had been intense but insubstantial. Last night had been solidly, spine-tinglingly real—violent, hot, and consuming.

But it was still Charlie. Lorenzo had no idea what last night meant to him, or what would happen now.

And he ached all over. He knew it wasn't from the crash; those injuries had healed almost instantly. This was something else.

Once he was done with the paperwork, he sent the pack lawyers on their way. A few moments later a knock came at the door, and he answered, assuming one of them had left a pen.

Charlie stood in his doorway, looking up at him with his big amber eyes, his lips parted.

They stared at each other for a long moment while the *we had sex last night* of it all just hung there, freezing everything.

Then Lorenzo shook his head slightly. Charlie cleared his throat. "Uh. Hi."

"Hello," Lorenzo said, standing aside so that Charlie could enter without any risk of touching him at all. He wanted to ask what he was doing here, but that would probably come out as hostile. So he said, "How are you feeling?"

Charlie's eyes widened. "After the crash," Lorenzo said gruffly. "Are you injured?"

"Oh! No, I'm—I'm good. A bit of whiplash, I think, but—I'm good." He touched his neck absently as he spoke, but it looked more like a nervous tic than anything else.

"Good," Lorenzo said.

"Um. I wanted to—" Charlie finally made eye contact with him, and broke off in a nervous grin. "I'm sorry," he said, scratching his neck and pulling a flyer out of his bag. "I wanted to show you this."

It was a flyer for an art show at a small local museum. "Why?"

"It looks like it's supernatural," Charlie said, leaning over to look at it with him. Lorenzo pulled back slightly, just enough to keep a plausible distance between them. "I mean, is it? I think I'm getting pretty good at telling."

He was so damn handsome when he got excited about something—his eyes lit up, his eyelashes fluttered, and his lips curved into a half smile that made Lorenzo feel like the floor was pitching underfoot.

He forced himself to examine the flyer more closely. When he realized what he was looking at, he frowned. "Well—it—yes," he said. "It's . . ."

"What?"

"It's . . . succubi," Lorenzo said grimly. "And incubi."

"Succubi," Charlie said, weighing the word carefully. "Like . . ."

There was a long, strained pause while they stared at each other, neither willing to put it into words. Charlie swallowed, his throat bobbing. Finally, Lorenzo managed, "Mm-hmm."

"So—it's an art show put on by . . ."

"Yes."

Charlie frowned, thinking this through. "Is it a live sex show?"

"No," Lorenzo said. "Well, a little. It—this is just a thing they do. They're very . . . artistic and high-minded." He sighed. "It's stupid, sexy art."

"I need to see this," Charlie declared.

"That's not a good idea," Lorenzo said.

Charlie looked up at him furtively. "Because of . . . ?" *Because of us?*

Lorenzo scowled. "No, because they can be dangerous to humans. They can influence human behavior, get inside your head."

"I thought it was an art show."

"Well, it is," Lorenzo said. "But . . ."

"Okay," Charlie said, starting to smile. "Then come with me."

Now Lorenzo was at a loss for words. Was Charlie asking

him out? Or was he just using him as a protector, distraction, guide? All of the above?

Why did it have to be a succubus exhibit?

Charlie was chewing on his lip, a nervous tic that belied his easy smile. "Just, y'know," he said, filling the silence that followed his invitation. "Like we've been . . . doing."

"Yes," Lorenzo found himself saying. "Okay. I'll go with you."

Charlie eyes lit up. "Great," he said.

They realized at the same time that they were both still holding the flyer, standing shoulder to shoulder.

Lorenzo let go first, taking a step back. Charlie blinked at him.

"So, uh," he said. "Do you . . . want to go now?"

Lorenzo's car was also on loan from the pack, as compensation for his beloved Ford Focus getting totaled. This one had a beige interior and smelled almost harshly brand new.

Nothing like the burning wreckage they'd turned his last car into. Charlie's skin had tasted like soot.

Lorenzo could smell him again now, close as he was in the passenger seat. He'd definitely showered, because the scent of last night was gone; now his skin had a distinctive soapy note. He smelled clean and familiar.

It was a shame they'd had sex for the first and probably last time outdoors. It had its appeal, of course, but Lorenzo couldn't help but feel like he'd missed out on the chance to fuck Charlie under the covers, somewhere warm and small where his scent would gather, and every one of Lorenzo's senses would be completely smothered by him.

Lorenzo swallowed. No one spoke for a long, long moment.
Then Charlie said, "We should talk about it."

Lorenzo jerked. "Uh," he said. "Talk about . . ."

Charlie quirked a flat eyebrow at him. "Last night?"

Lorenzo had no idea what to say. Thankfully, Charlie kept
going. "Thank you for saving my life," he said quietly.

Lorenzo tried to respond, but his *mm-hmm* came out more
like a grunt. "And um," Charlie said. "About the other . . .
stuff . . ."

Lorenzo bit his tongue again. What was there to say? That
he wanted to do it again, and he also thought it'd be a terrible
idea? It had been a mistake. A delicious, delirious mistake.

"I—it was fun," Charlie said. "Really fun. But, I think
maybe—"

"Just a one-time thing?" Lorenzo offered.

"Yes," Charlie said, deflating with relief, while Lorenzo tried
not to feel stung. "I mean—it really was fun."

"Yes," Lorenzo said, looking out at the road. *Fun.*

"Yep," Charlie said. "Just—okay."

It was the smart thing to do. Lorenzo still felt like he'd been
sent to bed without supper.

And he couldn't help but sneak a glance at Charlie.

The museum was gorgeous, sleek and modern—he'd been to
shows here before, and it was just as chic as he remembered. It
was after eleven, so the crowd wasn't overwhelming. Lorenzo
handed his keys to the valet and held the front door for Charlie.

The show, called *Need: A New Perspective*, began with a
collection of paintings and mixed-media pieces. Each had a
cluster of guests grouped around it discussing its merits, and
servers were passing glasses of champagne. Charlie grabbed one
and raised his eyebrows at Lorenzo. *Ready?*

He shook out his shoulders. It was just an art show; nothing had to be awkward.

Naturally, many of the paintings were erotic—classical oil paintings and faint, haunting watercolors. There were mixed-media pieces showing pornography and erotic art films, and sketches of the same woman, over and over again. Lorenzo couldn't always spot which pieces had been created via the succubi's powers, which had been hewn with other magic, and which were simply enthusiastic amateur attempts. If magic were truly intent, the intent behind the assembled exhibition so far reminded him most closely of that cake meme *congrats on the sex.* They turned a corner and found a massive field of balloons assembled to look like a strip club, complete with strangely enticing balloon dancers. Charlie chuckled when he spotted it, glancing back at Lorenzo with laughter in his eyes.

They passed into the next room and found a performance piece: a man and woman cuddled together on a soaking wet bed, the man sobbing into the woman's chest, while water poured onto them from the ceiling, draining into a deep circle around the edges. It was tremendously loud, and a faint mist from the water floated over the entire room. People stood along the sides and watched silently.

What the . . . ? Charlie mouthed to Lorenzo.

Lorenzo shrugged. They made their way into the next room.

It was large, but held only one exhibit on a slightly elevated platform: a vintage photo booth with a red velvet curtain and flashbulbs all along one side. Charlie smiled as soon as he saw it.

They drew closer to get a good look. Lorenzo asked, "Can you go in? There's no sign."

Charlie looked at him. "Do you want to take some pictures?"

Lorenzo hesitated. "I'm just kidding," Charlie said quickly. He looked back at the photo booth. "Why is this even at an art exhibit about sex?"

"I don't know," Lorenzo lied. "What's next?"

The next room was the sculpture room, and it took some getting used to. Every time Charlie was startled by something or burst into laughter, Lorenzo felt like he was being tugged a little closer to him, a little more irresistibly drawn in. Nothing here reminded him of last night, not really; every piece was so-phisticated or outrageous or elevated—sharp edges and refined palates.

Last night with Charlie hadn't been anything like that. It had been primal, dirty, and raw.

"So," he managed, when they were mostly through the sculptures. "What do you think?"

"About this one?"

"About all of it."

Charlie took a deep breath. "You were right," he said. "It is stupid, sexy art."

Lorenzo laughed, and Charlie grinned in response. *Danger-ous*, Lorenzo thought, and tried to control the errant fluttering in his chest.

Thankfully, they seemed to be near the end of the exhibit. They turned a corner and found an empty white room, but on the far side was a doorway—or at least, thick black curtains that presumably covered the exit. Lorenzo glanced at Charlie, who shrugged. They pushed past the curtain.

And they were inside the car crash from last night—everything, all of it, the starry night and fiery wreckage, the scent of blood and smoke in his nostrils, and the taste of Charlie's skin on his—all of it contained inside an empty room. Lorenzo stumbled backward, shocked. It was sort of like being inside his own memory, but at the same time seeing it from afar; like the way light warped through a crystal, it was real but not real at the same time, and it changed every time he blinked. It was as weightless as an image projected on a wall, but it was still burning hot like the twisted metal of his car, and he could almost feel Charlie's hands on him, the searing heat of Charlie's skin.

And then they wandered through a second set of black curtains, and found themselves in another empty hallway at the rear of the crisp white gallery. "Oh my god," Charlie wheezed.

A docent waved at them. "Thank you for coming!"

"What the hell was that?" Lorenzo demanded.

"Oh, our final exhibit—a one-second fully immersive sexual fantasy, pulled from your own subconscious," he answered. "One of our senior spell-bringers put it together. What did you think?"

They didn't attempt a response, and made their way swiftly out of the gallery.

Out on the sidewalk, Lorenzo gave the valet their ticket. Charlie didn't meet his eye when he turned around. "Uh," Lorenzo said, "this is awkward."

"Yeah, I know," Charlie said, sounding nervous. "And I didn't—"

"No, we couldn't have known they would re-create our memories from last night," Lorenzo reassured him.

Charlie frowned. "Last night?"

"Yes?" Lorenzo took a step toward him. "In that room, it was—it was like last night." He abruptly lowered his voice, because it felt like his words were suddenly touching Charlie somehow. "On my car," he said softly. "Wasn't it?"

Charlie licked his lips. "I saw the. Um," he rasped. "At the vampire party. When we were upstairs. When you pretended to . . ."

Lorenzo waited dumbly for him to finish his sentence, but Charlie just stared up at him with a look of deepening conviction. Someone honked at them. His beige car was here.

"Can we go back to your place," Charlie said neutrally.

"Mm-hmm," Lorenzo managed. "Yes."

The car ride was silent. Charlie got out when they parked.

"Want to come upstairs?" Lorenzo asked him.

"Mm-hmm," Charlie said, following quickly as he opened the door. "Yes."

They sprinted through a thankfully empty apartment up to Lorenzo's room, slamming the door behind them. Charlie had never been in his room before, but he didn't seem curious about it at all; he just kissed Lorenzo like they'd been interrupted, and he was desperate to keep going. Lorenzo kissed him back with more enthusiasm than finesse, fingers in his hair, and suddenly needed so many things at once. Charlie laughed as Lorenzo pushed his jacket off his shoulders and then abandoned it to grab him around the waist and drop him onto the bed. Lorenzo crawled over him and Charlie yanked his arms out of his jacket, running his hands over Lorenzo's back and biting his jaw, panting and slurring out half words between kisses, his human heart beating so hard, so fast.

Lorenzo couldn't stop touching him, couldn't imagine that anything would ever feel better than this. Charlie tugged at his clothes vengefully and caught Lorenzo's face for a deep kiss. When they broke apart, Charlie said, "I didn't eat anything today."

Lorenzo's throat seized. "What?"

"Just in case," Charlie said, blushing slightly. "If you want to."

"But you—you came here and said it wasn't . . . um . . ." It was hard to think straight with Charlie palming him through his pants. "That we shouldn't."

"I know," Charlie panted. "I'm a fucking liar." And he bit Lorenzo's lip, hard.

Lorenzo snaked forward and bit Charlie's neck—just with his square human teeth; a sharp but gentle nip.

Charlie went rigid, and his eyes were like pits as Lorenzo pulled back to peel his pants off.

Charlie shucked his shirt and then rolled onto his stomach. Lorenzo's vision went hazy for a minute at the sight of all that skin: the soft swell of his belly, his gorgeous, thick legs, the dips in his spine where sweat gleamed. Charlie propped himself up on one knee and looked over his shoulder. "You coming?"

Lorenzo ended up draped over Charlie's back, moving in small, careful, grinding motions that had Charlie gasping like he couldn't breathe. It was so good, just as hot as last night, but it wasn't as frantic—he wasn't blinking smoke out of his eyes or shaking with adrenaline. Last night Charlie had been a balm against the acrid scent of bloodlust and his own pulsing fear, but tonight everything was Charlie—there was nothing but his scent under the sheets, nothing but the heat of his skin and the sounds he was making enveloping Lorenzo as warmly as the blankets.

And of course he thought about biting Charlie. How could he not? He wasn't going to, for a million different reasons; but he could make a home for himself in the crook of Charlie's neck while they fucked, just kissing and nuzzling him there. The scent of his soft skin was so comforting, the pulse of his blood, and so what if Lorenzo drooled into the pillow a little. It was okay, while they were like this, to think about it; to fantasize about what it would be like if Lorenzo were brave enough to bite him.

Charlie gasped and Lorenzo thrust harder, trying to rattle every last sound out of him. "More," Charlie said.

"This is enough," Lorenzo grunted back.

Charlie reached up and grabbed his hair, grinding Lorenzo's face into his neck. Lorenzo kissed him, sucking on his skin deeply, but didn't pick up the pace.

"Fuck you," Charlie hissed, and dug his nails into the back of Lorenzo's neck, hard enough to draw blood. Lorenzo whimpered and came, crushing Charlie into the mattress.

When he recovered, he flipped Charlie over and sucked him off. They ended up sprawled diagonally halfway down the bed, staring up at the canopy, just starting to shiver as their sweat cooled.

And then Charlie said, "So I guess it's a two-time thing."

"It doesn't feel like a two-time thing," Lorenzo said, and winced immediately; he hadn't meant to say that out loud. He'd just been telling the truth—now that this had happened again, he didn't see himself mustering the willpower to stay away from Charlie. His whole body was tingling, and he could feel a drunken grin trying to fight its way onto his face.

Charlie rolled over to look at him. "I guess it doesn't," he said, smiling softly. "Um. Maybe we could keep doing what we've been doing—you taking me around to supernatural stuff—and we could do this too."

He crept closer until he was draped over Lorenzo's chest, his heart pounding right there above Lorenzo's still one. "You know," he whispered, brushing their lips together. "Some extra . . . education."

Lorenzo sat up a little. Is that what he was to Charlie? *Education?*

Is that what Lorenzo wanted to be to Charlie? Did he even know how to answer that question?

Charlie was biting his lip expectantly as he waited for Lorenzo to reply. There was sweat on his forehead, and his cheeks were flushed pink. He didn't seem sultry or calculating; he looked like he'd had just as much fun as Lorenzo and was reaching for any excuse to do it again. It didn't seem like he meant it.

But then again, Lorenzo had no idea if he could actually read Charlie or not.

Charlie tilted his head down and pressed small sucking kisses to Lorenzo's chest, licking up the sweat there. Lorenzo knew all the reasons not to do it; not to play some game with Charlie there was no way to win. But when Charlie flicked a look up at Lorenzo through his eyelashes, he knew he was already lost.

"I suppose," he said, "I did promise to teach you about supernatural-human relationships."

"Yes, you did," Charlie said, leaning forward to kiss him. "Lucky me."

From: braaaains@jmail.com
To: wiseoldcrone@midnight.com
Date: May 2, 11:42 AM
Subject: Horror Workplace

Dear Crone,

I think I'm being discriminated against at work because I'm a zombie. First they said that I should have to work more shifts than everyone else just because we don't sleep. Then they put a sign up in the break room saying "NO MICROWAVING BRAINS" even though I've never done that (I'm a zombie, not a monster). Someone even started a rumor that I deliberately became a zombie to discharge my student debt, because of how they changed the law so that vampires retain their debt but not other undead creatures. It's become a totally toxic workplace, but I'm also nervous about going on the job market again because last time I didn't have to deal with people staring at my gaping head wound during interviews. What should I do?

Sincerely,
Shuffling Toward the EEOC

From: sjarnathan@jmail.com
To: wiseoldcrone@midnight.com
Date: May 4, 9:06 AM
Subject: Sorceress Stalemate

Dear Crone,

I met a wonderful sorceress when a spell she was working on backfired and dropped her here from her own time 342 years ago. It's been a whirlwind romance, and I care about her a lot—and now that she's worked through her personal issues and her powers are back, she can undo the time-travel spell. There's just one problem: we can't decide where to go! She wants me to come back to her time, meet her friends and her family, which I totally understand—but I'm not exactly eager to go live in a time without modern medicine, women's suffrage, or the internet. On the other hand, she's not wild about climate change, nuclear power, or the internet. We're at a stalemate—maybe we could try to go even further in the future, or into another dimension entirely? We've pledged to abide by whatever you decide. Where should we go?

Sincerely,
Stop Living In the Past

Wise Old Crone

Should I Sell Out, or Keep the Magic Alive?
And how do werewolves deal with rejection?

June 16

Dear Crone,

I own a rare magical bookshop that's been in my family for generations. The local werewolf pack has offered to buy us out—I guess they want to bring our stock in-house as part of their collection of magical resources. If I accepted their offer, I could stay on as a kind of librarian or pack consultant, or I could take the money and walk away. Or, I could reject their offer and see how werewolves deal with disappointment. I love my store, and I don't want to see it changed ... but I also can't stop thinking about what I could do with that money. I could travel, pursue hobbies I've never had time for before, or maybe even start a new business. Every option feels dangerous. How do I even begin to decide what the right move is?

Sincerely,
Choosing My Own Adventure

Dear Bookshop Adventurer,

That's the thing about danger, isn't it? It's intoxicating.
All your options seem rich with possibility. Running a magical bookstore means being surrounded by knowledge, potential,

and imagination—but the kind that you can only ever put back on a shelf. Taking their offer and walking away would mean cracking the spine on your own life. No wonder it feels dangerous.

And speaking for myself, I understand the magnetic pull of the risky choice; the lure of giving in to temptation. After all, we only live once—or at least, humans do. It's romantic to think about fate picking us up like a leaf on the wind and depositing us wherever we're meant to be next. There's a relief in danger, isn't there? The relief of giving in; the freedom that comes with ignoring that cautious voice within.

All of which is to say that if walking away is what's calling to you, I'd give it serious consideration. I'd tell you to go with your gut, but I don't think instinct holds any particular wisdom. More to the point, I don't believe there are right answers to questions like this. You're not trying to figure out what's "correct" in any cosmic sense; you're choosing who you want to be.

In other words, if you're going to make the dangerous choice, make sure you do it with your eyes open.

Sincerely,
Crone

Chapter 17

♥

Over the next few weeks, Charlie became very familiar with Lorenzo's ceiling.

Really, he became familiar with the entirety of Lorenzo's bedroom, which was just as stunning as you'd expect a vampire's bedroom to be. The floor and walls were slick poured concrete, but the furniture was classically elegant, with the standout piece being his enormous four-poster bed, which had black cotton curtains whose edges wrapped around the posts of the bedframe like ivy on an old stone wall. The room was huge—it took up the entirety of the top floor of the apartment. There were bookcases everywhere, five separate dressers, and a fireplace big enough for Charlie to stand in. Thick, sun-proof black curtains covered every window.

The ceiling, however, was a mess. It looked as if it had been under construction for years or even decades, covered in a haphazard quilt of tarps and plywood, all of which were weathered with age. Sometimes Charlie worried it would collapse on them one day.

But he never did get around to asking Lorenzo about it, because, well—they'd been busy. Lorenzo kept taking him to meet new groups of supernatural creatures all over town: There were the river sprites who'd shown them some elemental water magic, resulting in sodden clothes they'd stripped off each other later. There was the magic historian who'd given them a lecture about the history of covens while Lorenzo and Charlie played footsie under his heavy table laden with spell books. And the werewolves had invited them back to witness the peace summit that was eventually convened between the packs after their brawl at the wedding. There had been lots of long, boring speeches about peace and familial duty, and Charlie hadn't been able to stop staring at Lorenzo all night, because the werewolf brawl was the first time he'd felt the strength in Lorenzo's arms as he'd whisked him away from danger, the first time he'd felt the urgency in how Lorenzo had touched him, how important it had been to Lorenzo to keep him safe.

They hadn't even made it back to Lorenzo's place that night; they'd fucked up against a tree in the woods half a mile from the werewolf grotto, the rough bark digging into Charlie's back, the stars spread out above them.

They hadn't been able to keep their hands off each other since the succubus art show. Every once in a while they abandoned Charlie's research quest entirely and stayed in, spending hours in Lorenzo's bed, reading and talking about nonsense when they weren't all over each other. Sometimes they would stay up past sunrise; Charlie had been mildly surprised to discover that vampires could do that, although it was difficult for them, and didn't last long. After sunrise, Lorenzo got drowsy and vulnerable in a grumbly way, which Charlie found adorable and kind of hot. He liked coaxing sunrise Lorenzo into fooling around with him before he drifted off to sleep for the day—it was the vampire version of morning sex, and he loved it.

He'd learned a lot about vampires since he'd started spending every night in Lorenzo's bed. He'd learned that vampires didn't need to breathe, but they still did sometimes in stressful or exciting situations—muscle memory, Lorenzo called it. He'd learned that vampires' cool skin could feel just as exciting as a human's warm touch, and that they actually did tend to warm up somewhat when they exerted themselves. His "education" with Lorenzo was working, and then some.

And every morning when he got back to his place, he wrote column after column, and sometimes even little short stories or essays that he had no idea what to do with. It was the most prolific he'd ever been, and he thought it might've been some of his best writing ever, or maybe he was just high on all the sex. Either way, his notifications as the Crone were insane—the column was a genuine hit. It was incredible to be recognized, and to be able to breathe for the first time in months, at least where his job was concerned. But he wasn't engaging with it—he'd abandoned almost all of his social media.

Because what if Lorenzo found his Insta or his TikTok, and figured out who he really was, and what he'd been doing?

Better to focus on how proud he was of the column, and how easy writing had been lately. The creative process felt joyous for the first time in years. *He* felt joyous.

He and Lorenzo had made a halfhearted effort to keep their situation a secret from the others, but it'd only been a few days before Rachel had stormed up the stairs one night and banged on the door for them to keep it down. Other than that, though, it hadn't really changed much about the group dynamic. Maggie mooned at them every chance she got and made horrible jokes about their portmanteau couple name; Lorenzo thought if they ignored her she'd eventually stop. Rachel and Isolde still seemed more interested in thinking up coldly polite but insulting things to say to each other than in Charlie and Lorenzo's relationship status.

Not that they were in a relationship. It was a change in their . . . well, some other status.

Charlie sighed. He was lying in Lorenzo's bed again, with Lorenzo snoring alongside him, but he couldn't sleep. He kept staring up at the ceiling, covered in half-finished detritus and cobwebs.

It couldn't hurt to look, right?

The only way he could reach the ceiling was by crawling up onto a dresser and standing on his toes until he could reach just high enough to pull one of the tarps down and peek under it. He craned his neck, straining to see. Eventually the moon came out from behind a cloud, bathing the ceiling in silver light, and Charlie realized it was—

A skylight. There was a skylight in Lorenzo's ceiling—and a nice one too. It took up almost half the area of the ceiling, with a sharp, triangular, art-deco-looking shape. It was made of wrought iron and that old glass that looked like it had just been poured, bubbled and wavy.

Lorenzo snored loudly and Charlie jumped, twitching the tarp back into place and crawling back into bed. But he still couldn't sleep, as the curtains flapped quietly.

Lorenzo was working his way up Charlie's body slowly, kissing his calves, rubbing his thighs, and nuzzling his hip bones as Charlie shifted impatiently. Then he turned and dipped his tongue into Charlie's belly button. It startled a giggle out of him, and he panted, "This is not what I thought sleeping with a vampire would be like."

Lorenzo lifted his head, raising an eyebrow at him.

"Shit, sorry, I—" Charlie winced. "I didn't mean that like it sounded."

"How did it sound?" Lorenzo asked. Before he could answer, Lorenzo trailed a finger down Charlie's inner thigh, and he gasped, distracted.

"I just meant—I didn't mean . . ." Charlie trailed off, entranced at the sight of Lorenzo drawing his tongue in lazy circles over Charlie's skin. "Fuck."

"You were saying?" Lorenzo asked.

"Why are you doing that," he panted, "if you want me to answer?"

"Maybe I want a straight answer," Lorenzo said. "I want your mind elsewhere so you won't lie."

The word *lie* sent a chill through him that chased off his lust. "Hey," Charlie said, sitting up and pushing Lorenzo back. "I wouldn't—"

Lorenzo was just staring at him, waiting for him to finish his sentence, and Charlie cursed, covering his eyes with his hand. "I didn't mean to—you're a very scary vampire," he said. "Very cool, and tough."

Lorenzo frowned. "Of course I am. What does that have to do with anything?"

Charlie hugged a knee to his chest. "I thought you were mad because you thought I was saying that you're not like what I thought a vampire would—or should—be like. Which—you are!" he added. "Or—I guess I was . . . there's obviously no one *right* way for a vampire to be, and . . ." He cleared his throat and lowered his voice. "When you . . . when you're gentle, and sweet, and silly, it's . . ."

He trailed off when he realized the shaking of Lorenzo's shoulders was laughter. "It's nice," he finished sharply. "What?!"

"I wasn't mad at you for impugning my scary vampire nature," Lorenzo said. He had a very, very nice smile that came out when they were like this—just the two of them in bed, talking shit and getting lost in roundabout conversations.

"Then what?" Charlie demanded.

The smile faded somewhat. "I was just . . . I was surprised to hear you say something like—that you had thought about what it would be like," Lorenzo said, not meeting his eye. "To be with a vampire."

"Oh. Really?" he asked. He was surprised Lorenzo was surprised—there must have been dozens of vampire groupies in his past. It wasn't exactly a rare fetish. "Hasn't everyone?"

Lorenzo didn't say anything, and as the silence stretched out, so did Charlie's anxiety. They'd started this whole thing with the understanding that it was *educational*. That was for the best—it kept everything simpler. More straightforward.

But Lorenzo had a look on his face that was anything but simple. Charlie wanted to reassure him, but what would he say?

He glanced at Lorenzo's ceiling again, thinking of the beautiful glass peaks underneath. It worried him more than he wanted to admit, thinking about how much sunlight must pour into Lorenzo's bedroom every morning, held at bay only by tarps and plywood.

But he couldn't ask about the skylight any more than he could ask about everything else unspoken in Lorenzo's life and past—any more than he could tell Lorenzo the truth about himself.

So instead he said, casually, "I've already learned so much about vampires from you."

He crawled into Lorenzo's lap, ignoring the way Lorenzo's eyes cut off to the side rather than look at him. "Like, the fact that vampires are ticklish."

He dug his fingers into Lorenzo's ribs, and Lorenzo huffed out a laugh as he wrestled Charlie's wrists away. There was still something dull and preoccupied in his smile, though.

"Or that vampires have very sensitive ears," he said, leaning forward to breathe hotly into the tender shell of Lorenzo's.

He shivered, running his hands over Charlie's hips and the small of his back. *"Charlie."*

"Or that vampires are allergic to cinnamon," Charlie said, pulling back to smile at him.

"That's not all vampires," Lorenzo said, scowling.

"I know," Charlie said, as his smile grew. "It's just you."

"And I'm not allergic. I just hate it."

A giggle burst up out of Charlie's throat. "That's so weird!"

"Why is it weird?" Lorenzo demanded.

"Because!" Charlie said. "Vampires, fall, Halloween? It's supposed to all be, y'know, connected."

"It's a stupid spice," Lorenzo muttered. "I hate PSL season."

"Hm," Charlie said, running his fingers through Lorenzo's hair and onto the back of his neck. "So."

He leaned forward and caught Lorenzo's lips in a soft, clinging kiss. "Thank you for educating me," he whispered.

Lorenzo went still, but Charlie kissed him again, and this time Lorenzo kissed him back.

Chapter 18

Rachel was going to court on one of her cases, and she'd asked Lorenzo and Maggie to watch her practice her opening statement. Charlie happened to be over that night—okay, Lorenzo had invited him; he knew he needed to cool it with Charlie, but it was so hard to resist—and at some point in the last few weeks, Charlie had become almost as close with Rachel and Maggie as Lorenzo was, despite his being their actual roommate. So when Charlie heard about Rachel's mock speech, he sat down to watch too.

She was a few lines into her second attempt when Isolde came home. As soon as Rachel saw her, she rolled her eyes and fumbled her words. "Start over," Maggie said encouragingly.

Rachel cleared her throat and started her speech again, and it went well until the sound of running water came from the kitchen. Her eye twitched a little, but she continued.

She managed to hold it together until Isolde reappeared, holding a glass of water. She turned toward her room, but then paused.

Rachel snapped. "Can I help you?"

"I was watching your speech," Isolde said.

"Okay," Rachel said. "Well, I'm trying to focus."

"Someone watching your speech unnerves you?" Isolde said levelly. "You do need practice."

Charlie winced and Maggie started to cut in, but Rachel spoke over her. "No comments about sin or degeneracy tonight?"

"Lorenzo and Charlie are sleeping together," Isolde said. "I thought you knew that."

"Y'know what—" Rachel seethed.

"Okay, hey!" Charlie said loudly. "Why don't we talk this out? Because this is . . ." He gestured widely, encompassing the whole room. "I mean it's great, but it's not healthy."

"I have nothing to say," Isolde said.

"Me neither," Rachel added.

"Okay, but like—you want to keep living like this?" Charlie asked.

No one said anything. Tentatively, Charlie said, "Maybe, Rachel, you could try to be less hostile, and Isolde, you could try to be more understanding."

"Of what?" Isolde demanded.

"Do you really not get why Rachel is uncomfortable when you talk about sex?" Charlie asked.

"I'm not uncomfortable!" Rachel objected. "*She's* weird. Focused on . . . purity and . . . rightness and . . . sin. When no one's—when it's not even—" she huffed out angrily through her teeth, and then stared Isolde down. "It's impolite," she said, almost pointedly.

Isolde crossed her arms.

"Okaay," Charlie said, indulgently, before turning back to Isolde. "Then—can you understand why Rachel might find it . . . impolite? You've been living here for a while, you must have picked up on some things."

"Her problem is with me, and with my people," Isolde said coldly. "Our very nature."

Charlie threw a hand up at Rachel before she could speak. "I get why you might feel that way," he told Isolde. "But you're also the one who chose to rent a room here, among all the humans and vampires and poltergeists. I mean, you left home."

Isolde said nothing, her gaze turned inward.

"You chose to come live among all of us, with all our . . . impurities," Charlie continued. "I'm sure there must have been some of your people who thought that was impure. The choice you made."

Isolde sat down next to him on the couch. She was silent for a moment, and then said, softly, "Yes."

An oppressive stillness overtook the room as they all simultaneously realized that they had no idea what to say. Rachel was still standing in the middle of the living room with her scripted cards, looking lost. "Well," Charlie said, glancing at Lorenzo. "That must've been . . . hard."

Maggie shuffled closer to Isolde on the couch, reaching out with her hand but then withdrawing it. "It was my choice to take on human form," Isolde said hollowly, staring at the floor. "Very few of us do. For most it would be unthinkable. This place is . . ." She paused, diplomatically, and then said: ". . . different from our Wood.

"But your world became hard to ignore after a while," she whispered. "And I was so curious."

Charlie nodded. "And then, ever since I came here, it's become so hard for me to find my way back to the Wood." She stared at her hands in her lap. "And even when I do, my people aren't there. I spend hours out there sometimes, but the wind is still. It's just . . . trees and rocks and water. And the Wood—our Wood—is gone." Very, very quietly, she said, "It's like they . . . they don't want me to find them."

Maggie murmured something Lorenzo couldn't hear, reaching out to rub Isolde's back. Rachel had stopped moving completely. "That sounds . . . really lonely, and confusing," Charlie said. "I probably can't . . . ever really understand, completely. But. I can always listen."

"No thank you," Isolde said, and she stood up abruptly, stalking over to her room. Rachel watched her go.

Charlie blew out a breath. "Sorry, Rachel," he said. "I—I didn't mean to derail your thing."

"No," she said gruffly. "I just, uh. I think I'm good. Need to stop thinking about this for a bit." She gestured to her cards, and then retreated to her own room.

Maggie left quietly after them. Charlie slumped back against the couch once they were alone, looking haunted. "Jesus," he said. "I had no idea."

"I don't think any of us did," Lorenzo replied.

"How awful."

Lorenzo nodded in agreement. He'd never been cast out by a group like the unicorns, but feeling isolated and adrift? That he could understand.

"I pushed her," Charlie was saying bitterly. "And now it's . . . I screwed it all up. Again."

Lorenzo wasn't generally inclined to support Charlie's interference in the personal lives of others, but his investment in whatever Rachel and Isolde were working through was touching. "You didn't screw it up," he said. "They're upset, but it's not about you."

Charlie scoffed, and Lorenzo rubbed his back. "Why are you being so hard on yourself?"

At that, Charlie flicked him a quick look that Lorenzo couldn't decipher. Then he shook his head, closed his eyes, and ground his knuckles against his brow.

"Hey, come here," Lorenzo said, putting an arm around him. Charlie still looked troubled, so Lorenzo kissed him. He could tell that Charlie barely noticed it with everything else running through his head, though; so he took Charlie's chin, turned his face, and kissed him again, deeply. And this time he could feel it through Charlie's skin and in the shift of his muscles, the way his anxiety faded and a breathlessness took over. He gasped when Lorenzo broke off the kiss.

"My room?" Lorenzo murmured.

Charlie nodded frantically.

Later, Lorenzo lay with his head on Charlie's chest, enjoying the rhythmic rise and fall of his breath and the swirling velvet sound of blood in his veins. Charlie's skin always smelled delicious after sex, hot and limber and sated, and he had to fight the urge to lick the warm sweat off him. Charlie was a temptation in many more ways than one.

Not for the first time, Lorenzo thought about how hard it was to have only part of this—to hold back so much even while they were together. Charlie had told him many times that their arrangement was "educational," and Lorenzo could follow those rules, he felt reasonably sure. Charlie said a lot with his eyes that he didn't say out loud, and so what if that ran in both directions—so what if he could never really tell what Charlie was thinking, could never hope to be as detached as him, as unaffected, as above it all? He could hope for the best and distract himself from the worst by jumping Charlie's bones—he seemed to want him for that much, if not more. Nothing ventured, nothing lost.

He ventured a gentle hand through Charlie's hair, and watched his eyelashes flutter closed against his cheeks. That was something gained, at least.

"Can I ask you something," Charlie whispered.

Lorenzo rested his chin on his knuckles, his hand splayed on Charlie's chest. "Yes?"

"Um. Do you . . . I mean . . ." Charlie was blushing, and shook his head after a moment, as if gathering his courage. Lorenzo waited with a slight prickling sense of unease, not sure where this was going.

Finally, Charlie blurted out, "Why don't you bite me?"

Lorenzo's mouth went dry. He was frozen in place for a moment before he rolled onto his back, away from Charlie.

Charlie had been thinking about this?

Wanting it?

A phantom ache swept through his mouth and throat, and he swallowed. Charlie had asked, so he tried to quiet the chanting of *bite bite bite* in his lizard brain and focus.

He couldn't look at Charlie while he said it, so he spoke to the ceiling. "A bite is . . . significant for vampires. A big step in a relationship."

Charlie rolled onto his side. "Really?" he asked. "Why?"

Lorenzo closed his eyes. He wasn't sure how to explain it to a human. He wasn't sure he even fully remembered what it had been like to *be* human, so how could he ever describe it in a way that made sense?

He glanced over at Charlie, and immediately regretted it. He looked so open and trusting, and Lorenzo could imagine it instantly: not just how Charlie would taste, or how he'd react to Lorenzo's bite; but how it would feel to consume Charlie in that way; to feel Charlie's lifeblood become a part of him and take root inside, somewhere deeper than he could ever reach.

"Vampires live on blood," Lorenzo whispered. "It makes us immortal. When you feed on someone—on a lover . . . when you take their life's blood inside of you, for your sustenance . . ." He sighed, hoping he was sounding somber instead of desperate. "It is . . . incredibly intimate."

Charlie was frowning slightly, his eyes still locked on Lorenzo. "Is it . . . I mean, is it always like that? When you bite someone for food?"

"No, of course not. It's . . . different when a bite happens between a vampire and a human they are involved with romantically. Or sexually," he hastened to add. "This . . . this essence you take of them, when you are already bonded in another way, it is . . ."

He sat up restlessly, drawing a knee up to his chest. "Some vampires don't treat it that way—they just bite indiscriminately. But most of us—we only bite a lover when it is someone we are—when it's serious." He paused, staring down at the sheets crumpled by his hand. "And I just . . . wasn't sure that's what we were doing."

Charlie nodded quickly. "No, you're right," he said. "This—that makes sense. Yeah." He cleared his throat, not looking at Lorenzo. "Thank you for telling me. I—I'm glad to know, for my, um. My research."

"Happy to help," Lorenzo said quietly.

Chapter 19

The hotel was large and luminous, but its parking garage was barricaded for some reason, and there was no street parking out front, so by the time Lorenzo managed to find a spot and get them into the hotel, he and Charlie were sniping at each other a little. "I don't understand why you're so desperate to meet witches," Lorenzo muttered.

"They're kind of—a big deal, aren't they?" Charlie asked. He always got a little nervous when Lorenzo harped on this; he could hardly say he was impersonating a crone on the internet and wanted to meet some in real life. "I mean, when it comes to supernatural creatures, aren't vampires, wolves, and witches kinda the big three?"

Lorenzo scoffed. "That's reductive."

The hotel's lobby was opulent but dated—it looked like it hadn't been dusted in a few months or maybe even years, and they were the only guests in sight. "Why did the coven want to meet here?" Charlie asked, examining a chintzy velvet and gold banquette.

"I assumed there was a restaurant," Lorenzo said, poking around. There weren't attendants at the front desk, or anywhere.

Charlie turned to ask him something else, and frowned as his shoe slipped on an unexpected texture on the floor. He glanced down, and realized it was part of a much larger shape underneath them—what looked like a massive rune, almost the size of the entire room, painted directly onto the hotel's marble floor. "Huh," he said, straightening up with some of the black paint on his fingers. "Is that . . . new?"

"Uh oh," Lorenzo said, as people in business suits emerged from the shadows and began chanting at them—at least six of them. Charlie was completely lost, but he was starting to get a bad feeling about this meeting Lorenzo had arranged.

"I condemn this vampire in the strongest terms!" intoned the businesspeople—witches?—in monotone unison, pointing at Lorenzo and Charlie. The rune under their feet was starting to hum. "I condemn any and all acts of bloodlust from all vampires! Your death fetish has no place in our magical commons!" They wobbled a bit on that last one, not all syncing up properly.

Lorenzo growled, making Charlie jump, and his eyes flashed red. Charlie shivered at the sight. It wasn't a bright, glowing red; it felt darker, like when you see a cat's eyes peering out at you from the darkness, and they have a flat sort of luminescence that seems to say *I can see you a lot better than you can see me*.

The mages gasped, and all but a few of them scattered. The remaining few continued their tepid chant, but it was clear that the loss of their comrades had overbalanced the spell somehow— Charlie could feel the air in the room boiling over, shifting, collapsing, and Lorenzo grabbed him and yanked him out of the circle just as the remaining witches chanted, *"Begone!"* and a cascade of blue-white sparks came down over everything.

Charlie landed with a thud in what he realized after a moment was an elevator. Lorenzo was pulling himself to his feet using the iron cage that surrounded the vintage cab. Back out in the lobby, the mages sounded locked in recriminations. *Fuck! Mark broke first. Fuck you, it was Claire! Your begone was weak. Look we all know it was the left flank— Wait, is the vampire still here? FUCK.*

By the time Charlie had gotten to his feet and dusted himself off, the witches had all fled. Lorenzo was pacing around the hotel lobby, growling lowly to himself, making sure they were gone. Charlie breathed out a little, shakily, and said, "Hey— thanks for saving us."

Lorenzo turned back to him, his eyes softening. "You're welcome."

Charlie shivered. And as Lorenzo drew closer, he frowned. "Are you okay?" Charlie asked. "You look a little . . ."

The same sort of realization was happening on Lorenzo's face, and Charlie glanced downward, where his forearm was still stinging slightly from the witches' spell.

"Oh," he said in a deep voice, as he watched his arm flicker in and out of reality. "Shit."

The hex seemed to have shifted them partially into another dimension—at least, that was Lorenzo's best guess. They were both translucent and had the vague sensation of standing on the edge of a cliff somewhere very cold. It seemed to be wearing off, though, a process that felt sort of like popping your ears, except every time Charlie popped, he could tell he was becoming more . . . real. He tried not to think about it too hard, and yawned as they finally got back to Lorenzo's apartment, prompting another pop.

"You should eat something," Lorenzo said, helping him pull off his jacket. "That might help."

"You too," Charlie said. Lorenzo scowled. He was so weird about drinking blood in front of Charlie, which bugged him to no end. And tonight, he definitely needed sustenance.

So Charlie dragged Lorenzo into the kitchen, shoved a blood bag into one hand and a mug into the other, and then started picking out some leftovers from the fridge, hoping whoever they belonged to wouldn't be mad at him.

"So that was an adventure," he said. As he watched, Lorenzo popped and became a little less translucent, his skin a little less gray and plasticine. Charlie grinned. Lorenzo put his blood in the microwave, and Charlie took a bite of his sandwich. He did start to pop a bit faster once he was eating. "Any other ideas for how we can meet witches?"

Lorenzo glared at him. "You want to try again? After this fiasco?"

"It's not that bad," Charlie said, waving one of his arms experimentally. It instantly popped. "See?"

"You have a death wish," Lorenzo said flatly.

"Well, I'm hanging out with the undead, aren't I?" He nudged Lorenzo's leg with his under the counter. They were solid enough now to do that, at least.

Lorenzo was glaring at him like he couldn't decide whether to be annoyed or turned on. Charlie's heart fluttered.

A moment later the front door slammed, and Rachel joined them in the kitchen, looking first-date cute. Charlie perked up as soon as he saw her. "How was it?"

"Meh," she said, putting her clutch on the counter. "Maybe next time."

Charlie *tsk*ed and shook his head, but Lorenzo frowned. "You're giving him another shot?"

"She means next time with someone new," Charlie told him.

He waited for Rachel to chime in, and looked up just in time to catch her flinch. "Rachel," he said, in his best not-angry-just-disappointed voice.

Before she could respond, Isolde joined them. Rachel stiffened. "Oh. Hi."

"Hello," Isolde said calmly. Peering at Lorenzo and Charlie, she said, "Did you know you're not fully in our dimension?"

"Yeah, it's wearing off," Charlie said, shrugging his shoulder pointedly and making it pop.

"No way," Rachel said, coming over to poke at him. "What happened?"

Charlie told the story, and he didn't even mind when Lorenzo jumped in at the best part to tell the punchline they'd workshopped in the car, because he did it so well. He glanced at Charlie when the girls laughed, and Charlie couldn't look away. He wanted to live in Lorenzo's smile. He was getting addicted to it.

When they'd finished the story, Isolde nodded solemnly and said, "A harrowing tale."

Rachel snorted. "A harrowing tale," she said, smiling. "That's funny."

Isolde narrowed her eyes at her. "How is it funny?"

Rachel's face went slack with alarm. "I didn't mean it like that," she said. "It was a—a good turn of phrase. Really."

Isolde continued to glare at her. "Well, hopefully it wears off soon," Lorenzo said.

"Yes, and more importantly," Charlie said, turning back to Rachel, "don't go out with this guy again."

"Guy?" Isolde asked.

"We really—don't . . ." Rachel said, squirming. "It's—"

Charlie cut her off, explaining, "Rachel had a *meh* date and wants to give him a second chance."

"Are you okay with us talking about . . . dating things?" Lorenzo asked Isolde. "Things potentially related to . . . sex?"

Isolde drew herself up. "Yes. I am." Turning to Rachel, she said, slowly and diplomatically: "And . . . ah . . . I agree with Charlie that if this person does not please you, you should look elsewhere. Because you are a nice, attractive human host for a poltergeist, and you deserve a fitting mate."

Rachel was blinking rapidly. "Um," she replied.

"And you're here," Isolde added. "Which means that this person didn't tempt you to give in to carnal lust."

Rachel had frozen completely. "So," Isolde said, raising an eyebrow. "That's a bad sign, right?"

Rachel exploded. It sounded kind of like a pillow going *whump*, and the next moment the entire kitchen was covered in cobwebs. As Charlie started to blink his eyes back open, he saw Lorenzo and Isolde picking cobwebs out of their hair and brushing them off their clothes, but Rachel was gone. "Rachel?" Lorenzo called out. The webbing on his sleeves was starting to disintegrate already, fading back out of reality as soon as it moved.

"Sorry," Rachel called from her room, her voice muffled. "I'm fine."

Isolde was brushing the last few cobwebs off her shoulders in stiff, precise movements. Once the path out of the kitchen was clear, she left without a word.

"What was *that*?" Charlie breathed, trying not to freak out.

Most of the webs on him had shaken off already, and the kitchen was almost back to normal, but he still felt chilly all over.

Lorenzo seemed far less affected. "Poltergeist thing, I guess," he said, picking up his mug of blood.

"You guess?" Charlie demanded. "That's the first time that's happened?"

"This specific thing?" Lorenzo asked. When Charlie just gaped at him, he said, "These poltergeists, you know, they do all sorts of strange things."

Charlie laughed to keep from shrieking. "Okay. So—speaking of strange. How can we find a real witch coven to talk to us?"

Lorenzo tipped his head back and sighed deeply. "Charlie."

"Come on," he said, taking a step closer to Lorenzo. Lorenzo looked away and didn't move at all as Charlie slowly invaded his space. "You have to admit, curse aside—"

"It's a hex," he muttered.

"You've been—you've been so helpful to me," Charlie said, finally letting his hands rest gently on Lorenzo's chest. "Introducing me to all these people, taking me to a—a werewolf wedding, a druid initiation. You know everyone." He smiled, no longer sure if he was buttering Lorenzo up or just thinking out loud. "I'm so lucky I ran into you."

Lorenzo had a strange, sour look on his face. "Yes, well," he said, and he shifted away from Charlie, ostensibly to rinse his mug in the sink. "I'm pleased my connections from decades spent doing nothing are of use to you."

Charlie frowned at him. "You haven't spent decades doing nothing."

Lorenzo rolled his eyes. Charlie got the feeling he wished he hadn't brought any of this up. "Don't worry about it," he said, as he shook out his arm, making it pop, and then looked at his hand. It still wasn't back all the way; the tips of his fingers were barely there as Lorenzo slowly wiggled them back and forth.

How could Lorenzo describe his life as *nothing*?

"You are a very cool person," Charlie said.

Lorenzo glanced up at him, something barbed in his eyes. "Charlie—"

"What?" he asked defensively. "You are. You're a vampire. You've done everything. You know all kinds of cool people."

"Thank you," Lorenzo said stiffly.

Charlie nudged him. "What's bugging you?"

"Nothing."

"I think you have a much cooler life than you might think you do," Charlie told him. "Which is understandable, because . . . it's your life. And it's easy to take it for granted."

That got Lorenzo to turn around and glare at him, though he could tell his heart wasn't in it. "You're the expert, huh?"

"You're a vampire with a bunch of cool supernatural friends," Charlie said. "You have this . . . community."

"It's not a community," Lorenzo snapped. Charlie thought he was probably trying to sound angry, but it didn't come out that way; he sounded exhausted and grim. "We're all from different—they're not—" He sighed. "We're not the same. It's not like that. It's just . . . I know people. But it's not a community."

Charlie thought about every time Lorenzo had introduced him to someone for his nonexistent thesis, and the way they'd all been unfailingly happy to see him. "It could be."

That seemed to give Lorenzo pause, though he didn't respond. A moment later Charlie popped again, and then a strange feeling of sudden, blissful rightness washed all over him. It was not unlike the first few notes of a Sade song, or being under a weighted blanket. "Oh," he said, "I think I'm done popping." He looked down at his hand, trying to see if it looked different. "I think I'm back."

"Good," Lorenzo said, smiling faintly. The tips of his fingers were still slightly blurred.

Charlie took Lorenzo's hand in his, lacing their fingers together. "I'll wait with you."

Charlie had almost completely acclimated to a nocturnal schedule by now, and one of his favorite parts of his new routine was the sunrise walk home. He didn't always walk; his apartment was kind of far from Lorenzo's, but when the weather was just right, he enjoyed it. The streets were quiet, and the soft pink light made everything feel magical.

His phone ringing interrupted the serene beauty. He frowned at the unfamiliar number, but his phone wasn't tagging it as spam. Curious, he answered.

"Why aren't you returning my calls?" Ava demanded.

The surprise of hearing her voice sent a wave of nausea through him. He looked at the number on his phone again, and Ava correctly interpreted his silence. "It's Henry's phone," she said. "I was wondering if it was me you were dodging or everyone. Guess I have my answer!"

"Jesus, Ava," Charlie said. "Are you watching *Killing Eve* again?"

She giggled. "Yeah, I'm a spy. So . . ."

He swallowed, saying nothing, and she sighed. "Listen—we need to talk about the column!"

"It's doing well," he said, reflexively. He had the jittery feeling that he needed to get off the phone as soon as possible, which didn't really make any sense. But every second the conversation ticked on, he felt a little closer to crawling out of his skin.

"It's doing *incredibly* well," Ava said, pride radiating through the phone. "That's why we need to capitalize on it!"

"Capitalize," Charlie said. "Yeah. What do you, um."

"I mean, anything!" Ava said. "For one thing, I feel like you need to come in and do a victory lap around the office. You know boomers don't think anyone's real unless they see them, in person, wearing a suit."

Charlie laughed thinly. "I guess."

"But it's not just that," Ava gushed. "You're crushing it lately! People love the Crone. We could get you on some panels, or—you could write a book!"

"A book?" His voice echoed off the sleepy streets around him, sounding unnaturally loud.

"Whatever you want, Charlie," Ava said. "I just don't want you to waste what you have right now. People are finally paying attention! Let's show 'em what you've got."

"Right," Charlie said. He felt dizzy. "I'll, uh, think about it."

"You should," Ava said. "If we play our cards right, you could even get an offer from somewhere else."

"Somewhere else?" Charlie asked. "What do you mean?"

"I mean, you've been kicking such ass, some other site might want to steal you away." She sounded positively smug about the idea. "To move your column—or, you, really—your services as an advice writer, to some other platform. For a big cash payout."

He laughed a little, hollowly. "That's not a real thing."

"Um, it totally is," Ava said. "You'd be an amazing get for a lot of places. *Midnight* might not be big enough for you anymore."

Charlie scoffed.

"And listen, on that topic, I feel like we should put a meeting on the books about your latest Crone columns, in terms of voice," Ava said.

Charlie paused. "What do you mean, voice?"

"Oh, I don't know," she said, sounding distracted. "Normally as the Crone you kind of ham it up, but some of your latest columns have been sounding a lot like a regular twentysomething gay guy."

"I am a regular twentysomething gay guy," he said flatly. An early-morning jogger gave him a funny look as he passed by.

"Right, I just mean that's not usually the Crone's voice," Ava said. "You were talking about, like, *circling back* in one of your columns. That's not really a Crone thing."

It was beginning to feel like there was a fire in Charlie's chest, slowly smoldering and eating everything away. Maybe it had been there ever since he'd started his column; because of what it meant to him, how lucky he knew he was, and how much he had at stake. But that fire was burning harder than ever now with everything he was keeping from Lorenzo, and Charlie felt like he was losing more and more of himself to crumbling ash.

"In another column I think you said *speaking for myself*," Ava said. "You don't usually—"

"Speak for myself?" Charlie snapped.

"Babe," Ava said, sounding like he'd suddenly caught her attention. "Are you feeling like a change in persona? Because we can talk about that—"

He hadn't heard anything after the word *persona*, which swamped him with shame. "Ava, I gotta go," he choked out.

"Charlie, wait—" Ava said, but he hung up on her. He slid his phone into his pocket, then pulled it back out, after a moment, to block her husband's number.

From: shellmer@jmail.com
To: wiseoldcrone@midnight.com
Date: May 28, 11:23 AM
Subject: Next Week on Mad Men

Dear Crone,

My partner and I have been together for six years and it's
going really well—I love him deeply, and he really understands me. He has one bad habit though that's driving
me crazy: as a psychic, he always knows what's going to
happen on every single show we watch together, and he
keeps spoiling them for me! He claims it's because it's
hard to distinguish between what he's actually seen and
what he sees when the muse visits him, but I'm sick of
having every great plot point on all of our shows ruined!
What should I do?

Sincerely,
Foretold Fights

From: lewisknef@jmail.com
To: wiseoldcrone@midnight.com

Date: May 6, 4:12 PM
Subject: Penne a la Regret

Dear Wise Old Crone,

My roommate is part of a hive of magical interconnected spores stretching across the entire continent. He's polite and a great roommate, and I can see us being friends. Or at least, I could—but last night I got super drunk and accidentally ordered this pasta dish from my favorite Italian restaurant down the street, and I got it *with mushrooms*. Now he's not talking to me, and I feel awful. The kitchen is like a crime scene. How can I apologize?

Sincerely,
Fungi Faux Pas

Wise Old Crone

Am I Wild Enough to Date a Wolf?
Who could ever learn to love a bookworm?

June 23

Dear Crone,

I'm in a new relationship with a great guy—he's funny, sexy, and treats me really well. The problem is that apparently no one "gets" us as a couple. I'm known to be kind of uptight, I guess—I'm definitely type A, and not really that adventurous—

and my new boyfriend is a werewolf. My friends keep asking me how the relationship "works"—like, whether he's "supposed" to be dating another werewolf, or if I ever feel overwhelmed by his "animalistic nature." (They've even asked if we have sex in the woods!!) Even acquaintances or work colleagues seem surprised—in an unflattering way—when they learn I'm dating a wolf, I guess because I'm so bland by comparison. My boyfriend is kind and gentle, not a toxic "alpha" type at all, but these comments make me feel so bad about myself. I love this man, but I've never dated a nonhuman before, and I'm nervous for our future. Is it true that a werewolf could never be happy with a quiet human, one who prefers staying in with a good book to howling at the moon?

Sincerely,
Not Wolf Enough

Dear Bookworm,

Allow the Crone to recap: you have a hunky, sweet, adoring boyfriend who makes you happy. What's the problem?

Seriously, fuck every single person who's made snide comments about your relationship. They are clearly jealous. And why wouldn't they be? Whether you really are getting busy out in the woods or staying in to scrapbook together, it sounds like this is working for you. Who cares what anyone else thinks?

It is understandable to have anxieties early in a relationship—to wonder about the person we're dating, what they're looking for and what they need, and what being with them might mean about us. It's especially understandable to feel out of your depth when it comes to the supernatural, if this is your first such relationship.

But to be clear: of course a werewolf could happily date a human, even a "bland" one (which I doubt you are). I personally know many werewolves who don't fit the dated stereotypes your friends are relying on—I've seen senior werewolves play like pups, and met type A werewolves who could probably out-organize you. The truth is, there are humans who behave like beasts, and werewolves who'd probably love to curl up beside you while you read *The Call of the Wild*.

If you're wondering about your relationship, think about the **person** you're dating, not his species. Does he make you laugh? Can you pass hours or days together and still want more? Do you think about him when you're not together?

Are you happy—not just content, but deliriously, giddily, uncontrollably happy? If the answer to that is yes, don't let anything else phase you.

And if anyone makes a shitty comment to you again, you have my permission to maul them.

Sincerely,
Crone

Chapter 20

Charlie and Lorenzo had started the evening on perfectly respectable ends of the couch. But Charlie hadn't made plans for the night yet, and the longer he spent on his phone trying to find something for them to do, the closer Lorenzo crept. Eventually he got Charlie sprawled over him, his back to Lorenzo's chest, while Lorenzo nuzzled at Charlie's neck and Charlie for some reason insisted on pretending that they were still going out. He seemed to take offense at the idea of staying in for the night, as if that meant he wasn't creative enough to make plans for them. Lorenzo stroked the soft skin of Charlie's neck with his fingers, his mouth watering, and tried to change his mind.

"You're sure the Masons aren't a satanic group," Charlie asked, as Lorenzo massaged his shoulders and the nape of his neck.

"As far as I am aware, no," he replied. "They are humans."

"QVC salespeople?"

Lorenzo grinned, and pressed a kiss to the nape of Charlie's neck. "Also humans."

"Area 51?"

Lorenzo pulled back so that Charlie could see how crestfallen he was. "How would I know if the U.S. government is hiding aliens?"

"I dunno," he giggled. "Ooh, what about the Mall of America? The Mall of America has to be haunted."

"We can't make it to the Mall of America tonight," Lorenzo muttered, ducking down to suck on Charlie's neck lightly. "It's hours away."

Charlie was finally rolling back against him. He obviously couldn't see his phone anymore. "How far?"

"Give up," Lorenzo told him, but before he could kiss Charlie properly, there was a hammering at the door.

They both jumped, staring at each other in confusion as the noise continued without stopping—someone on the other end was pounding at the door relentlessly, as if there were an emergency. Lorenzo jumped up and yanked the door open, not sure what to expect—and revealed a staggering, disheveled . . . "Gray?"

"Oh good," he said in a distracted sort of tone, pitching forward over the threshold. "Do you have wolfsbane?"

Charlie was staring at him, his mouth open. Lorenzo shut his when he was hit with the overwhelming scents of dirty wolf and alcohol. "I—" he started.

Before he could continue, Gray pushed past both of them into the kitchen, where he started tearing through every drawer and cabinet. "Hang on," Lorenzo said, following him. Gray was dressed horribly by his own standards, in a wrinkled collared shirt and frumpy jeans. "What's—hey!" he pulled a bottle of mirin out of Gray's hand. "What's going on?"

Gray squinted at them blearily, as if he'd forgotten they were there, and then drew himself up. "I have been . . . um . . . separated. Terminated." He paused, and then added, "Shitcanned."

"What . . ."

"The pack?" Charlie asked. And then, in an insufficiently quiet aside, he muttered, "You can get fired from a werewolf pack?"

Lorenzo glared at him.

"Oh yes," Gray said breezily, as he started rummaging through Lorenzo's kitchen again, leaving cabinets open and rattling dishes. "Especially when the wedding you spent *months* of your life arranging becomes a bloodbath."

Lorenzo winced. "They blamed you for that?"

"Mm-hmm," he said. "It was part of the peace talks with the other pack—they couldn't hold anyone *important* accountable for the mess, so they decided it was my fault." He gasped in happiness as he found a fifth of something in the back of a cabinet, but upon his squinted examination in the light, he sighed and tossed it into the sink. "Now I'm blacklisted everywhere. Okay, do you—where is it?"

"I don't have any," Lorenzo told him.

Gray grumbled at him and resumed his search. The commotion had drawn Rachel and Isolde out of their rooms, and they hovered at the edge of the kitchen, watching Gray warily. "Any what?" Charlie asked.

"Wolfsbane," Lorenzo explained. "It's—wolves heal too quickly to become intoxicated, so they make special alcohol infused with wolfsbane so they can . . ." He trailed off as Gray seemed to exhaust his search, sliding against the wall to sit on the floor in an ungainly heap. "Not heal," he finished.

"What kind of self-respecting werewolf doesn't have any wolfsbane?" Gray asked plaintively.

"I'm a vampire."

"Right. Right. Oh!" Gray said, perking up—he'd spotted the cabinet in the dining room, which held at least a few bottles of wine visible through the glass doors. He jumped up and pushed past Rachel and Isolde to reach it, shoving Isolde into Rachel's arms in the process.

Rachel jerked and shoved her away just as quickly, making Isolde frown. "What's your problem?"

Rachel stood there awkwardly for a moment, just as Lorenzo caught a strong, unfurling scent of decay. Then he noticed the bruises all over Rachel's skin, growing and spreading until she was a putrid, deep soft red all over. The color darkened to purple, then black, and then she liquified into a puddle of blood, just as there was a thump and rattle inside Rachel's room, presumably from her rematerializing.

In the corner of his eye, Lorenzo saw that Charlie was white and shaking, his eyes wide. He clapped him on the shoulder and gave him what he hoped was a reassuring hand gesture. Isolde, though, just looked annoyed, seething down at the blood smear Rachel had left before stomping off, muttering, "That is *so* immature."

"I," Charlie whimpered. "I don't . . ."

"It's okay," Lorenzo said, pulling him into a hug and rubbing his shoulders until he stopped shaking.

Gray, who had finished going through the cabinet, cried, "Gin? Ugh," in a miserable tone, and collapsed onto the floor again. Charlie and Lorenzo both went to sit next to him.

"Gray," Lorenzo said. "When did they . . ."

He closed his eyes. "Few days after the wedding."

"Why didn't you tell us?"

"I was at home, drinking all my wolfsbane," he explained,

with a hollow sort of cheeriness. "Then I ran out, and I can't go to a single wolf bar because I'm . . ." He thunked his head back against the wall behind him. His voice was starting to sound thick. "I'm a lone wolf now."

Lorenzo stood up. "Gray," he said, "I am truly sorry to hear of your misfortune."

Gray sighed. "Thank you, friend."

"I have no wolfsbane, for which I apologize," he said graciously, offering Gray a hand to help him up. "Let's go to a bar."

Gray sniffed. "They're all owned by one of the big packs. Any bar that has wolfsbane, anyway."

"There has to be an unaffiliated supe bar somewhere that has it," Charlie said with completely unearned confidence. Lorenzo glared at him doubtfully as Charlie got out his phone once again.

This time Charlie's research proved fruitful, as he discovered a casino forty minutes out of town that he claimed had what Gray was looking for. The neon and fluorescent lighting, and the sense that one could get lost in the slots and never emerge, were chilling. And while the resort didn't appear to be supernaturally owned or affiliated, one of the small bars on the basement level did, in fact, have wolfsbane.

They kept pace with Gray for a while, but split off on their own once he got sufficiently hammered and started ranting at the bartender about men's tailoring. They played a few electronic betting games, lost some money, and then found themselves wandering the shopping area, which had many suspiciously overpriced luxury stores that Charlie thought must be a front for something.

The only store Charlie was interested in was a cavernous, touristy place that exclusively sold tacky and completely useless knickknacks. Charlie delighted in examining each one, shoving several into a basket that Lorenzo was carrying, and informing him which pieces would look good in his apartment and where.

Despite the fact that he was evidently having a fantastic time, Lorenzo still felt compelled to apologize. "Sorry this derailed our evening in."

"It wasn't an evening in," Charlie said, looking at a refrigerator magnet of the pope. "I was going to pick something. But this is fun."

"Mm," Lorenzo said, pulling the magnet out of Charlie's hands so he could kiss him.

"Gray's lucky. You're a good friend," Charlie said when they broke apart, smiling and winding his arms around Lorenzo's shoulders.

"You're a good—" *boyfriend*, he almost said, and nearly physically flinched as he grasped to redirect the sentence. "Friend of a friend," he managed. "For coming with us."

For a brief moment there was a blip of something that looked like panic in Charlie's eyes, as if he'd noticed Lorenzo's near miss, but it was gone in a second, and then he smiled. Lorenzo kissed him again, trying to push past the knot of embarrassment and anxiety in his gut, trying not to think about the way they were still dancing around each other, keeping their distance, not risking anything.

Charlie made a small, hurt noise in the back of his throat when Lorenzo deepened the kiss, and he shivered from head to toe. *Fuck not risking anything.*

Charlie pulled back, licking his lips, his cheeks bright pink, and Lorenzo shoved a tchotchke back into his hands before they got themselves thrown out of the casino. Charlie took it gratefully, and Lorenzo hovered over his shoulder as he went back to browsing.

"So," he said, once he felt more in control of himself. "How is your thesis going?"

Charlie froze, turned, and blinked at him. "Uh. Well. Really well. I've been turning in chapters to my—my advisor, and, um. She really seems to like them."

Lorenzo couldn't figure out why Charlie seemed nervous. Maybe he was worried about the *educational* aspect to their relationship, but Lorenzo wasn't feeling sensitive about that today, so he tried to reassure him with a smile. "So I've been helpful?"

Charlie's anxiety, whatever the source, melted into a warm smile. "Very helpful."

Lorenzo walked down the aisle, looking at some discount candles. "And . . . what's the timeline?" he asked. "When do you finish it, or turn it in, or whatever?"

"Uh . . ." Charlie said, poking around on the opposite shelf. "A few more months, I think. Then it'll be done."

"And then what?"

"Then what . . . what?" Charlie asked.

"You get a teaching job?" Lorenzo asked. "That's what people do with advanced degrees, right?"

"Yeah," Charlie said vaguely. "I mean—maybe."

"You should probably think about that," Lorenzo said, smiling at him. "If you're going to be done in a few months."

"Yeah," Charlie said, rubbing his neck. "I've never been great at planning."

Lorenzo sighed. He didn't know what Charlie wasn't telling him, but that wasn't really the point. He clearly didn't want to include Lorenzo in whatever it was. So he stopped asking questions, and a stilted silence fell.

Then Charlie said, abruptly, "But, uh—I know they're never really hiring here, at the university."

"Oh," Lorenzo said, frowning. "So—"

"So I'll have to move," Charlie said, darting a glance at him. "Eventually."

"Okay," he said slowly. He remembered something about Charlie's father being a professor at the university, but he was guessing he wouldn't want to talk about that. Charlie always clammed up anytime they were talking and the subject started to drift toward his family.

Charlie was moving?

"Yeah," he was saying. "I mean, everyone wants to live here—I mean, in Brookville," he said with a grin. "Not this . . . incredible casino."

"Yes," Lorenzo said softly. Jobs were hard to come by in Brookville; it was a popular town, and graduates of the university were always looking to return. Lots of people wanted to live there. But Charlie wasn't one of them.

He was moving after he graduated. Lorenzo felt like an idiot. He'd seen this coming with Olivia. Why not now?

Because he's already taken root in you, a cruel voice whispered. *There'll be nothing left when he's gone.*

Charlie glanced back up at him. His soft brown eyes seemed so full of emotion, but Lorenzo couldn't be sure. Sometimes he felt like he could see Charlie—really see him—and other times it felt like trying to know him was like trying to hold the sky in his hands.

"It's really competitive," Charlie said. "So I'll probably be looking at jobs in New York. Or, uh, elsewhere."

What was the point in Lorenzo holding back from biting him? He would already be torn apart when Charlie left.

"Right," he said. "Okay."

Then again—hadn't he always expected to lose Charlie somehow?

Chapter 21

It was incredible having an affair with a vampire over the summer. As June wound into July it had only gotten hotter; the kind of discomfiting, sweltering heat that lasted long into the evening.

Charlie grinned to himself and pressed his leg against Lorenzo's, as he lay next to him snoring. Being with Lorenzo was like having a cool side of the pillow he could snuggle any time he wanted. It was amazing.

Dawn was still hours away, but Charlie was always flattered when Lorenzo passed out after sex, and he knew he'd be up again soon. He liked being alone like this with Lorenzo sometimes—being able to stare at his sleeping form unobserved, and daydream.

He wondered what the winter would be like. Lorenzo's cool skin would be less of a perk, but night was longer in the winter; that would be fun. And it would be a neat sort of challenge, trying to keep Lorenzo warm. Either all vampires got cold easily or it was just Lorenzo, but the man loved his chunky sweaters and reading books by the fire and taking long, hot baths in the gorgeous antique bathtub that Charlie's plumber had repaired. He liked reminding Lorenzo of that fact when they were in there together.

He'd need a lot of baths in the winter. Charlie could get behind that.

He sat up in bed, suddenly feeling queasy.

He was thinking long-term with Lorenzo. He couldn't afford to do that.

He glanced at Lorenzo, who was still dead to the world. His face looked more open in sleep; he lost that broodiness that was either all vampires' or just Lorenzo's, and looked . . . vulnerable.

Charlie pulled his shorts on and snuck downstairs, looking for a snack or something to distract him.

The first floor was dark, but he fumbled his way to the kitchen and turned on the light. There were plenty of human snacks in the pantry despite the complete lack of actual humans who lived there, but none of it looked good. Charlie slumped against the pantry door, fighting off a wave of mild panic.

He couldn't remember why he wasn't supposed to be thinking long-term with Lorenzo. Which is to say that of course he knew why: the column was doing so well, soon he'd be able to move back to New York and reclaim the kind of life he'd always wanted. That was the plan.

He just couldn't remember what it felt like to want that anymore.

It would be childish and stupid to stay in Brookville forever. Who did that? Just because his memories of New York were growing gray and washed out, while his life now had never felt more vibrant? He liked Lorenzo's roommates. He liked everything about Lorenzo. He liked who he was here.

But it was a lie. And staying was impossible.

He worried less and less now about Lorenzo figuring out his big secret. He worried more about how he'd take it when Charlie left.

Glumly, he abandoned his quest for snacks and retreated back toward Lorenzo's room. But on his way down to the kitchen the lights had all been out; now, with the dim light of the kitchen illuminating the hallway, Charlie saw it: a smoky, translucent ooze covering the ceiling outside Isolde's room.

He slowed to a stop, horror and curiosity crowding for his attention. As he got closer, he realized that the ooze had eyes; dozens and dozens of eyes, blinking asynchronously, looking at nothing and everything as its membranes slowly rippled.

He swallowed back a scream. "Uh," he said, manfully. "Rach?"

"Oh. Hey Charlie," Rachel said. He slumped at the familiar sound of her voice, though it sounded echoey and distant.

"Yeah. Uh," he said. "Whatcha doin'?"

"Just, y'know." She sounded distracted, or maybe stoned. The ooze pulsed indecisively. "Looking at my phone."

"Uh-huh," Charlie gritted out, fighting the urge to run. The eyes had started to look at him. "Uh, Rach? Could we talk, y'know—human form to human form?"

"Oh," she said, "sure." The ooze dropped to the floor like a bucket of water being poured out, making Charlie flinch backward; but then it was gone, and Rachel was standing there, looking gaunt with exhaustion, in a ratty purple robe. She still had a few extra eyes on her face. Charlie grimaced and tried not to look.

"What's up," Rachel asked, still seeming dazed.

"Rach, are you okay?" Charlie asked. "You've been really . . . um. Really poltergeist-y lately."

Something a little more human flickered in Rachel's eyes, and she stood a bit straighter. "Oh yeah. Sorry about that." She cleared her throat. "I didn't mean to scare you."

"It's fine, I don't care," Charlie said. "I mean, I'm a wimp, y'know?"

Rachel smiled a little, and he said, "Seriously, is everything okay?"

Rachel glanced at Isolde's door. "It's fine," she said. "I just need to get some sleep. Later."

He watched her trudge back to her room in silent contemplation. He thought often of Lorenzo's maxim that *magic is intent*. It was both profound and profoundly unhelpful, because as he'd learned in his many years as an advice columnist, nothing was more mercurial or inscrutable than intent. He had a lot of theories on what was going on with Rachel, but he wasn't ready to commit to one yet. In real life, unlike his column, people didn't just come out and tell him exactly what was bothering them, what choices they were staring down, what was haunting them, and what they had to lose.

And he wasn't sure how helpful he was even when they did. More than once he'd made the tension between Rachel and Isolde worse; if he tried again now, he didn't like to think what nightmarish horrors he might unleash.

And this was supposed to be what he was good at. His calling, or whatever.

But these were real people he knew, unlike the people who wrote into his column. Oh, the letters the Crone got were real (at least, he hoped)—but Charlie never met the people who wrote them. Nor did he really think about them after he hit publish. Not until Ava texted him to tell him how well the column was doing.

Maybe he'd never really cared about helping people. Maybe it had all always been about helping himself.

He swallowed a twist of shame in his throat and jogged back up the stairs to Lorenzo's room.

Lorenzo was awake when he got there, and the smile on his face when he saw Charlie washed away most of his lingering unease. "Hi," Charlie said, sitting on the bed to give him a kiss.

"Mm," Lorenzo said, still shaking off sleep. "Where were you?"

"Getting a snack," Charlie said. Lorenzo glanced at his empty hands and smirked.

"I got distracted," Charlie said, climbing into the bed so he could tuck himself against Lorenzo. "Rachel was . . . I don't even know. Manifesting horrors that I wish were beyond my comprehension."

"What did she do?" Lorenzo asked idly, carding his fingers through Charlie's hair. He sighed and slumped further against him.

"I think she was haunting Isolde," he said slowly.

"Really."

"Mm."

"You think they're fighting again?" Lorenzo asked.

"Yeah," he said. "Maybe."

"Charlie?" Lorenzo said, sounding suspicious.

"What was it like when Isolde first moved in?" Charlie asked him.

"What do you mean?"

"Was Rachel annoyed with her from the start, or was . . ." He trailed off as he felt Lorenzo stiffen beneath him, and pulled back. "What?"

"Why are you asking me about this?" Lorenzo asked, his expression stormy.

"I'm curious," Charlie said.

Lorenzo glared at him.

"Oookay," Charlie said, and went back to snuggling Lorenzo's chest. "We don't have to talk."

"You mean gossip," Lorenzo said flatly.

"What's wrong with a little gossip?"

"Hm," Lorenzo said. "What about a little meddling?"

"Who's meddling?" Charlie shot back.

Lorenzo grumbled but said nothing, and Charlie's eyes fluttered closed.

"Y'know," Lorenzo said, "we wouldn't have any problems with Rachel or Isolde if we stayed at your place."

His eyes flew open. The reason they never stayed at his place was that he was paranoid Lorenzo would see the grimy apartment he was subletting and somehow discover all of his secrets. He liked it here, with Maggie and Rachel and Isolde; his place was small and dark and cramped, and reminded him of what his life really was.

He pulled back again, trying to read Lorenzo, who was waiting for a response with a cool, distant look on his face. Did Lorenzo *want* to see his place, or was this some kind of test? If so, did he suspect Charlie was hiding something from him? Or was this all more basic?

Charlie forced a playful smile and pushed up on his elbow, grinning at Lorenzo cockily. "Is that your way of asking to come over?"

Lorenzo shrugged, closing his eyes.

"My place sucks," Charlie whispered, leaning in close to him. "It's grad student living—not this ritzy."

Lorenzo said nothing, even as Charlie pressed kisses to his chest and up his jaw. He wasn't ignoring Charlie, moving slightly against him in a warm, pleased sort of way, but he hadn't responded yet either.

"I mean, I don't have this bed," Charlie said between kisses. "Or your bathroom. Or . . ."

That skylight, he thought. And suddenly he *did* want to invite Lorenzo over to his place, badly. He thought of Lorenzo lying in this bed, day in and day out, under an enormous glass pane, and he wanted him safe. Wanted to offer him someplace different.

Which scared the shit out of him.

"Or what?" Lorenzo asked, finally looking at him.

Charlie's heart was hammering. He kissed Lorenzo, scrambling into his lap, to distract him.

And Lorenzo let him.

Chapter 22

It stormed badly on Sunday night. Normally Lorenzo liked the rain, but tonight he was annoyed because he'd found a faerie circle that he'd been looking forward to taking Charlie to. He would have been shocked, because Lorenzo always complained and dragged his feet when Charlie came up with an idea for one of his "educational" excursions. He'd have been surprised and maybe even delighted by Lorenzo bringing an idea to him. Lorenzo had been looking forward to that—discombobulating Charlie. Exciting him.

But the damn faerie circle got rained out, so they were stuck inside. It was early, before midnight, but Lorenzo already felt like crawling the walls.

They'd taken over the living room, thinking they were the only ones home, when Maggie came out of her room to get something from the kitchen. Charlie roped her into sitting on the couch with them, and after a long meandering conversation, Charlie brought them around to talking about Rachel and Isolde. Lorenzo stiffened.

He didn't know why Charlie's curiosity about them bothered him, but it did. When Charlie got like this, he reminded Lorenzo of the man he'd met five years ago. Shallow. Judgmental. Manipulative.

Caring. Invested. Sensitive, his brain chirped back at him. And he knew that was true; he knew that Charlie cared about Rachel and Isolde. He knew he was only trying to help.

A touch on his knee startled him. Without interrupting the story he was telling Maggie, Charlie dragged Lorenzo's bare feet into his lap and started giving him a foot rub.

He'd noticed Lorenzo's discomfort and responded to it without being asked. And his thumbs felt amazing pressed firmly into Lorenzo's soles. He melted into the couch a little, closed his eyes, and tried to let the conversation wash over him.

"Did you really vote for someone else, instead of Isolde?" Charlie was asking.

"Well, there was this supercool gremlin dude who built these elaborate sets for D&D," Maggie said.

Lorenzo could feel Charlie turning to look at him, and opened his eyes. "So you were the deciding vote?" Charlie asked. "Why'd you vote for Isolde?"

Lorenzo shrugged. After a moment, a look of scandalized understanding took over Charlie's face. "Because she's hot?" he demanded.

Lorenzo smiled sheepishly, and Charlie doubled over with laughter. Maggie grinned, curling her legs up into her chair.

"Wow," Charlie said, sitting back against the couch. Turning back to Maggie, he asked, "So why do you think Rachel voted for her?"

"I don't know," Maggie said cautiously. "Why do you ask?"

"Well, because things have been super weird with them lately," Charlie said. "You can't tell me you haven't noticed."

Lorenzo pulled his feet back from Charlie's lap and got up off the couch, stretching his legs. Charlie looked after him in confusion, but was distracted when Maggie said, "I think they just get on each other's nerves sometimes. They could do a better job communicating."

"Yeah. Yeah," Charlie said doubtfully. "I wonder the best way to get them to talk. Y'know, really talk."

"If they want to talk, they'll talk," Lorenzo snapped. "You can't make that happen."

Charlie blinked, his eyes going wide. "No, I know," he said. Lorenzo realized he was shaking finely, his muscles jittery with adrenaline. "I'm just saying—"

"Well don't," he said harshly.

"Don't . . . what?"

Maggie quietly left the room, and Charlie leaned back over the couch to try to reason with him. "Lorenzo—"

"You are meddling," Lorenzo hissed.

"I'm—we're just talking," Charlie said defensively.

"Behind their backs," Lorenzo said. He knew it was a rationalization, but he was angry—so angry—and he was willing to hold on to anything, regardless of whether it made sense.

"I was just asking her opinion—" Charlie started.

"No," he said, "you're trying to—you're trying to shape this situation to your own desires."

"Lorenzo—"

"And I know you think you're helping, but you're not," Lorenzo said. "This isn't your business."

"I know it's not my business. But I can—I can do this,

okay?" Charlie said earnestly. "I mean, this is what my—my thesis is about. I write about relationships and interpersonal stuff just like this, and I can help them sort through their issues. I'm good at this."

"No, you're not!" Lorenzo barked.

Charlie's face went blank with shock and hurt, and Lorenzo instantly wished he could take the words back. But he couldn't, because he was still scared. This was what had scared him about Charlie the last time they'd known each other—that he was smarter than everyone else, and he knew it. That he would try to butt in and control things.

And he *knew* that version of Charlie had probably never existed, and that that wasn't what was going on now. But he couldn't shake the fear, and words just kept tumbling out of his mouth. "You think this is fun!" he shouted. "And I know you think you want to help, but you get too—too—and you end up ruining things, just like when you told Olivia to leave me!"

Agonized embarrassment hit him like a freight train. He stiffened and turned his back on Charlie, mortified. What was *wrong* with him? He felt like a child—bringing that up *now*, out of the blue . . .

And then he heard Charlie's voice, quiet but distinct: "I was right."

Lorenzo froze. He turned to face Charlie slowly. "What did you just say?"

Charlie stood up from the couch and walked around to stand directly in front of him. "I was right to tell Olivia to leave you."

Disbelieving—furious—Lorenzo said, "You apologized for that. When we first ran into each other, you—"

"I know," Charlie said firmly. "And I—I am sorry that it hurt you, but—"

"I can't believe you are taking back your apology," Lorenzo thundered. Charlie was still talking, his voice ramping up, but Lorenzo kept shouting over him. "—and are standing here before me to say—"

"*She wasn't into you!*" Charlie shouted.

His harsh breathing was deafening in the silence that followed.

"I know I was—I was a dick about it back then, and I shouldn't have been," Charlie said, his chest heaving. "But Olivia came to me, talking about her future and her life—and then she said she felt like she *had* to try the long-distance thing with you. And I could tell that her heart wasn't in it."

An echo of heartache twisted in Lorenzo's gut; shame and anger and a perverse, aching need for Charlie to keep talking. "And yeah, at the time I was probably only thinking about Olivia, not about you," Charlie said. "And I told her not to be with someone if she wasn't all in. But you deserved better than that too."

Lorenzo shuddered. Charlie took a step toward him. "You deserve someone who wants you. All of you," he said quietly. "You deserve someone . . . who can't be dissuaded by some bullshit advice."

Lorenzo husked out a laugh. Charlie took another step closer, cupping Lorenzo's face in his palm. "You deserve . . ."

Lorenzo waited, hanging on every expression that flickered over Charlie's face. He could swear his heart was pounding.

No, pounding was what human hearts did. His seemed to be trying to writhe and spasm and pour its way through his dead rib cage straight to Charlie.

Charlie still hadn't said anything. He was just staring at Lorenzo's lips, and Lorenzo wasn't sure whether he wanted him to finish his sentence or kiss him.

"Done fighting?" Maggie asked in a meek voice, peeking from around the edge of the kitchen wall.

Charlie slumped into Lorenzo's chest. "Done fighting," he shouted back, his voice muffled. Lorenzo brought his arms up around Charlie and felt the tension drain out of him.

Maggie was clinking as she shuffled awkwardly back into the living room. "Well, while you guys were occupied," she said obliquely, "I got all my hot sauces together."

"Your hot sauces?" Charlie asked. His throat sounded thick.

"Oh yeah, I have almost everything from *Hot Ones*," she said, laying them all out on the table. "And—" She was interrupted by a beep from the kitchen. "And I thought we could experiment," she called back. "See which one tastes best."

"You want to make wings?" Charlie asked, looking at one of the bottles.

"No," Maggie said, coming back into the living room with an enormous bowl of popcorn. "We'll try it on this."

Charlie laughed, and Maggie's smile lit up her weather-beaten face. *Thank goodness for Maggie.*

"It'll be awesome," she said. "Now, let's start with this one."

Chapter 23

In an incredibly sweet gesture, Lorenzo let Charlie set up a mini home office in his bedroom. It was just a little secretary desk that he could tell Lorenzo never used—sort of a vanity without the mirror—but he'd let Charlie lay claim to it, keep his water bottle and box of tissues there, and that's where he'd set up his laptop when he was going to be spending a while at Lorenzo's and wanted to be able to work a bit. Sometimes he'd get to Lorenzo's place before the sun had set and putter around the room while Lorenzo lay in bed, still all corpse-like; he'd shower and get some writing done, eat a snack, and wait for Lorenzo to arise.

At the moment, he was scrolling aimlessly in front of a blank page. According to the new widget he had on his home screen, sunset had been six minutes ago, but Lorenzo was still lodged under the covers and showed no signs of stirring. He sighed.

An email pinged as it arrived—Ava, probably wanting to know where his next column was. The only downside of the column being a smash hit was Ava and their bosses breathing down his neck, always looking for the next installment. He was still dodging her calls.

He loved writing the columns—he wasn't sure that would ever change—but hitting publish every week was getting harder and harder. The bigger the column got, the more inescapable it became—all the things he needed to do, and everything he had to answer for.

He clicked on Ava's email anyway, out of resigned guilt.

She was not checking in on his next column. He saw the words *Advance Media*, a conglomerate that owned hundreds of outlets worldwide. And he saw the word *offer*.

Panic choked his throat, and he shut his laptop before he finished the email.

From the bed there was a soft rustle of sheets, and he looked up to find Lorenzo, blearily awake and looking at him, drowsy eyes peeking out from over the crest of a pillow. He couldn't see the rest of Lorenzo's face, but he could tell he was smiling, and his chest gave a little happy clench at the sight, his anxiety about his job and the column melting away.

"Good evening," Charlie said, and came to sit on the bed next to him. He threaded his fingers through Lorenzo's hair, petting him as he stretched and groaned, throwing some of the covers back.

"Hmm," Lorenzo said. "When did you get here?"

"A little while ago."

Lorenzo sat up and kissed him undemandingly. Then he yawned, stretched again until Charlie could hear something pop, and mumbled "Let me brush my teeth" against Charlie's lips.

Charlie flopped back onto the bed while Lorenzo trudged off to the bathroom. He felt warm and tingly all over, like he might start purring. The sheets were cool and silky, and he could feel himself melting into the mattress. "Have I said enough that I love your place?" he shouted to Lorenzo.

There was the sound of water running, on and off. Charlie frowned as the silence stretched, but he still heard little echoing noises as Lorenzo moved around the bathroom, so he waited patiently. Eventually, Lorenzo came back and sat next to him on the bed. "Yes," he said, though he looked distant.

"What's wrong?" Charlie asked.

Lorenzo smiled at him faintly. "I like that you're here."

"Me too," he said, disarming the non sequitur. "But . . . ?"

Lorenzo glanced around. "This place just—it can feel a little lonely sometimes."

"This place?" Charlie said skeptically. "It's a palace. And you have your roommates."

"That's true," Lorenzo said unconvincingly.

Charlie glanced up at the ceiling, the one incongruous element in the entire room—in the entire building, for that matter. "I don't remember," he murmured, and held his breath as he said, "How did you end up living here in Brookville, anyway?"

Lorenzo sighed. "This house . . . belonged to a descendant of mine."

"Oh," Charlie said. "Wow, your—okay." *Descendants.* That would mean that, when he was still human, Lorenzo had . . .

He cleared his throat. "How did you . . . find them? I mean, what made you want to look for them?"

"I was just so bored," Lorenzo said, flopping back onto the bed. "I was made a vampire while I was still living in Sardinia—as you know—and I spent much of that first century in Europe, living . . . wildly. Carousing, drinking from people—sometimes, er . . . violently." He flicked a nervous look at Charlie, but he just nodded and motioned for him to go on.

"But after a hundred years of that sort of thing, it gets a bit old. I came over to America in the nineteen . . ." He squinted. "Was it the 1900s? 1910s? I'm not sure. But here in the New World it was much the same as it was at home. So much meaningless revelry. Drudgery."

He sounded exhausted. "Eventually I began to yearn for something more to my undead existence."

"So," Charlie said, "you found out that you had a great-great-grandchild in Brookville?"

"A great-great-granddaughter," Lorenzo said softly. "Dorothy."

The name sounded lovely in his accent, formal and fond. Charlie waited for him to go on. "I could never figure out why she wasn't afraid of me," Lorenzo said, sitting up. "By the time I found her, she was a little old lady—a widow, no children, living alone in this mansion. And then I appeared on her doorstep, a mysterious, dangerous stranger, and I turned out to be an actual monster, and she . . . didn't care."

"She knew what you were?"

"She wasn't a mark," Lorenzo said, smiling, his eyes gone distant and warm. "That's what she'd say. She was—gorgeous. A tiny bit cruel, just enough to be good fun. She invited me to live here, and she was never scared of me. She—" He laughed, rubbing the back of his neck self-consciously. "Well, she told me what to wear. Vampires dress to impress, she'd say. Elegant, not tasteless. She scolded me when I forgot my manners, but she also . . ." He grinned. "She loved lying to the police anytime a human said they'd spotted something spooky or strange. And by that point in her life, she didn't sleep much, so we'd stay up late, looking out the window. She'd poke me and point at passersby, and tell me who to bite."

Charlie raised his eyebrows, delighted by the mental picture. "She picked the people that you . . . ?"

Lorenzo scoffed, looking genuinely offended—maybe even horrified. "I wouldn't feed on someone my—"

He stopped, abruptly, and it felt like it punched all the air out of Charlie's lungs. "She told people I was her grandson," Lorenzo said in a helpless, empty voice. "And at a certain point I could just—it wasn't a lie, for her, anymore. I was her grandson."

Charlie said nothing. He could feel it building up in his throat, dread and fondness and misery, and part of him hoped Lorenzo wouldn't finish the story.

But of course he did. "I was living here with her," Lorenzo said. "So when she passed away in 1972, it came to me."

Charlie glanced up at the mess of wood and rags covering the ceiling. "Was this her room?"

Lorenzo nodded. Charlie felt his throat closing up.

"I know it's silly," Lorenzo muttered. "I should just sell it. But . . . I can't sell it."

"Of course not," Charlie said. "You—"

"No, it is foolish of me." He'd started to sound angry.

"It's not—"

"Why?" Lorenzo demanded. "Because I am honoring her memory by staying here? Her memory is gone. I watched it happen. It's been fifty years since she left, and no one remembers Dorothy. No one but me."

"But—" Charlie's voice was growing thick. "You—"

"I watched her be forgotten," Lorenzo said. "This town—this community—this place that Dorothy loved—it forgot about her. It was so easy for her to just fade away."

He looked up at Charlie, and there were tears slowly making their way down the sides of his nose, leaving small trails of steam rising from his skin. "You don't have to be dead to be forgotten," he whispered. "Actually dead, I mean. I'm still here, and I can feel myself being forgotten every day."

"Hey, hey," Charlie said, going to his knees in front of Lorenzo, hugging him around the waist, holding him tight. "You are not disappearing, okay? You're right here, with me."

"I am, though," Lorenzo said brokenly. "Look at me. What do I do, Charlie? What do I contribute?"

"You're not a . . . machine," Charlie pleaded with him. "You don't have to contribute something to matter."

"You don't understand," Lorenzo said. "Every year, it goes faster. It all— Why can't I . . ."

Charlie waited urgently for him to continue, but Lorenzo just shuddered. Charlie felt cold all over, desperate to reach Lorenzo somehow, to bring him out of this funk and into the version of himself that Charlie could see. The warm, funny, wonderful guy who Charlie couldn't get enough of. "I think you're just . . . in a rut," he tried.

In a rut. What did that mean? He was so bad at this.

He leaned closer, took one of Lorenzo's shoulders in his palm, and stilled the small tremors that were running through him. "You're right, you've been alive—or undead—a long time, it's no wonder you might feel . . . aimless," he said lowly. "So— why don't you pick an aim?"

"An aim?"

"Yeah, like a goal, or a project or something," Charlie said. He ran his fingers through Lorenzo's hair, tucking it back behind his ears. "My mom read me this book when I was little—it was about this woman who went around planting flowers everywhere. Purple flowers. And when they went into bloom every year, she was the reason. That was her thing. The flower lady."

"You want me to plant flowers?" Lorenzo asked. His small, confused glare through reddened eyes made Charlie's breath catch.

"I think you should plant something," he said softly. "You have so much going for you, I think you just need to look around and see it. I mean, look at all the supernatural creatures you're friends with."

"You mean that I work for."

"Okay, but, that's kind of cool too," Charlie said. "I mean, they all seem pretty segregated. You're the guy who knows everyone. That's interesting."

"It's not—"

"What if you—formalized it?" Charlie suggested.

"Formalized what?"

"What if you started, like, a club? For the supernatural creatures of Brookville."

"Like a support group?" Lorenzo asked doubtfully.

"Like anything," Charlie said. "I'm just saying. Maybe you're not the only one feeling this way."

"I'd rather plant flowers," Lorenzo muttered.

"Mm," Charlie said, levering himself up to sit next to Lorenzo on the bed, moving his arms from Lorenzo's shoulders to his waist. "They were pretty. I think they were called lupines."

Lorenzo scowled at him. "What?"

"The flowers."

"You want me to plant werewolf flowers?"

"What if you had a party," Charlie said. "With all your friends—everyone you've introduced me to over the last few weeks, and anyone else you can think of?"

"For what?"

Charlie shrugged. "To see if it . . . feels like something."

Lorenzo rolled his eyes. Charlie crawled into Lorenzo's lap, lifting his jaw gently until Lorenzo looked at him. "And for the record," he said, "you do contribute. You contribute to your roommates being happy. You contribute to the overall hotness in the town of Brookville."

Lorenzo scoffed.

"And you contribute to me being happy," Charlie said quietly. "Very happy. And having lots of orgasms."

Lorenzo was watching him again, his eyes inscrutable. His cheeks were still steaming slightly from the last of his tears. "And you contribute to my knowledge of the world around us," Charlie said. "Like that vampires tears are . . . acidic?"

Lorenzo frowned, then swiped at the tears on his face, swearing a little. "Not acidic," he said. "Or . . . just to us. To vampires."

Charlie lifted a hand and touched Lorenzo's face hesitantly, and found that the tear tracks on Lorenzo's handsome nose felt just as he might have expected them to—soft and harmless. Damp. Human.

Holy water, he thought. Maybe this was where the myth came from—vampires could be burned, not by religious faith, but by sorrow, or regret, or vulnerability.

"It's kind of . . . beautiful," Charlie said.

Lorenzo shrugged.

"I know no one wants to hear that they look good crying, but . . . you really do look hot crying," Charlie added.

Lorenzo hiccupped out a laugh, and Charlie kissed him to chase it.

Chapter 24

Saturday night Charlie took Lorenzo out to dinner. It wasn't a supernatural-affiliated restaurant, and he didn't bring up a single harebrained scheme to befriend some huldra or a flock of selkie. By all appearances, it seemed to just be a date.

Lorenzo tried not to let on how much it pleased him, but he felt fizzy all evening. He'd thought Charlie might pull back a little after everything Lorenzo had told him about his past and the house—he wouldn't have blamed him if he'd needed some space. But Charlie didn't seem distant at all; they weren't exactly baring their souls over dinner, but Charlie had been warm and funny and seductive all evening. Lorenzo was acutely conscious of trying not to grasp on to it too firmly, worried he might startle it away.

Once they'd paid the check and were standing on the cobblestone street outside, and he realized they had the whole night ahead of them, he had to physically fight a wide grin.

"So what next?" he asked, leaning closer to Charlie. "There's this art house movie theater around the corner. Or if you want to rest for a bit we could go back to my place, and then—"

"Actually, I was thinking," Charlie said, and he paused to flash Lorenzo an apologetic look for jumping in. "I mean, I was just thinking—if you wanted, you could come over to my place."

Lorenzo knew he hadn't hidden his excitement quickly enough, because Charlie was already smiling, small and relieved. "Really?"

"Yeah. If you want," Charlie said, glancing down at his shoes, like he was nervous. "I mean, it's not as nice as yours. But. If you want."

"Yes," Lorenzo said. "I want."

Charlie's apartment was on the second floor of a small, squat building. The door jammed a little as Charlie opened it—the building was newer than Lorenzo's, but it was neglected and dim, and smelled of mildew.

Charlie rubbed a hand on the back of his neck as Lorenzo took in the foyer in its dark, dusty glory. The place was barely decorated, and most of the furniture was utilitarian. It might even have been IKEA.

Lorenzo whistled. "Wow. It's . . ."

"Like I said, it's not as nice as your place."

"No, it's not," Lorenzo said, poking around Charlie's coffee table with great interest. "Why do you have so little furniture?"

"I dunno," Charlie said after a moment. "Just not much of a decorator, I guess."

"Clearly not," Lorenzo said, disgusted and fascinated as he explored what constituted the kitchen.

Eventually they reached the bedroom. The bed was made, the final clue that Charlie's offer hadn't been spontaneous, but

Lorenzo said nothing. The furniture was just as awful and sparse in there as in the rest of the house, but the bed was a queen, and it looked sturdy.

Charlie was looking like he'd put up with Lorenzo's insults for the rest of the apartment just so he could lure him in here. "Oh, is that your bed?" he asked, wandering around the other side.

"Yes it is," Charlie said, following him.

He leaned in for a kiss, and Lorenzo stopped him with a finger to his lips, nodding at the nearby window, which was covered in cheap aluminum blinds. Charlie followed his gaze and winced.

"I forgot," he breathed, staring up at Lorenzo's lips and biting his own.

"Well, I can't spend the day here," Lorenzo said. "Not with it like this."

"We can be done before daybreak," Charlie said, pulling Lorenzo closer.

"Wow," Lorenzo said, acting utterly appalled as Charlie leaned up to press kisses to his neck. "You don't want to make your apartment vampire-safe so we can . . ."

He took Charlie's face in his, leaned down, and whispered against Charlie's lips: ". . . take our time?"

There was a big-box store five minutes away that was still open at one a.m., and Lorenzo and Charlie couldn't stop giggling as they made out in the home furnishings section. There was a big display with dozens of curtain fabrics hung up side by side, and they got tangled up in them as they sampled different kinds, shoving each other around and getting entirely too carried away with their necking for a public place. The lights were screaming bright fluorescents, tinny Chappell Roan was beating down from the store's speakers, and Lorenzo felt drunk on Charlie, on the way he made fluorescent light and suburban errands feel enchanting, wondrous. Magical.

When they finally made it to the cashier with their blackout curtains, Charlie couldn't stop blushing. Every time their eyes met, all Lorenzo could think about was staying in bed with Charlie until high noon. The curtains being rung up might as well have been condoms. "You don't have to pay for them," Charlie said, his voice tight with giddy, delicious shame.

"Let me," Lorenzo purred back. "Your sad apartment needs them. And besides—I am the one who will benefit." He leaned over Charlie, hungry for a kiss.

The cashier was desperately uninterested in them. "The chip reader's not working guys, just touch it."

Lorenzo snatched his card and the curtains back from her and manhandled Charlie out of the store.

They drank and listened to music while putting up the curtain rods and then the curtains, and then Lorenzo tackled Charlie back onto his queen mattress; not as big as Lorenzo's, but perfectly adequate.

They fell asleep for a while, but Lorenzo woke first. He was perfectly content to scroll on his phone as Charlie slept, but he blinked awake soon too. Charlie smiled and rolled over to snuggle him more thoroughly, and Lorenzo put his phone away. They lay in silence for a moment, and then Lorenzo said, "Can I ask you something?"

"Mmm?"

"Your father," he said, and he felt Charlie tense. "He's a professor at the university, isn't he? A prominent one?"

"Yes," he said, after a moment.

"So I assume he—makes good money?"

"Yeah?" Charlie said. "And?"

"So I'm surprised you'd rather live here than at home," Lorenzo said.

"I'm an adult," Charlie said petulantly.

"Yes, but Charlie, these quarters are . . ."

"They're not that bad."

"Hm," Lorenzo said, in a tone that conveyed that Charlie was obviously wrong, but they didn't have to discuss it more if he didn't wish to.

After a moment, though, Charlie spoke again. "We're not close," he said flatly. "My dad and me."

"Why not?"

"I don't know. We just . . . aren't." He paused. "He doesn't really approve of my . . . my graduate degree."

"Your thesis?" Lorenzo asked, frowning. "Why not?"

Charlie laughed hollowly. "He's an economist. Me writing about people's relationships and friendships and sex lives? I think he's embarrassed by it all."

"Well—that's ridiculous," Lorenzo said firmly. "You're an academic, just like him."

Charlie said nothing. Lorenzo thought he'd said the wrong thing somehow, and grasped to right himself. "If your father makes you feel ashamed of yourself, he's a fool," he said, hoping Charlie could hear how fervently he believed it. "You are smart, and capable, and kind."

Softly, Charlie said, "Thanks, Lorenzo."

He had another question, but this one was much more delicate, and he wondered if he should quit while he was ahead. Eventually, however, his curiosity won out, and he asked gently, "What about your mother?"

He watched the shadows creep across the room as the

silence stretched out. After a while Charlie shook his head, and Lorenzo thought that was the most he could do. He pulled Charlie's head down into his chest more firmly, holding him tight, letting him know that it was okay.

But then he said, in a thin, bare voice, "She died when I was seventeen."

"Oh, Charlie," he whispered.

"Yeah. It was, um . . . I mean, I had time to say goodbye," he said. "Not a lot. It was pancreatic."

Lorenzo just held him and stroked his arm, from his shoulder down to his elbow. "What was her name?"

"Ali," he said quietly. "Alison."

Lorenzo kept stroking Charlie's arms, his back, steadily and firm, like he could knead comfort into his muscles and his bones. "What was she like?"

"She was . . . fun," Charlie said. "She was so much fun."

He took a deep breath. "Her room used to be filled with all these—like, trinkets, stuff from random shops, and prizes we'd won at fairs, and beads from Mardi Gras. She just liked having that stuff around, to remind her of the good times. And she loved telling stories, especially ones where she did something stupid or embarrassing." He sighed a little, his body molding itself even closer to Lorenzo. "I know I can be a . . . a really prideful person," he said, his voice small. "But I think I turned out okay because . . . she taught me to laugh at myself. She loved to laugh at herself."

He paused again, for a while this time. "She helped you see the world for what it was—ridiculous and often disappointing and always fun. She was just so . . . happy," he said. "She made you forget why life wasn't like that all the time." After a moment, he added, "My dad got—quieter, after she was gone."

Lorenzo kissed his forehead.

"Y'know what's so weird about it," Charlie rambled on. "Once you've . . . been through something like that, it's like you suddenly become a member of this . . . club. The—the nightmare scenario club. Because—people who aren't in the club—people who haven't had to go through that—I mean, they—" He scoffed a little. "They just don't have a fucking clue. But once you're in the club, you can—you can see other people who're in the club. And you can help them," he whispered. "You can be like—I've been there too, I know what it's like when your . . . your whole world falls apart. Because mine did too."

"Yeah?" Lorenzo asked, even though he knew it was true. He'd been a member of the club for two centuries.

"Yeah," Charlie said. "And it's . . . it's the only good thing about it. Feeling useful like that. Feeling like you're able to do that for someone else."

Even as he said it, a frown twisted Lorenzo's face. Charlie was talking about something horrible but lovely, a silver lining on the darkest cloud, but he didn't sound sad in that way; he sounded twisted up and bitter. Like he was talking about something he'd lost, aside from his mother. "You're a good person, Charlie," Lorenzo whispered.

Charlie huffed a laugh and turned his face away. "I don't know about that."

Lorenzo hummed and rubbed Charlie's back more. Speaking aloud as the thought came to him, he said, "Well, with your mother gone, and you living in this . . . squalid hole, maybe the time is right for you and your father to reconnect."

Charlie sighed. "Lorenzo . . ."

He knew that Charlie had been working tirelessly on his thesis—that was what had brought them together, after all, and even with all the time they'd been spending together lately, he'd seen Charlie hard at work on his laptop, and knew he toiled away during the sunlight hours as well. Perhaps all that hard work wasn't enough; perhaps he struggled with self-doubt, and the situation with his father no doubt fed into that.

Maybe, if they could resolve things, Charlie would feel better.

"What if . . . you invited him to the party?" Lorenzo asked tentatively.

Charlie frowned. "The party?"

"Our party," Lorenzo said. "The thing at my place, for the—all my supernatural, y'know. Contacts."

"Oh," Charlie said. He seemed odd suddenly—almost breathless. "Yeah—I—sure. That's not a bad idea. Sure."

It was tepid, but Lorenzo would take it; he'd pushed enough for tonight. So he just cuddled Charlie closer to him in the small, dark room, kissed the top of his head, and said, "Good."

Chapter 25

Charlie dreamed he was back home, in his childhood bedroom. Everything was the same—posters on the wall, school papers on his desk, bed neatly made. It was dark outside, and the house was still.

Lorenzo was there with him, though he wasn't sure where. He stood up from his desk chair, and he could feel Lorenzo emerging from the shadows behind him. He walked over to his childhood closet, pressing at the uneven paint on the door, and the hairs on the back of his neck stood up as Lorenzo drew closer.

He felt a soft touch at his waist—Lorenzo's hands, taking hold of him and pushing him gently forward. He kept going until Charlie was pressed against the wall, his hands splayed, with Lorenzo all along his back. He breathed heavily against the wallpaper, and felt Lorenzo's hands wandering, still with that firm pressure keeping him in place. And all the while Lorenzo leaned closer, his lips drawing nearer and nearer to the pulse pounding in his throat.

"Tell me to stop," Lorenzo said into his ear, whisper-soft.

Don't stop, Charlie wanted to say. Did say? The dream was thick with his own hazy longing, and he couldn't tell if he'd said the words or just thought them.

But Lorenzo heard. He fisted a hand in Charlie's hair, tugged his head to the side, and leaned in, fangs bared.

Charlie woke up all at once, still panting. He glanced at his phone—it was barely past ten. He was at Lorenzo's place, and he couldn't believe he'd nodded off so early—it was the beginning of the day for Lorenzo.

He looked over at him, propped up in bed with a book open on his stomach, smiling at Charlie softly. "You woke up."

"Yeah," Charlie said roughly, rubbing his eyes. "Sorry about that—I guess I'm still not fully adjusted to the nocturnal lifestyle."

"It's okay," Lorenzo said. And he was smiling at Charlie so warmly, and the dream was still coursing through Charlie's veins, so he sat up, pushed the book off Lorenzo's lap, and kissed him.

Lorenzo laughed into the kiss, though he returned it. "Hello."

"Hi," Charlie said, pushing his hands under Lorenzo's soft shirt.

"What has you in such an amorous mood?" Lorenzo asked.

Charlie pulled back, his mind full of visions of Lorenzo's teeth sinking into his neck. "Uh, I . . . I dreamed about you," he said.

He'd expected Lorenzo to be flattered or excited, but instead his expression dimmed. "What's wrong?" Charlie asked.

Lorenzo sat up straighter in bed and pushed Charlie away from him—not cruelly, but more like he had something on his mind. "I have to tell you something," he said.

He looked sick to his stomach. Charlie's heart skipped a beat. "Okay," he said, hesitant.

"I mean—you should know this, for your thesis," Lorenzo rambled, and Charlie tried to ignore the icy flush of guilt that swept over his skin.

Lorenzo sighed and said, "Vampires can . . . enter humans' dreams."

This was not what Charlie had been expecting to hear at all. "Okay," he said doubtfully. "I— What does that mean?"

"It means . . . we can travel through the ether and actually . . . *be* in your dreams, just as if we were entering a room with you in it," Lorenzo said. "Except the room is . . . your mind. Or, your dream."

Charlie was still confused. "Okay," he said again.

Lorenzo lifted his eyes to Charlie's, looking like a kicked dog. "So, when we first ran into each other a few months ago, I—I really wanted you to leave me alone, at first," he said. "And . . . I thought maybe if I scared you off . . ."

It took Charlie a second, but then he remembered—the nightmare of a dark alley that had become something stranger. Tighter. Hotter. "That was you?" he demanded. "In the—like— actually *you*?"

"Yes," Lorenzo said miserably. "I'm sorry."

Charlie clambered off the bed, pacing back and forth. He couldn't deny that this knowledge felt a bit—well, a bit like being violated. If what Lorenzo was saying was true, that would mean that Lorenzo had been *inside* his mind. "That's . . . what the hell!"

"I know!" Lorenzo said, gazing at him, stricken. "I know."

Charlie stopped pacing and narrowed his eyes at Lorenzo. "That was a sexy dream."

Through the haze of guilt and worry, a slight sheepish grin crept onto Lorenzo's face. "I know."

Charlie sat heavily in the chair by his desk and opened his laptop, typing furiously. After a moment, Lorenzo asked hesitantly, "What are you doing?"

"Like you said," Charlie said, in a petulantly flat tone. "Gotta get this all down."

"Are you," Lorenzo asked. "Mad?"

Charlie finished writing and glanced at his desktop behind the blank page he'd opened to jot this all down—at a folder full of his finished columns. All at once, any lingering traces of shock or anger seeped away, and he shut his laptop. "No," he said. "I guess not."

"I'm really sorry," Lorenzo said, sitting up on his knees in bed.

Charlie sat down on the bed next to him. "It's fine," he said with a sigh. "Thank you for telling me, though."

Lorenzo bit his lip, and he looked so concerned, so guilty, that Charlie couldn't help but touch him. He put a palm on his thigh, feeling the tension in Lorenzo's muscles ease a bit the instant he made contact. "I guess it's just a . . . weird . . . somewhat intrusive way of flirting," he said.

That sheepishness came back into Lorenzo's eyes. "You were the one flirting with *me*," he said. "I went there to scare you. Your subconscious made it all . . . sexy."

Charlie found himself grinning. "Yeah, well, you're pretty sexy."

"I haven't done it at all since," Lorenzo added, as if this had just occurred to him. "Your dream just now, that was all you."

Heat stole over Charlie's skin at the memory; Lorenzo

surrounding him, his hands on his waist, on his shoulders; his lips at his neck, fangs breaking the fragile skin of his throat.

Lorenzo saw him blush, his eyes tracking his face closely. "What were you dreaming about?"

Tell me to stop. Charlie's heart hammered wildly. He couldn't tell Lorenzo. Sweet, trusting Lorenzo, who'd made it clear that a bite was meaningful for him, not something he'd do with a casual partner.

And definitely not one who was lying to him.

He glanced at Lorenzo's lips, his hands, the curve of his neck and shoulder. What had he said? When a vampire drank from a human, that human stayed with them forever. His neck throbbed at the thought.

It was an act of intimacy and vulnerability. He couldn't let Lorenzo do that, not with him.

No matter how much he wanted it.

"Charlie?" Lorenzo asked, his big brown eyes sharp and concerned.

Tell me to stop.

"I dr—I dreamed about you biting me," Charlie breathed.

Lorenzo's eyes darkened. He shuffled slightly in the blankets to face him. "Do you want me to?"

Charlie felt like he was falling, drawn toward Lorenzo as inexorably as if by gravity. "I—I would," he managed.

Lorenzo kissed him as he added, "I mean, you don't—you don't have to." They fell backward onto the bed together, Charlie's fingers tangled in Lorenzo's hair, as Lorenzo pressed lush kisses to his chin, his collarbone, his temple, his neck. Charlie gasped out, drowning in sensation, and said again, "O-only if you want to."

"I want you," Lorenzo said, panting against his skin. "I always want you."

He pulled at Charlie's clothes eagerly, kissing Charlie all up his arms and along his collarbone and chest but coming back often to kiss him properly, like he craved the taste of Charlie's lips and the symmetry of their bodies like this. Charlie felt like he was bubbling over, like with every item of clothing Lorenzo peeled away he was unraveling just a bit more, heat-flushed and reckless. "Please," he whispered against Lorenzo's skin, burning up.

When Charlie was naked, Lorenzo pulled back and gave him a long, considering, hungry look. Charlie shivered. Whatever Lorenzo read in his face, he seemed to come to some kind of decision, and Charlie caught his breath at the dark confidence in his gaze. But when he bent down, it wasn't toward Charlie's neck, but to his chest, where he kissed him again, hot and slow. Charlie squirmed, grinding his hips up against Lorenzo's.

Lorenzo trailed his mouth down Charlie's stomach, then pushed his left thigh up and out with one big hand. Charlie jerked his head up from the pillow. "Are you going to bite me there?"

Lorenzo just flicked a dark look up at him, ducking his head down to kiss Charlie gently right on his glans. Charlie gasped, and Lorenzo swirled his tongue and lowered down, at just the right angle for Charlie to catch the flash of his fangs as they scraped his cock wetly. He whimpered as his neck snapped, his head hitting the pillow.

But despite the excellence of Lorenzo's mouth on him, it continued to be just that—Lorenzo's lips and cheeks and tongue, with only the occasional, dull scrape of teeth—not at all the bite (or location of the bite) Charlie had wanted. He realized quickly that Lorenzo was doing it on purpose—he could feel him smiling, feel the way Lorenzo was toying with him. He knew this wasn't where Charlie wanted his mouth, but Charlie couldn't muster the strength to ask him to stop, not when Lorenzo *felt like that*—wet and deep and perfect, as he hummed contentedly to himself.

So Charlie panted and squirmed, making a fool of himself but too far gone to care. He was so dazed that he missed it when Lorenzo grabbed the lube, but his thumb was slick and cool when it slid inside. Charlie moaned and ground back against Lorenzo, his shoulders slick under Charlie's grasping hands. He was on fire, frantic; already so close just from the wild heat between them, the knowledge that Lorenzo wanted him, wanted this, and the fact that he'd finally stopped resisting.

He protested when Lorenzo pulled away—too lost for words, so it was more like a grumpy moan—but he was only grabbing the lube again, and this time he got it everywhere, all over their stomachs and dicks and thighs, and then he was laying down on top of him, grinding down against Charlie, gloriously heavy and slick. Charlie gasped, raking his nails down Lorenzo's back. *This* was perfect—finding their pleasure like this, messily, greedily. The sight of it was nearly enough to drive him over the edge. Lorenzo's other hand was still on Charlie's ass, his thumb grinding into him, their bodies working together, and Lorenzo's mouth was now finally—*finally*—lined up with Charlie's neck.

But he still didn't bite. Maddeningly, even as they ground together, getting rough with each other, Lorenzo's lips were gentle, kissing him tenderly, seeming to differentiate each inch of his neck and throat as worthy of attention. "Come on," Charlie begged, scoring Lorenzo's ass with his nails.

Lorenzo just licked his neck, then sucked a bit of it into his mouth. Charlie moaned, lost for him, lost in the dream of it, the pure pleasure.

It was torture—Lorenzo all over him, around him, the intense but imprecise pressure on his dick, the thumb behind, and Lorenzo's mouth slowly tenderizing his neck. The skin there was growing hot and sensitive, tingling now under gentle rolls of Lorenzo's jaw, as if he were testing the give of Charlie's skin between his teeth. Charlie moaned something hoarse and protesting. Finally, Lorenzo began to bite him—but slowly, carefully, not hard enough to break the skin. Not hard enough for Charlie.

It hurt; it all hurt, in the urgent pulse of his body, and the stinging ache of his abused skin, and the place deep inside where he still feared that Lorenzo would leave him without this bite that he now needed—that he was aching for—that he craved. Charlie shuddered, digging his nails into Lorenzo's back, and tried not to listen to the things he was saying—broken begging and drunken, reckless praise falling from his lips to Lorenzo's skin unthought and too honest.

And finally, when Charlie's skin was damp and tender and abused, his body sore, and his throat nearly hoarse from crying out for it, Lorenzo snarled, his fangs snapped into place, and he bit.

It was indescribable.

The pain was like a metal spike through his orgasm, bliss wrapped in electric wire; it made everything harder, brighter, wetter, more dizzying. He felt anchored; he felt unleashed.

Lorenzo was touching him everywhere; his mouth was locked into Charlie's neck, their bodies pressed together, Lorenzo's arms around him, fingers carded through his hair, and he was making little happy wet noises as he drank. Charlie shuddered, riding it out, and then sank pleasantly into the afterglow, feeling drowsier than usual after sex in the best possible way. He loved the smell of Lorenzo's skin. He was warm.

He slept again, for a few minutes at least. Then he woke to see Lorenzo looking down at him, naked and adorably disheveled, his hair sticking up in every direction. "So," he said, with a shy smile. "Did it, uh. Live up to the hype?"

"You're ridiculous," Charlie whispered, pulling him close. His mouth tasted faintly of iron, and the kiss made his head spin.

Lorenzo settled into bed, sprawled over Charlie until their noses were a hair's breadth apart. "So how was I," he said, his breath teasing against Charlie's lips. "On a scale of one to ten fangs."

"One to ten?" Charlie asked, giggling breathlessly. "You only have two fangs. It should be a scale of zero to two."

"No," Lorenzo said. His eyes were a soft brown blur, his eyelashes tickling Charlie's cheek. "I want you to rate my biting on a one-to-ten fang scale. Including half fangs."

Charlie laughed, obsessed with Lorenzo's bubbly, arrogant grin, and thought *I love you.*

Then he sat bolt upright as something belatedly occurred to him. "Vampires can't, uh, read minds," he asked. "Can you?"

Lorenzo blinked up at him, then smiled slowly. "No," he said, whisper-soft.

Shit. "Oh," Charlie said, stupidly, and shuffled back down onto the bed. His heart was pounding.

Lorenzo was still looking at him, radiating fond happiness, growing warmer by the moment. Charlie felt like the air had turned to water. Panicking, he kissed Lorenzo, trying to ignore the ghost of a smile on his lips.

As Charlie got his arm under him, he felt a twinge in his neck and fell backward, hissing. Lorenzo glanced at his neck, looking concerned, and touched his bite mark with incredible gentleness. "Sorry," he whispered.

"It's okay," Charlie told him.

Lorenzo maneuvered them until Charlie was lying back against him, so Lorenzo could kiss the bite and massage Charlie's shoulders. He tried to get his breathing under control.

It was fine. Scary—embarrassing—but at least now he knew.

And he knew what he had to do.

He was going to tell Lorenzo the truth. He wasn't sure how or when, but he knew now that he had to.

He had to figure out if this could be real.

Chapter 26

"I can't believe you're calling it a *soft launch*," Lorenzo grumbled, his hands slipping under Charlie's shirt.

"That was in one text!" Charlie protested. They were in a quiet corner of the kitchen, avoiding their guests so Lorenzo could berate Charlie. And grope him.

"Three texts," he muttered, stroking Charlie's skin.

"It was the same text to three different people," Charlie said. "My point is, it *is* a soft launch."

Lorenzo had, at long last, agreed to have a party and invite all of his supernatural—well, mostly his clients and acquaintances, and only potentially friends. It was part of Charlie's idea for Lorenzo to embrace the idea of community, which he felt was a bit hacky and probably unrealistic, but. He didn't hate parties; and he didn't hate Charlie pushing and prodding him, and taking an interest in his life that felt real.

But a *soft launch*? "How dare you," he said, drawing closer to Charlie, intoxicated by his body heat. "I should threaten to rip your throat out just for that."

"Please," Charlie whispered, pulling him close.

"Mmmm," Lorenzo said. "We have people here."

"I don't care," Charlie breathed into Lorenzo's mouth.

So far, their rudeness aside, the soft-launch-slash-regular-party was actually going well. Gray had come, thankfully no longer reeking of wolfsbane; so had a few of the succubi Lorenzo had met briefly at their art show; and a few of Kenny's pack. The young druid they'd watched bomb his initiation was there—he was a necromancer, apparently; not something particularly welcomed by the nature-worshippers. Sal was there, the bartender from the demon pub, and he was chatting with one of the werewolves in a way that made Lorenzo think he'd dumped his fae girlfriend after all. Lorenzo had also invited Roberta, mostly because he'd been worried no one else would show, and she was happily eating most of the finger sandwiches Maggie had helped him make.

It was a bit of a motley crew, but they all seemed to be mingling happily; and Charlie was smiling up at him even as Lorenzo forced his hands to behave and tried to put a respectable amount of distance between them.

The party could have been a total disaster, and he probably wouldn't have noticed.

Charlie was wearing a collared shirt, but Lorenzo had watched him put it on; he knew his bite mark was there, just below the collar. Charlie had *asked* Lorenzo to bite him.

He knew a lot of vampires thought of the whole idea of bites between lovers as mere superstition. But Lorenzo could swear there was a magnetic pull between them that hadn't been there before. Charlie was a part of him now, like a hook under his ribs, drawing him close. This party was a terrible idea, he decided suddenly. He should have canceled all their plans and kept Charlie close all night, all week, all month.

Isolde cleared her throat loudly, making him realize that she was standing right next to them, by the sink. "Could you two keep it down, please?" she said, sounding irritated.

Lorenzo was mortified. To someone like Isolde, who sensed sexual energies, he and Charlie must have been excruciating. "Sorry."

"It's fine. It's just . . . like you're shouting right next to my ear," she said, imitating the woman from *Clue* with the flames on her face.

The image made him smile, and he hid his face in Charlie's neck while Charlie swatted him away. Isolde winced. "Have you seen Rachel?" she asked in a strained voice.

"No."

She sighed and wandered away, and Lorenzo took the opportunity to drag Charlie out of the kitchen and to the edge of the living room, so they wouldn't be at risk of fully humiliating themselves. They got drinks and took in the atmosphere. "So," Charlie said, grinning. "This is going well."

"Seems like it."

"Do you think you should," he said, and waved a hand vaguely at the room. "Y'know?"

"What?"

"Give a speech?" Charlie asked. "Or something?"

"A speech?" Lorenzo asked, his stomach plummeting.

"Yeah. Just—welcome everyone," Charlie said. "Tell them why they're here."

"I, uh . . ." Lorenzo said.

"You don't have to," Charlie said quietly, and he took one of

Lorenzo's hands in his. He instantly felt steadied. "But I think you'd be good at it."

He sighed, and Charlie leaned up to kiss him on the cheek. From that angle, Lorenzo could see his bite mark on Charlie's throat below his collar. His cheek was still warm after Charlie pulled away.

It quieted his nerves enough for him to raise his glass, gathering everyone's attention and waiting for the noise to die down.

"Okay," he said. "Uh, hello, everyone. Thank you for coming. And, uh, welcome. I don't . . ."

A dozen faces looked at him expectantly, and he took a calming breath. "I've, uh, known most of you for years," he said. "And. I feel sort of . . . silly . . ."

He trailed off again, but a few feet away, Charlie nodded at him firmly. *You can do this.*

"I just thought it would be nice to get together a group of—um, well."

It all sounded so stupid when it was time to say it out loud. He took a deep breath and started again. "It can be a lonely thing, sometimes. Being one of us. We're not human—though we welcome our human allies."

Charlie *woo*ed quietly, pumping his fist.

"Um . . . but we're . . ." He sighed. How to put words to the feeling of being an unaging artifact of foul magic; a silly pretense of immortality, when all his many years had afforded him was a view of how vast it all was, and how insignificant he was in comparison?

"Sometimes, even if you're a powerful immortal being, or a creature that everyone has read about and whispered about and watched in movies," he began, cautiously, "it can still be lonely. You can feel like you don't belong."

He glanced at Isolde, stone-faced in the back of the room. "Maybe you're . . . not welcome among your kind."

Rachel looked lost in thought, staring down into her drink.

"Or maybe you . . . maybe you just feel like you've lost your way."

He swallowed. "Maybe you feel like you live in the shadow of this . . . this idea . . ."

He caught Charlie's eye again, and then it was just the two of them in the room, Lorenzo's words safe in the sudden silence, spoken just for Charlie. "This idea of—everything you could be. And you feel like you're just not doing it right."

He blinked, and suddenly felt ridiculous; they weren't alone, and he was being sorrowful and dour, bringing down the mood of the party. But . . . the guests didn't seem discouraged. They were staring at him. Waiting for him. Listening to him. Other strange creatures like him, coming together in this world that was cruel at best and at worst, indifferent and impossibly empty.

Why shouldn't he ramble about his sad nonsense and see if anyone else felt the same? Discover if anyone else shared this mournful feeling in his soul that he just couldn't shake?

Correction, he thought, as he met Charlie's softly smiling eyes. *Had* trouble shaking.

"Well . . ." He raised his glass. "Here's to dealing with all that, with all of you."

He toasted, and the room joined him. And suddenly he was very glad he'd hosted this silly party.

Charlie bounded over to him and wrapped him in a hug. "That was great!"

"It was stupid," he mumbled, blushing.

"No, it was perfect," Charlie said, and leaned in to kiss him again.

Lorenzo wrapped his arms around Charlie and deepened the kiss, even though his rational brain knew he shouldn't maul him in the middle of a crowded room. He pulled back and nuzzled at Charlie's neck, thinking this a fair compromise, before he realized he was snuffling at Charlie's bite. It was healing nicely, though the mark was still a lovely, vivid red. His mouth watered.

He wondered if Charlie would be up for another bite tonight—maybe from his leg. He wanted as much of Charlie as he'd give. Charlie looked up at him, his amber eyes dark, and he knew he was thinking the same thing.

Then Charlie stiffened, and Lorenzo pulled back. He was startled to see Charlie's face frozen in a horrified grimace. Lorenzo looked behind him and saw a middle-aged man who'd just arrived to the party; and after a moment, Lorenzo put Charlie's horror in context and realized who the man must be. "Oh, wow," he said. "He came."

Charlie jerked toward him. "What—you—"

Lorenzo frowned. "Didn't you say you were going to invite your father?"

"I," Charlie stammered, as his father spotted them and started heading their way. "I didn't—actually—"

"Oh, is that your dad?" Maggie asked, wandering over. "Lorenzo told me you'd invited him, so I added him to the Facebook group."

"You made a Facebook events page?" Rachel asked scornfully. "Jesus, you sound a thousand years old."

"I'm only four hundred. And it's helpful to give people a heads-up about food allergies and stuff," Maggie was saying, though Lorenzo had tuned them both out. Charlie looked beyond strange—he was stock-still, almost as if he were frozen in panic.

Maybe Lorenzo had been wrong to push this idea on him. He had just hated the thought of Charlie feeling as lonesome in his own family as Lorenzo did in the world. He'd thought maybe they could even fix both things at once, if Charlie brought someone from his own life to this silly little party he'd made Lorenzo throw, in a genuinely sweet attempt by Charlie to fix *Lorenzo's* life.

But Charlie did not look happy; in fact, the blood had drained from his face. "You . . ."

"Do you want me to ask him to leave?" Lorenzo asked.

Before Charlie could answer, his father approached them. He looked just like his photo on the UB faculty page—like an older, faded version of Charlie, with curly salt-and-pepper hair at his temples and deep creases around his sharp eyes. He seemed wary as he approached them. "Charles."

"Hi Dad," Charlie said quietly. Under Lorenzo's palm, his back felt tense as a bowstring. Lorenzo silently cursed himself, realizing how misguided this suggestion had been. He could only hope Charlie would forgive him.

"Lorenzo?" George asked, and shook his hand. "Thank you for the social media invitation. What a . . . lovely home you have."

The slight pause before *lovely* conveyed just how hard he'd had to reach for the compliment. Lorenzo smiled politely and said, "Thank you."

"Dad," Charlie interrupted, "can we—"

"I didn't know you were back in town," George said to him. Lorenzo frowned. "Back?"

"Yeah. Well," Charlie said shortly. "I didn't know you'd be coming tonight."

"I see," George said frostily.

"Lorenzo," Charlie said. If he didn't know better, he'd think he sounded desperate. "Can you get my dad a drink?"

"Oh, that reminds me," George said, holding up an expensive-looking bottle of wine. "I brought this for the host."

"Thank you," Lorenzo said, taking it. Charlie was acting very strange—more than just awkward or tense, he seemed fidgety. He was almost twitching.

"Charles," George said heavily, taking a deep breath. "There's something I wanted to tell you. I've, well—I've been reading your column."

Charlie's eyes closed.

"Your column?" Lorenzo asked.

Charlie was staring at the ground as his father spoke, but Lorenzo could see the color leaching out of his face. "I'm one of your subscribers, actually," George said. *Subscribers?* "I don't really go in for that sort of thing usually, but—well, I was thinking of you, and I started reading them, and . . . they're quite good, I think. I mean, you could be doing more with your life than writing relationship advice for strangers on the internet. But, for what they are . . ."

Lorenzo stared at Charlie, waiting for him to make sense of this. But Charlie still wouldn't look at him. He hadn't looked at him once since he'd spotted his father at the party.

"What are you talking about?" Lorenzo asked quietly.

"You don't know?" George said. He took his phone out—an old flip phone, but it seemed to have web browsing. "I have to say, they're really quite well-written for, ah, a *Dear Abby* sort of thing. Where's the latest one—oh, I liked this part."

He tilted his phone so that Lorenzo could see the screen, and read the chunks of text out loud.

What does it mean that your partner glows while he's dreaming? I'm sorry to say that there's no satisfying answer here. I recently learned that vampires are burned by their own tears—likely a progenitor of the holy water myth. How often magic seems to feel cruel in that way, mirroring our inner lives with gut-punch accuracy: turning regret or yearning into mercuric acid or literal phosphorescence. It's tempting for us humans to treat these signs and omens as representing some sort of inherent truth about the supernatural creatures we associate them with, but that's where we go astray. Magic isn't an exact scientific equation so much as a dusty relic of everyday life; for all the symbolism baked into their very essence, paranormal people are disappointingly, inspiringly, and reliably still just people. In other words, as I've been reminded so often lately: magic is intent.

So what does it mean about your partner? It could mean anything. Intent is as complex and murky as the human heart—or anyone's. There could be as many reasons for a glowing faerie as for a vampire's tears.

Charlie remembered when he'd written that one. He'd been proud of himself for what he'd thought was a well-written piece, and for telling his readers that supernatural people were just people. After all, he thought of Lorenzo as a *vampire* less and less; more and more, he was just the guy he was seeing, who happened to be a vampire.

The guy he'd fallen in love with.

And he hadn't been able to resist using the part about his tears, because it was so beautiful; how could he not?

"I never knew that," his dad was saying. "The thing about vampire's tears. Isn't that clever? Oh, sure."

"Wise . . . Old Crone," Lorenzo muttered blankly as he took the phone from Charlie's father, using the keys to scroll up and down. Charlie's heart was pounding.

"Ah, yes, his *nom de plume*," his dad said, nauseatingly. "Isn't that smart? It's his initials backward—Charles Owen Wever."

Lorenzo still hadn't moved, except for his eyes flicking over the tiny screen. For a second, a wildly optimistic part of Charlie thought that maybe he wouldn't be mad. Surprised, sure, maybe a little thrown, but—maybe he'd be proud. Maybe he'd be impressed.

Then Lorenzo looked up at him.

"I—I was going to tell you," Charlie said, the words scraped out of him like they didn't want to be heard. He was ashamed to even say it.

"This is what you were doing?" Lorenzo asked. Quietly. Brittle.

"I can explain," he said.

"You wrote about me?" There was almost a gentle curiosity to the question, like he couldn't quite believe it. "You wrote about me . . . crying?"

"I . . ." Charlie said. "I . . ."

What was there to say? He'd been lying to Lorenzo for months—mining his most sensitive, intimate moments as fodder for his career. Spilling his secrets to the whole world, if not by name.

There was nothing—absolutely nothing—to say in his own defense.

"Wait," Rachel said, peering over Lorenzo's shoulder and then back at Charlie. "*You're* Wise Old Crone?"

Charlie felt like his skin was shrinking around him, turning to ice. Others at the party were starting to notice the tension building between them. Charlie's dad frowned. "Charles? What's going on?"

Maggie put a hand on Lorenzo's arm. "Lorenzo? What's wrong?"

Lorenzo swallowed. "I have to go."

He shoved Charlie's dad's phone back to him and walked away—from his own party—from his own house. Charlie was frozen solid as he watched him go, barely hearing his dad say, "Charles? What is it?"

His dad put a hand on his shoulder, and that finally broke the spell. He shoved him away, snarling, "Leave me alone."

And he ran.

He didn't find Lorenzo until he got all the way down to the street. It was dark, most of the shops having closed hours ago, and only a few streetlights pierced the gloom. They were all there—Maggie, Isolde, and Rachel all standing around Lorenzo, talking swiftly in hushed voices he couldn't hear.

Lorenzo saw him first and physically recoiled—jerking and turning away immediately, walking down the street. "Lorenzo!" he shouted.

He heard Rachel say his name in a warning tone, but then she shook her head, turning to follow Lorenzo. Isolde was rubbing his back.

"Lorenzo, wait—" he said, desperately. "Let me explain, please—"

It was Maggie who stood in his way, stopping him with an outstretched hand. He looked past her to where Lorenzo was waiting in the shadows, his back turned, Rachel and Isolde hovering around him.

"Please," he said to Maggie. "I just need to—to—" If he could just get to him, stand in front of him, look into his eyes, maybe that would change something. Maybe that would give him some clue of what to say, how to make it right. If he could just touch Lorenzo, and make him understand—

"Charlie," Maggie said quietly, "go away."

He finally looked at her. "Maggie . . ."

There was no warmth left in her eyes, no humor in the grooves of her face. She said with simple finality, "You need to leave."

"But—"

"Fucking go, Charlie," Maggie said, looking down at him. "We don't want you here."

She turned and walked back to the others, leaving Charlie alone on the street.

Chapter 27

Lorenzo may have been a vampire, but he wasn't a cliché. Not every single moment he spent in bed with Charlie was spent doing . . . that.

In fact, for the last few minutes he'd been ranting about the snap election in Italy. He trailed off, however, when he realized that Charlie was staring at him with a familiar, hungry expression. "What?" he asked, self-conscious.

"Sorry," Charlie said, blushing a little. "Just, hearing you say all those—those names, and phrases—"

He did sometimes slip into Italian when he was ranting. "Oh," he said. "Yeah?"

Charlie scooted closer on the bed, gazing up at him impatiently. "It was hot."

Lorenzo rolled his eyes.

"Say something else," Charlie urged.

"No."

"C'mon, say something," Charlie said. He begged and wheedled until Lorenzo found himself propped up on his elbow over Charlie, who was fairly squirming with excitement.

He couldn't deny him. In Italian, he said, "It's ridiculous that you think this is sexy."

Charlie lit up as soon as the first word left his mouth. "What did you say?" he breathed.

"I said," Lorenzo said, staring down at him, hopelessly lost, ". . . you're cute."

"I don't think that is what you said," Charlie said, laughing and snuggling closer to him. "Say something else."

He was always performing for Charlie, in some sense. The seductive vampire. The worldly heartbreaker, the one who wouldn't get too attached. Someone cool enough for Charlie to want. Someone who could hold back from wanting him just enough that, maybe, he could trick Charlie into wanting Lorenzo back.

Like this, though, in his native tongue, he could speak freely. "Io . . ." he said, "vorrei che potessimo . . ."

Sensing that he'd stopped, Charlie whispered, "What?"

Between one blink and the next, Lorenzo woke up.

It was still daytime; the air in the room was hot and still. He was alone in bed, of course. He took a deep, shaking breath, put an arm over his eyes, and tried not to collapse completely.

Dorothy's skylight was above him, all boarded up and covered over. He remembered telling Charlie about her. Breaking down in front of him.

He flipped over, lying flat against the mattress and tensing all his muscles. Maybe if he could just hold himself still for long enough, get his body into the right configuration, he wouldn't cry again.

But then it just burned all over, deep inside, even when the tears didn't come.

Around sunset, there was a knock at his door. He ignored

it, but after a moment it creaked open anyway. "Hey," Maggie said quietly.

She came over to the bed, and he heard a soft clunk on his bedside table. He opened one eye just enough to see that she'd brought him a steaming cup of blood. He closed his eyes again. He wasn't hungry.

Maggie seemed to understand. "Well, just thought I'd bring you something." He felt the bed dip a little as she sat down. "Do you want to . . . talk?"

He didn't trust himself to speak. Eventually, he croaked, "Nothing to say."

"Yeah."

There was another long pause, and then the bed creaked again as Maggie climbed in fully, laying down next to him, her on her back, him on his stomach. She folded her hands on her rib cage, looking up at where the skylight would be, her craggy features relaxed. Dorothy would have loved Maggie, he thought. And Maggie would have adored Dorothy.

At length, Maggie said, "What a . . . jerk."

He snorted—an involuntary, outraged giggle that started in his stomach and almost made it past his throat. The bed shook. *What a jerk.* The understatement wasn't funny, exactly, but it made him laugh. Maggie smiled, seeing it.

"Want me to fuck him up?" she asked. "We're a savage race, we trolls, you know."

She was so lovely, looking at him with a soft smile on her face. It felt a bit like sunshine—that cold sunshine in the morning he barely remembered; a bloom of light on the horizon, brushing away the cobwebs and dew. And he felt suddenly very ashamed for not having realized what Maggie was to him—to have missed, somehow, how precious she was—his oldest roommate and best friend. He wondered how he'd gone so long without seeing it. Her slim weight on the bed next to him felt like a lifeline he didn't realize he'd been grasping on to. He wasn't adrift. Or maybe he was, but he wasn't alone.

Then he heard Charlie's voice in his head. *I think your life is better than you think it is.*

Maggie frowned at whatever she saw on his face. "He's a jerk," she said again, low and heartfelt and a little wet. "Seriously, he . . ."

Lorenzo grunted again and pressed his face into the mattress. "Why don't you come out and watch a movie with everyone," she said.

He didn't even bother grunting that time.

"Come on, you can lie face down on the couch instead of the bed."

Twenty minutes of cajoling later, Lorenzo grudgingly got into the shower and pulled on some fresh clothes. He wandered downstairs warily, not wanting to be accosted by everyone's well-wishes all at once, but it was strangely quiet in the living room. He'd just sort of assumed they'd all be there.

Maggie came out of the kitchen and smiled when she saw he'd cleaned up a bit. "So—what're we watching?" she asked, bouncing onto the couch. "My go-to cheer-up show is *GLOW*."

He sighed, sitting next to her and putting his face in his hands. "But it got canceled. Everything is the worst."

Maggie leaned in. Before she could suggest an alternative, the doorbell rang. They glanced at each other and then got up to answer it together.

A delivery woman was waving as she walked back down the hall, something that smelled like butter chicken wafting temptingly from a small plastic bag left in front of the door. Maggie grabbed it and glanced at the receipt. "Rachel's. Where is she?"

It didn't occur to Lorenzo that the apartment was in fact *suspiciously* quiet until Maggie went to drop Rachel's food off and absentmindedly shouldered open her bedroom door, and they found themselves in a whimsical faerie greenhouse. It looked like the sort of lush yet artificial space where they'd stage a coercive Netflix dating show or a modestly expensive wedding. Fireflies were hovering in the marshes, moonlight lit the trees, and the stench of death seemed to be everywhere—verdant, like overripe figs.

And Rachel had Isolde backed up against a huge dark tree, their skin an urgent blur, lips fused together, damp breaths heaving between them, and Rachel's hands—Lorenzo jerked his eyes away, throwing an arm in front of his face. He didn't want to see where her hands were.

Maggie let out a mortified yelp. "What are you guys doing?" she wailed, hastening to follow Lorenzo's example and block her eyes.

He could make out just enough to see them spring apart. "We—you—" Rachel stuttered, her lips shiny and wet.

Around them, the illusion was crumbling like crepe paper wilting after a long party—the greenhouse was disappearing, becoming Rachel's room again. The tree was now just Rachel's closet door, where Isolde seemed to have frozen, her face bright purple, her lower lip slack.

"We have your chicken," Lorenzo managed.

For whatever reason, that was what prompted Rachel and Isolde to share a long, weighty look—and then flee in opposite directions.

Maggie turned to him with a frozen scream that was part embarrassment, part glee, and all horror. Lorenzo felt like his head was swimming. He didn't like drama.

Especially when the one person he would have wanted to tell all about this was—gone.

No. Especially when that person had never been there; not really.

Lorenzo took a step backward, the implications hitting him successively. Charlie had claimed he was worried about Rachel and the way she'd seemed obsessed with Isolde—haunting her, stalking her, exploding around her. Maybe that was just how a poltergeist had a crush. And it had all started when Charlie had gotten them to talk, or at least helped Isolde open up.

Because he'd wanted to help them.

Maggie was looking at him, a careful, worried look on her face. "Lorenzo?"

He shook his head, and trudged back up to his dark, quiet room.

Chapter 28

Charlie woke up in his childhood bedroom. He didn't move for a long while. Didn't want to remember.

The morning after the party, he'd gone over to his dad's place to explain everything. He'd felt awkward about his dad getting caught up in all the drama, and a small part of him felt like he owed him an explanation for having been back in town for months without saying anything.

His dad didn't mention any of that, though; he just made a sour expression as Charlie explained, in as clipped and detached a way as possible, what had happened with Lorenzo. When he was done, his father had apologized for causing a *commotion*.

No, Charlie had told him. *It was my fault.*

Things had only gotten more uncomfortable from there, so he'd left quickly.

But then he'd gone back to his place—his stupid little sublet apartment—which was empty and quiet. Someone else's home, not his. The only personal stamp he'd made on it was the black-out curtains he'd put up with Lorenzo.

So he'd shoved his toiletries and computer and a few other things into a bag and gone back to his dad's place. His dad saw his bag and let him in without comment.

And now he'd been here a week. Ava had called him a few billion times; texted, DMed, and emailed. He was leaving her on read—not just about the column, but about the Advance Media offer, about everything. He hadn't turned in a column in weeks. He wasn't sure he'd ever write again. One of the emails in his inbox right now might have been a pink slip.

He didn't care. He didn't give a shit about any of it. Nothing mattered.

His eye caught on an old poster leaning rolled up against the corner of his room, faded orange and black. It was a fan-made vintage *X-Files* poster, a stylized version of the shot in the credits of Mulder and Scully swinging their flashlights around. His mom had gotten it for him his senior year of high school—for his dorm room, she'd said. He'd called her silly for saying that, when they didn't even know where he'd be going to college yet. He hadn't even known where he'd gotten in, though his dad had already been mentioning the UB faculty tuition break every other day by that point.

But his mom had just smiled and said she knew he was going to get in somewhere great, and that he'd need a cool poster for his dorm. That was one of the last good days they'd had before she was diagnosed.

When it actually came time to move into his room at UB, Charlie put the poster up himself. He unpacked his clothes himself, plugged his mini-fridge in himself, and downloaded all the stupid apps himself. He also met his roommate, wandered through a decently fun freshman orientation street fair, and

ended up making friends with a big group of other new fresh-
men at the pub.

But when he got back to his room—his roommate hadn't
come home yet; good for him—that *X-Files* poster was still
there, and Charlie was alone.

To be fair, his dad had called. The academic conference he'd
been booked at that week was too important for him to miss,
and besides, Charlie was an adult now, he'd said; he could move
himself into college alone. And he'd still called at the end of the
day to hear all about it, about the dorms and new friends and all
the exciting new possibilities.

He'd been distracted, though, on the phone—thinking about
the conference, maybe; Charlie couldn't remember. In the months
after his mom died, it had been like his dad was still around, but
not quite all of him. And how much of him had there been to
begin with, really?

Maybe there had always been something missing in his
father; but maybe not, Charlie reflected, as he stared at the poor
abandoned poster, rolled up now and abandoned in this room.
He knew his mother and father had been good together. They'd
brought out something special in each other. And he'd seen exactly what was left of his father when that stopped.

If someone can be flawed, and be saved by love, they can
also become a hollowed-out shell of a person when that love is
gone. Right?

He went downstairs without brushing his teeth and poured
some cereal into a bowl, then sat next to his dad, who was reading the paper. He glanced at Charlie's bowl as he started eating.
"Don't you want milk?"

Charlie shook his head.

Sounding testy, his dad asked, "What are your plans for the day?"

He didn't answer. His dad sighed and put his paper down. "Charles," he said. "Do I need to be concerned?"

"Why?"

"Are you . . ."

Charlie looked at him when he trailed off. To his surprise, his dad actually seemed concerned. "Do you want to talk about . . . anything?"

He scoffed. "No."

"Well, you can't stay here forever."

"Why?" he shot back. "You're gonna kick me out for my own good? I have money. I'm just here because . . ."

His dad raised a bushy eyebrow. "Because . . . ?"

He said nothing. His dad didn't push, and for a while he thought that was the end of it.

After a moment, though, his dad said quietly, "Are you sorry?"

Charlie scraped his spoon against his bowl, taking small, precise bites, keeping his mouth full.

"Did you tell him that?" his dad added.

"Dad," he snapped, pushing away from the table, "I don't want to—"

"Fine, okay!" he said, holding his hands up in surrender.

They ate in silence for another moment. "It was a beautiful column," he said. "The one about—the one about him."

Charlie shook his head roughly, willing himself to be okay. "I don't care."

"You should."

"I hurt him," Charlie said. "I betrayed him."

"Yes, you did," his dad said, nodding slowly. "But your work was excellent."

Charlie's chair scraped as he stood up. "I don't care," he spat. "Do you understand? It wasn't worth it."

"I understand more than you," his dad said, looking up at him with cold sincerity, "because I know that you do care. That's why you did it. And I understand that." He shook his head, his lips thinning. "I know what it's like to . . . to not let anything stop you. To be . . . consumed by it."

Across the kitchen, almost entirely in shadow, Charlie spotted a painting his mom had made. They'd done one of those guided art classes together years ago, before she got sick. They'd all been supposed to paint the same sunset scene, but Mom had ignored the directions and tried to paint Patrick from *Sponge-Bob*, because Charlie had loved him as a kid and she never let him forget it. It was more an impressionistic red smear than a recognizable starfish, but he loved the painting. He was surprised his dad still had it.

He sat back down slowly. "I know you do, Dad," he said. "I know."

His dad reached over and took his hand, and they sat like that for a while, in the quiet, empty house.

Eventually, his dad said, "You should say you're sorry. Just tell him again. It'll get through."

Charlie swallowed back everything bleak and wrong he wanted to say back, and just said, "Thanks."

Chapter 29

Eventually, after Lorenzo had managed to make it out of his room and then even out of the apartment a few times, Maggie bullied him into throwing another party. She'd pointed out that it was unlikely this next one would crash and burn quite as spectacularly as the first one had, which he had to concede was true. Charlie wouldn't be there.

There was no one to betray him anymore.

And though the last thing Lorenzo wanted to do was anything that would remind him of Charlie, Maggie thought the supernatural support group, or whatever they were calling it, was a good idea. So he found himself staring sullenly at a shrink-wrapped set of paper plates, procrastinating in his duties as host while Maggie buzzed around him, setting up drinks and cheese plates and everything else one needed to entertain. She'd even brought out some succulents and faux flowers to decorate the apartment—because it needed to be *homey*, she insisted, not *festive*.

He wasn't sure the difference. He wasn't sure this was a

good idea. There was a decent chance he'd end up back in his sweats, under the covers, before the guests finished arriving.

Maggie nudged him, bringing him back into reality, and he sighed and began unwrapping the plates. "Don't mope," she told him. "This is already going better than last time—look how many people showed up!"

Sure enough, there were already enough guests to fill the apartment with the pleasant sound of chatter. There were plenty of people from the last time, and a few new faces. They'd set things up this time as more of a discussion circle than a party, but folks were still mingling and chatting amiably with each other as they grabbed snacks and seats.

Maggie had just put the finishing touches on a carefully arranged charcuterie plate when Rachel arrived, grabbing a large chunk of cheese and shoving it into her face. "Hey!" Maggie objected.

"Bleh," Rachel said. "What is this? Where's the cursed stuff?"

Maggie indicated another wedge of cheese, this one with a slightly more ominous odor, and Rachel dug into it eagerly. "Sure, go right ahead," Maggie sighed.

Rachel's eyes were darting around the apartment. "Isolde's not here, is she?"

"I invited her," Maggie said sternly, unwrapping some new blocks of cheese. "And you said you weren't going to be weird."

"I'm not weird," Rachel said, her mouth full. "There's nothing—"

She jumped at the sound of glass tinkling, but it was just some goblins in a corner of the room toasting each other. Maggie glared at her, and she swallowed her cheese shamefully before giving Lorenzo an apologetic smile. "I'll just—help you guys set up."

They worked in silence for a moment, setting out bottles and napkins, until Rachel seemed to notice Lorenzo's subdued mood. "Hey," she said. "You doing okay?"

He grunted something by way of reply.

"Has he called?" she asked. "Or texted?"

"No."

"He probably thinks you don't want to talk to him."

"I don't want to talk to him."

"Okay," Rachel said in a tone that got under Lorenzo's skin.

"You think I should?" he asked.

"I don't know," she said. "I mean, no, I guess not. Not if you don't want to."

"Why would I."

Rachel and Maggie exchanged a look. Then Rachel took a deep breath and said, "Look, I know what he did was—awful—monstrous—"

"He lied to me from the minute we met," Lorenzo snapped. "Both times."

"I know," Rachel said. "And I'm Team Lorenzo here, a hundred thousand percent. I will literally kill him if you want me to." He started to object, and she waved him down impatiently. "But . . . it kinda seems like—maybe he just—"

"What."

"I think he lied to you because . . . well, because people are shitheads sometimes—most of the time," Rachel said. "And then I think the whole thing just snowballed. I don't think he ever meant for it to go this far."

"But it did," Lorenzo said.

"Yeah, it did," Rachel said softly. "But . . . I don't think he *meant* to hurt you. People . . ." she sighed. "People fuck up.

They make mistakes." Her eyes went distant. "They reach for what they shouldn't."

"Mistakes," Lorenzo scoffed. "He deceived me."

"He made a bad call," Rachel said softly. "He—for whatever reason, he lied to you, and that was wrong. But he obviously cared about you."

Lorenzo shook his head.

"He didn't mean to betray you," Rachel said.

"But he did," he snapped.

"Yeah," Rachel said, deflating a bit. "I know."

Then she spotted Isolde across the room, and her entire body stiffened.

"And look what he did to you two," Lorenzo muttered. "Meddling, butting in, and . . . ruining things."

"It's not Charlie's fault," Rachel said with a sigh, her eyes never leaving Isolde. "If anything, he . . ."

"What?" Lorenzo demanded.

Rachel was silent a moment. "I don't know," she said at length, chewing her lower lip. "I guess you're right. I probably never would have kissed her if it wasn't for him."

Lorenzo looked from Isolde's perfect, glimmering form back to Rachel, who had a dark, complicated look on her face as she gazed at the other woman. "And that's . . . bad," he said.

"Yeah," she said, sounding distracted. "I gotta go get . . . something."

She flitted away, and Maggie rubbed him on the back comfortingly. "Why don't you go take a quick breather?" she suggested. "It's filling up fast."

Lorenzo sighed and went to straighten the drinks table. He went through the motions of the gracious host—introducing folks who hadn't met, keeping the music going, making small talk.

He was counting down the minutes until he could be alone with his sorrow again.

A while later he found himself in a quiet corner with Isolde. She looked a bit less glittery than usual, wrapped in a silky soft sweater, her hair in a neat, flat braid along one shoulder. And though her skin still held the secret glow of the evening forest, she chewed on a nail as she flicked a glance at the rest of the party over Lorenzo's shoulder. "Rachel's not here, is she?"

"You *both* promised to not be weird," he reminded her.

Isolde slumped a bit and said, ". . . okay."

A glum silence fell. "You're sad about Charlie," Isolde said.

"You can sense that?" he asked.

"No," she said. "I just noticed."

He grunted.

"Human emotions are complicated," she went on. He started to clarify that he was not, in fact, human, but she continued, ignoring him. "They're fractal. Little Matryoshka dolls of . . . doubt and fantasy. Desire and . . . torment."

"That's true," Lorenzo said lowly. They nodded, united for a moment in their morose contemplation.

Then something occurred to Lorenzo. "Hang on," he said. "You read people. You read auras. You never got anything off of Charlie that he was—" He swallowed. "That he was lying to everyone?"

In a tone that was slow and a bit embarrassed, as if Lorenzo had asked her what color the sky was, Isolde said, "I sensed he was holding himself back from you in some way. And that he felt . . . ashamed."

She flicked her eyes back up to his. "But I felt the same from you."

"He used me," he said.

"Yes," she agreed. "But he regrets that."

"No he doesn't," Lorenzo hissed.

"I told you," Isolde insisted. "I felt your shame when you were holding yourselves apart, each of you. And I saw that shame fade away, these last few weeks."

"So?"

"So," she said, blinking a bit. "That's love."

"That's not how your powers work," Lorenzo snarled. "Sensing purity and shame isn't the same thing as—as—"

"Lorenzo—"

"You're still new to human emotions," he said sharply. "You said so yourself. This isn't something you could understand."

Isolde flinched—just a bit, just in the depths of her eyes where he could glimpse something other than otherworldly terror. "I guess I don't," she said quietly. "I just . . ."

He held his breath, but she merely shrugged. "You seemed happy."

He clenched his teeth as she walked away.

Lorenzo returned to the small indignities of hosting until it became clear that it was once again time for him to kick things off, so to speak.

Only this time, Charlie wasn't there to prompt him.

He cleared his throat and shoved those thoughts out of his head. "Welcome everyone," he said. "Thank you for coming. I, um . . . I talked about this a little bit at the—the last party, but I just . . . want this to be a place where people feel . . ."

He looked around the room at everyone who'd come—werewolves and necromancers; demons and succubi; a unicorn and a human poltergeist; even one of Sebastian's vampire flunkies had shown up, looking hesitant and a bit ashamed, but Lorenzo hadn't had the heart to make him leave.

They were all here, looking to him.

"A sense of community," he said. "And . . . I'm not sure exactly what that should look like, but . . . I'm open to suggestions."

He sat. There was a slightly awkward silence.

Then Eugene—the teenage druid who was actually a necromancer—spoke up. "Well, I'm glad to be here!" he said. "Hi all. I'm uh—well, my coven thinks my powers are scary. But I *don't* reanimate corpses! Or—human corpses. Just small rodents."

This silence was considerably more awkward. Lorenzo decided to push past it. "Great, thank you, Eugene," he said. "Anyone else?"

Gray talked about the wrongful termination suit he was planning against his former pack. A young woman who hadn't been at the first party spoke hesitantly about the fear and isolation that came with being a siren. Sal, the bartender, talked about the arguments he'd had with his fellow demons about whether to risk a potentially fatal trip to their home dimension or try to make a living here.

The loneliness and unease they described was never the same; sometimes it was big and intentional and harsh; sometimes they sounded just like Lorenzo—drifting. Listless.

But talking about it felt good—*he* felt good, for the first time in a while. Like he was taking charge of his life instead of just letting it happen to him. Because these stories of sadness and loneliness were being met with nods and support, and he'd made it all happen.

I'm proud of you, he heard Charlie whisper. He shook his head to dispel it.

When the speeches seemed to come to a natural close, Lorenzo stood and toasted everyone. "Well, I think we can call our first formal meeting a success."

From over by the drinks table, Roberta said, "The first meeting of—what are we calling this thing?"

They all looked at each other expectantly. "Paranormals Anonymous," Eugene said.

"The supernatural squad," the other vampire suggested.

"The supernatural support network," Gray said.

"The Lupines," Lorenzo said. He hadn't known he was going to say it until it came out.

There were frowns among the group. "Well, *I* like it," Gray said, "but—"

"Not lupines like wolves," Lorenzo said. "The purple flower. The Lupines."

"Works for me," Roberta said. She lifted her glass. "The Lupines."

The rest of them toasted. From the back of the room, Maggie smiled at him sadly.

Chapter 30

Eventually, Charlie started reading his emails again. A few days later he video called Ava. "Hey stranger," she greeted him, looking happy and a bit surprised. She was at home, in her Brooklyn brownstone. "Thanks for taking the call."

"Is this real?" he asked her. She snorted.

Apparently, while Charlie's life had been crashing and burning, *Wise Old Crone* had been doing so well that Advance Media had bumped *up* their initial offer. Just as Ava had predicted, they wanted to buy Charlie's column, along with Charlie and Ava to run it. They'd have much more editorial control and the kind of money he'd thought was a typo at first. It was in every way his dream job.

"Yes, it's real," she said, beaming. "And you deserve it. Congratulations, Charlie!"

"Thanks."

She sat forward, her forehead filling up the screen. "Thanks? That's all the reaction I get? I thought you'd at least scream, or throw up, or something."

He tried to smile. "It is a lot of money."

"Yeah," Ava said, looking increasingly concerned. "It is." When Charlie didn't respond, she said, "Okay, what's wrong?"

He rubbed his face with his hands. He hadn't showered in days, and he was suddenly regretting taking this call in the first place. "Uh, nothing. I met someone while I was living here," he said. "And it . . . it didn't work out."

"Oh," Ava said softly. "I'm sorry."

"Yeah."

"Do you want to talk about it?"

"No."

"Okay, well," she said, "let's sublimate the heartache by focusing on work. Like, talking about this amazing deal!"

Charlie rubbed his eyes. He felt numb. "You're sure it's real?"

She laughed again. "Yes, and I think we should move quickly. You're overdue with your *Crone* columns, and I want to close this thing before we get any pushback from management here."

"Right," he said, more out of muscle memory than anything else.

In his peripheral vision, he could see Ava staring at him through the screen, trying to puzzle him out. "You and me running the whole thing," she said. "It's going to be amazing. Independence, status, and—y'know, the money."

He sighed. "I don't know, Ava."

"You don't know what?" she asked. "Do you want to counter? Are you worried about their ownership of your work—"

"No," he said, "I don't know if I want to do this anymore."

"This," she asked, "like . . . write?"

He put his head in his hands, feeling like he was collapsing inward. "I don't know."

"Charlie, babe," Ava said softly, "I'm sorry for what you're going through right now, but that's nuts! You're a great writer. Look at what you've accomplished! You took what they *did to you*—and you thrived. *Wise Old Crone* is doing better than ever! You're a total Cinderella story!"

"So I should be proud of this?" he asked sharply.

Ava sat back in confusion. "Why wouldn't you?"

"Because it's not—because it's bullshit," Charlie snapped. He felt like everything inside him was tying itself into knots, the pressure building and building. "Like, what do I—I'm just using people's lives and drama for my own benefit."

"Well, you're getting paid," Ava said doubtfully, "but I don't think you're—"

"Taking a huge deal, that you arranged?" he spat. "Just to, what, like—hurt people? Is that what you want me to do?"

Calmly, Ava said, "Why are you yelling at me right now."

Charlie took a breath. "I wasn't—"

"Charlie," she said, and it pierced the last of his pride and defensiveness. He sighed again, his eyes burning, and didn't try to talk anymore.

"What's going on?" Ava asked quietly. "Because you're acting like I did something wrong by trying to get you paid for your work."

"I'm sorry," he muttered.

"Hm?" she prompted.

Louder, and properly, he said, "I'm sorry."

Ava waited.

"I'm not mad at you," Charlie said, taking a deep, shuddering breath. "I'm . . . I'm mad at myself."

Ava sat forward. "What is going on?"

Half an hour later, he'd crawled into bed, taking Ava

with him under the covers. She'd slumped over at her desk, in absorbed listening mode—all he could see was an ear. He sniffed, hating how congested he got when he cried.

"Oh man," Ava said softly. "So—what are you going to do?"

"I don't know," Charlie said. "I want to fix it. But I can't."

"Have you talked to him?"

"I want to fix it more than that," Charlie said, forcefully. "I want to . . ."

"Take it back?" Ava asked.

Quietly, Charlie said, "No." Then he shook his head. "I don't know."

Ava said nothing, just sitting with him while the sounds from her apartment filtered out into the cocoon Charlie had made.

"I just want . . ." He took a shaky breath before the tears started again. ". . . to do right by him."

"What would you say if this was you writing in to the column?"

Miserably, Charlie choked out, "I'd tell him to dump me." He squeezed his eyes shut against a fresh sob fighting its way up his throat.

"Not if it was him writing in," Ava was saying. "What would you tell *you* to do?"

Charlie took a deep breath and thought, and Ava waited with him.

Chapter 31

Two weeks later, Charlie texted him.

By then, Lorenzo had finally gotten around to reading all of Charlie's columns, or at least the ones he'd written since they'd started hanging out. To his relief, there weren't any other horrifying details about his private life—aside from the one about him crying, which he still couldn't read—but some of the jokes or little turns of phrase were hauntingly familiar. It was clear that Charlie had been inspired by their time together—by the places and people Lorenzo had shown him.

The writing sounded like Charlie. He could almost hear him reading each one aloud. It was beyond strange to read the column and realize that he was seeing a side of Charlie he hadn't known existed. Something that Charlie had kept from him, deliberately. It hurt.

But it didn't just hurt; it made him miss Charlie. So when he got the text, in a moment of weakness, he agreed to meet him in the same coffee shop where they'd run into each other months ago.

It was nearly empty when he got there, which was a relief. Charlie was sitting at a table in the back, but he stood up when he saw Lorenzo. He was dressed nicely, but he looked gaunt. There were dark circles under his eyes.

And he was still so goddamned handsome. A nervous smile lit up his face when he saw Lorenzo, and the hesitation in his amber eyes melted into soft, tentative happiness with every second that Lorenzo didn't turn around and bolt.

He was fighting the urge.

But he didn't run. He could still feel it behind his ribs— that knot drawn messy, painful, and tight, urging him closer to Charlie. Some ineffable trace of Charlie's blood still running through his veins, tying them together. Braiding Charlie into him.

He shook his head, schooling his features into an impassive mask, and sat at the table. Charlie's smile wavered a bit, but he still looked relieved. "Hi," he said. "Thank you for coming."

Lorenzo said nothing, glancing up at Charlie only as long as he could bear it.

"I wanted to, um," Charlie said, sounding unsure. "I wanted to tell you about . . . my column."

This time, he waited Lorenzo out. "What about it?" he finally grunted, crossing his arms.

The last traces of charm melted out of Charlie's demeanor, leaving just nerves. He bit his lips. "I want to give it to you," he said.

Lorenzo frowned. "What? What are you talking about?"

"I spun it off from the site. Cut ties with everyone there. Well, everyone except my editor, but she's—she's on board," he said, quickly, like he was nervous that Lorenzo wouldn't believe him. Or that he'd get up and leave. "So it's ours now. I mean, we have no money, but we won't have to answer to anyone but ourselves. And we spent the last few days building out the infrastructure, so now it has a—well, a forum, basically. Like a beefed-up comments section."

"Hang on," Lorenzo said.

"I thought the—if people could talk and connect—it could be like a digital counterpart to your group," he said. "And the original column is successful enough by now that—I mean, I think it'll have reach and visibility. So supernatural folks could find support and community anywhere—all over the world. But it's not just—" He sighed. "I also put some feelers out to other writers—supernatural writers. So they can keep the column going if you don't . . ."

He trailed off, his rant suddenly out of steam. Lorenzo stared at him. Charlie's breathing evened out as he waited for a response.

Lorenzo wasn't sure what to say.

"I wanted to make it better," Charlie said. "So it wouldn't be . . . um . . ."

He petered out again. And this time, when he looked back up at Lorenzo, he could see all the hope and fear in Charlie's eyes.

"You want to . . . give me your column," he said.

"Yes," Charlie answered immediately.

"Your life's work," Lorenzo said carefully.

Charlie flinched and looked away. "I mean—it's . . ."

Lorenzo waited. Charlie sighed, took a deep breath, and said, "I don't think I was . . . doing it for the right reasons. Not anymore. I did—I do want to help people. Give them advice that's useful. But . . . I got so caught up in 'making it,'" he said bitterly. "Getting the column, being published, being known. Living in New York, being able to call myself a writer. I felt successful. And that's what I—that's what I was trying to hang on to. And I don't want to do that anymore.

"Meeting you, and Rachel and Maggie and Isolde—it reminded me of who I want to be," he said quietly. "So . . . I'm giving it to you."

"And what would you do?"

He shrugged jerkily. "I don't know. But I won't—this thing I created, it won't be—it'll be better."

Lorenzo didn't know what to say. He stared at Charlie, and Charlie stared at him.

The bell over the coffee shop door jangled as a large group came in, laughing loudly. Charlie and Lorenzo shared a look, then got up from their table and stepped over to the sliding glass door at the back of the shop.

There was a small patio out back, fenced in from the property next door, that was just big enough for two tables. Tonight, there were paint cans and plywood boxes stacked everywhere, and large tarps draped over most of the furniture and walls. Lorenzo turned and saw that a mural had just been painted on the back of the shop: a vision of the Blue Ridge Mountains—a hillside covered in riotous, bright wildflowers.

Charlie cleared his throat, and Lorenzo tried to take a step back, but the painting equipment didn't leave them much room. Charlie suddenly felt a million miles closer. *Touchable.*

"So," Charlie said nervously. "What do you think?"

"I—I don't know," Lorenzo said. "I've never . . . run an advice column—forum—before."

"You'd be great at it."

"Charlie," Lorenzo said quietly, and Charlie looked up at him.

He took a steadying breath, like a skittish human, and then made himself ask. "Why did you do it?"

"Which part?" Charlie whispered. Lorenzo was close enough now to make out the texture of his stubble where he hadn't shaved, and the dark, delicate skin under his eyes.

He didn't answer Charlie's question. Charlie swallowed and said, his voice small and hoarse and painfully familiar: "Because I didn't want you to stop liking me."

Lorenzo looked away and clenched his fists. Charlie stepped closer, even in the cramped space on the patio. Lorenzo didn't back away.

Staring up at Lorenzo, he said lowly, "I'm so sorry. I love you, and I screwed up."

Lorenzo closed his eyes. He could feel the warmth rolling off Charlie's body, but he felt icy all over. He longed to touch him, and was dying to turn and run. He felt screaming and leaden; suffused with fear and sick with hope.

He hadn't known Charlie was lying before. What if he was lying now?

Charlie was craning his head like he wanted to close the space between them. Lorenzo's eyes flickered over his neck and caught at the edge of his collar.

He lifted a hand to touch Charlie there, making him gasp. But Lorenzo just leaned in and gently pushed on the collar of Charlie's shirt, brushing back the fabric far enough to see his bite mark.

It was still there. In fact, it looked as fresh and tender as the day Lorenzo had given it to him. "Oh, I'm—I'm sorry," Charlie said breathlessly. His heart thumped, sending blood flooding through his body, just under his fine skin. "I wore a collared shirt because I—I wasn't sure if you wanted to see it."

Lorenzo stared at the two ripe blooms of red on Charlie's

skin, remembering the night he'd made it. The night Charlie had asked for it. The taste of Charlie's blood. The openness in his face.

Vampire bites heal quickly. Vampires are predators that look just like their prey; they're meant to blend in among humans, and quick-healing bites help allay suspicion. Most bites like this would have been gone a day or two later.

But Charlie's looked like he'd gotten it last night.

Lorenzo was close enough now to feel the warmth every time Charlie exhaled, a violent gust against the backdrop of soft heat that rolled off his body all the time; the brush of his shirt, the tickle of his hair at Lorenzo's temple; and his pulse was right there, the familiar tempo of it like a song he'd gone too long without hearing. "I read online that vampire bites usually fade pretty fast," Charlie said quietly, standing still as Lorenzo pulled back just a hair, just enough to look him in the eye. "But . . . every day I woke up and saw that it was still there . . ." His voice dropped to a whisper. "I was so happy. I didn't want it to go away."

Magic is intent.

And Lorenzo had forgotten that humans had their own magic too, sometimes, if they wanted something badly enough.

"Magic," he whispered.

Charlie laughed a little, almost nervously. "What?" he asked, blinking up at him, just as lost as Lorenzo was.

Lorenzo came closer, giving Charlie a chance to back up or object. But he didn't; he held still, looked up at Lorenzo, and then swayed closer; and Lorenzo kissed him, slowly, carefully, and fully.

When they broke apart they were both panting like humans.

Charlie clapped a hand to his bite mark, swallowing, and Lorenzo cradled his face in his hands.

"Okay," he said. "Okay."

And he brought their lips together again, Charlie's fist tight in his shirt, not letting go, and Charlie's pulse warm and steady and perfect under his palm.

Chapter 32

Five Months Later

It shouldn't have been surprising that when they got to the air-port, they discovered that there was something wrong with their reservation.

"Welcome, and thank you for flying with us," the agent at check-in told them, once Charlie had given her their names. "I see one first-class coffin and one business-class seat."

Charlie blinked. "No, I booked two seats in first class—one coffin, one daybed—so we'd be together." He shot a small smile at Lorenzo, who was still waking up—they had to fly at the very crack of sunset, and he'd grumbled about it more than once in the car ride over.

"I'm sorry, sir, I see separate seats here," the agent said, typing rapidly.

"That must be a mistake," Charlie said.

"I'll see what I can do," the agent said, "but—"

"You suggest," Lorenzo said slowly, taking a step closer to

the counter, "that I would have intentionally seated my chosen human companion away from my coffin?"

The agent looked flummoxed, her hands frozen over the terminal. "You think I should do such a thing as we take to the sun-drenched skies in this magnificent beast?" Lorenzo went on, gesturing at the planes on the tarmac. The pitch of his voice had dropped to something volcanic and dark. "Be separated from the call of his blood?"

The agent blinked rapidly, and then said, "Uh . . . no, sir. Let me—let me just get my manager."

Lorenzo broke into a goofy grin as soon as she left the podium. "I just love doing stuff like that."

After they'd secured their seats and gone through security, they got snacks. Well, Charlie got snacks—there was a stall by the moving walkway that had truffle fries, and he loved truffle fries, he didn't care how basic it made him. But Lorenzo wasn't feeling anything they'd passed yet, so they'd found their seats at the gate, and Lorenzo had asked Charlie to watch his bags while he stretched his legs and poked around.

Charlie took in the terminal slowly, savoring his snack and trying to resist the urge to check his phone. They were on vacation, and besides, where else but an airport could you engage in some true people watching in this day and age?

A millennial couple on the other side of the gate were arguing quietly about something on the woman's phone. He watched patiently, trying to see if he could suss out anything about the fight from their body language—the man was pointing at the phone vigorously, but the woman kept shaking her head and mouthing something Charlie couldn't quite decipher. Sitting closer to him was a woman with a dog in her purse—it was too snuggled up for him to make out the breed—and a girl who looked like a student, who had very cool iridescent snakes coiled neatly on her head.

But he decided to stick with the arguing couple. He loved a good fight. He wanted to see if he could figure it out.

"You look deep in thought," Lorenzo said, settling into the seat next to him. He was holding a pair of Reese's cups, and started to unwrap them.

"Just snooping. You know me," Charlie said lightly. Lorenzo grunted, but not in a way that gave Charlie anything to work with when it came to reading his mood. He hadn't always had the best reaction to Charlie's curiosity about others.

Then Lorenzo slid him a glance. "The girl with the dog, or the fight?"

Charlie's heart bloomed a bit. "The couple. What are they fighting about?"

Lorenzo's eyes glazed over as he tuned in to the distant voices. It always turned Charlie on when he did this, every single time. Just imagining the things he could hear . . . the sounds Charlie could make so quietly that only Lorenzo would hear them . . .

He was lost in thought when Lorenzo reported back, flatly, "Backsplash."

"Ugh," Charlie sighed, stuffing his face with truffle oil. Lorenzo leaned over and snagged a few fries before he'd even unwrapped either of his candies. He licked his thumb when he was done, and Charlie giggled at him.

Then his phone buzzed twice, and Charlie slid it from his pocket without thinking.

"No," Lorenzo said sternly, leaning over to grab it from him and immediately getting greasy fingerprints all over the screen. Charlie sighed, looking pointedly at the smudges.

"We said," Lorenzo defended himself.

And it was true—they'd badly needed this getaway. Relaunching the column and the rest of the site after turning down Advance Media's offer had been a herculean task. They'd gone from the meager support he'd had as Wise Old Crone to doing absolutely everything themselves—the kind of legal, administrative, and technical minutiae that turned Lorenzo's eyes red and gave Charlie panic attacks. But slowly, painfully, they'd gotten the new site up and running—Charlie's column, and eventually a few other regular contributors' pages, plus some fun new features—and the forum. The forum had been a *ton* of work, but it was so worth it to see people start signing up and chatting. They posted about stuff Charlie had written, and issues he hadn't had a chance to write about, and about things he'd never heard of—creatures and rituals and places that even Lorenzo hadn't encountered.

They weren't getting a lot of sleep—along with Ava, Rachel, Maggie, Isolde, Gray, and the few other friends they'd press-ganged into service. But all those sleepless nights and stumbling blocks had been worth it, because the site was starting to thrive. They'd attracted a decent number of subscribers, and they had five other regular contributors now, including Rachel and Gray. People were getting paid, they had enough money to hire more staff, and Charlie and Lorenzo had even done a mini tour, helping to get in-person supernatural groups set up in other cities, which was incredibly gratifying and fully exhausting.

They'd called the new site *The Lupine*. The forum they'd called Green Shoots. Wise Old Crone was gone, dead, and Charlie didn't give her a second thought. (Like other mystical old crones, though, he wasn't counting on her *staying* dead forever.)

Ava said she'd always known it was headed here, but Charlie

knew it hadn't been. He and Lorenzo had had to work to make the site successful—to make it into something they could be proud of.

But they'd left all that turmoil and stress and hard work back home, and on this trip, they'd pledged not to think about it even a little.

At the changeover in New York, Charlie kept watching the movie he'd started on the first plane, while Lorenzo flicked through the news. Eventually Charlie noticed that Lorenzo had put his phone away and was staring somewhat blankly at his own screen. Charlie grinned and offered him one of his earbuds. Lorenzo's answering smile was full of warmth, like a sunrise.

It was so strange to think that there might have been a time that Charlie would have dreaded Lorenzo taking a peek at his phone. Sharing screens was a sign of trust—and more, he supposed, as Lorenzo tucked his head into Charlie's neck, already getting wrapped up in the film.

They'd spent a lot of time in the last few months working on themselves and their relationship, rebuilding the trust that had been lost. Charlie had shown Lorenzo the parts of himself he'd kept hidden before—when he'd first wanted to be a writer; landing the gig at *Midnight* and crafting his Crone voice; the kind of artistic projects he'd long dreamt of but never dared to say out loud. He could whisper those things to Lorenzo in the middle of the night on a random Tuesday and feel like no one heard them, because he was speaking directly into the universe via the slow, even way Lorenzo stroked his hair as he listened to Charlie.

Charlie apologized in many different ways and different languages, both love and literal, for violating Lorenzo's trust.

They reread and dissected every column he'd written since moving back to Brookville. They had long meandering conversations that went until five a.m. and were often half crying, and they had nonsensical, barely coherent conversations about love and trust and meaning and honor while they were still short of breath and glued to each other, watching some inane movie on mute in the dark of Charlie's room.

They stayed at Charlie's place more.

But they were at a good place with the roommates again. Charlie was in a good place with Maggie again, thank Satan. And it was just at that moment that a text from Rachel popped up on Charlie's phone, blocking the top third of the movie.

Charlie winced when he saw Isolde's name. Without even opening it all the way, he looked at Lorenzo, who had a weary look on his face.

Charlie swiped the notification away, unread.

"Cold," Lorenzo murmured, though he was starting to smile.

"We're on vacation," Charlie said. "And I'm not touching that mess with a ten-foot pole."

An echoing voice reminded them that it was almost time to board, so Charlie turned off the movie and started getting his things together. "How many more flights?" Lorenzo asked, staring at the gate with dread. To hear him tell it, plane coffins ran the gamut from tolerable to medieval torture device.

"Just one," Charlie reassured him. "And then a teeny tiny boat."

Lorenzo perked up at that.

"Hm," Charlie said, as they stepped into the accordion-like boarding apparatus. He was pointing at a sign. "What does that say?"

Lorenzo sighed happily and translated for him. "Keep seat-belts and coffins fastened."

One flight, one boat, and one sunset later, Charlie and Lorenzo were in the heated pool. By the time the sky was fully dark, they were well on their way to hammered.

The hotel was gorgeous, a thoroughly modern glass and steel enclave set right onto the pebbled beach. It had the standard-issue infinity pool with a huge swim-up bar, close enough to hear the waves crashing in the dark.

And Charlie and Lorenzo were being every inch the obnoxious American tourists, laughing too loudly and falling over each other and making out without a care in the world for who could see. There weren't even that many other guests out at this time of night, but those that were must have been judging them. Charlie just couldn't find it in himself to care.

He'd almost lost this.

The hotel was in Cagliari, a big, bustling city all the way across the island from Lorenzo's hometown. Italy from the U.S. was already a long trip, so they were stopping along the way, and he didn't want those stops to necessarily be laden with meaning, not if Lorenzo wasn't ready for that. He'd have time to show Charlie everything here that meant something to him, everything he might've touched or seen centuries ago, but that was tomorrow. Tonight, they could take a night off in a luxury hotel that was younger than Charlie.

"Hang on, hang on," Charlie said, only slurring a little. "Watch this."

He was trying to tie a cherry stem into a knot with his

tongue, but it was difficult with Lorenzo standing just behind him in the pool, his hands roving all over Charlie's body, practically drooling onto Charlie's shoulder as he scented his latest bite.

Lorenzo had bitten him in a number of fun places by now, but Charlie's favorite would always be the bite on his neck. After he and Lorenzo had gotten back together, it had finally healed, though it never went away completely; Charlie knew the two shiny, thick scars on his neck would never fade. He loved rubbing at his bite absently, or in the mornings, when he missed Lorenzo; the reminder that he belonged to him; that they were bound together by this messy, painful connection they shared; that they'd chosen.

Lorenzo's fingers drifted over Charlie's nipple, and he shivered, turning to kiss Lorenzo with his sticky-sweet cherry mouth. Lorenzo's lips were shining when he pulled back.

Charlie went on his back in the pool, looking up at the stars. Lorenzo kept a hand under his back and helped him float, pushing and pulling gently so he was rocking in the water. "Can vampires float?" Charlie asked him.

"Yes."

"Can you drown?"

"No."

"I already know you can hold your breath for a really long time."

Lorenzo quirked an eyebrow down at him, but didn't bother dignifying the remark with a response.

Charlie stretched and then stood up again, water rolling off his shoulders, and put his hands on Lorenzo's hips. "What's the worst part about it?"

They both knew why he was really asking, but they weren't

talking about that directly just quite yet. He appreciated that Lorenzo wasn't rushing him. He knew Charlie would tell him when he was ready.

Lorenzo thought about Charlie's question carefully, and said, "No sunlight." Charlie hummed. "Being stereotyped by vampire fiction." Charlie laughed. "Obsessive advice columnists."

Smiling, Charlie asked, "And what do you do with those?"

"I'm a vampire," Lorenzo said softly, catching Charlie's jaw in his palm. "I seduce them."

And they kissed under the moonlight, surrounded by the ocean and a whole unknown world waiting just for them.

ACKNOWLEDGMENTS

The book about the lupines is *Miss Rumphius* by Barbara Cooney.

Brookville is a thinly fictionalized version of Charlottesville, Virginia, which is a lovely town that deserves much better than to be forever associated with the shit-eating nazis that terrorized it. If you're ever there, please check out El Puerto—my favorite restaurant, and the inspo for Charlie's.

The druids' drive-in movie theater is based on the Delsea Drive-In in Vineland, New Jersey.

Lastly, this entire book is inspired by *What We Do in the Shadows* (the film and show), which if for some reason you haven't seen, you should remedy!

Now the actual people to thank for this book existing. Any such list must begin with my wonderful agent, Laura Zats, for listening to my early half-formed ideas for a vampire romance and encouraging me to actually write the rest of it. (And then selling it!)

I am overwhelmed with gratitude to Ava Wilder, Tim Janovsky, S. A. MacLean, Emily Ohanjanians, Merren Tait, Chip Pons, and Erin La Rosa for their kind words of praise blurbing the book.

And, of course, this book would not exist without the talented folks at St. Martin's Griffin who acquired it and brought it to life, especially my editor, Alexandra Sehulster, and editorial assistants Ashley Quintana and Cassidy Graham. The full list of folks at St. Martin's Publishing Group who helped publish this book is below.

Thank you to Mildred for keeping me sane long enough to write this book.

Finally, thank you to my family for their love and support. Grammy, I hope you enjoyed the scam-artist fortune teller to whom I gave your name. Grampy, I know I owe you a character now, but I just don't think I'm talented enough to write a heist book. We'll see.

Thank you to April for the trash cans and the reset. Thank you, Mom, for always keeping me in baked goods and supportive talks. Thanks, Molly, for being the best nerdy kid sister a nerdy girl could ever ask for.

And thank you to Chris and Ollie for showing me that magic is, indeed, quite real; in every hug, every joke, every fight, and every day. I love you.

St. Martin's Publishing Group—*Thirsty* Team

Alexandra Sehulster . . . . Executive Editor
Ashley Quintana . . . . Editorial Assistant
Cassidy Graham . . . . Editorial Assistant
Chrisinda Lynch . . . . Managing Editor
Layla Yuro . . . . Production Editor
Amy Carbo . . . . Copyeditor
Julie Gutin . . . . Proofreader
Dakota Griffin . . . . Cold Reader

Janna Dokos . . . . Production Manager

Gabriel Guma . . . . Designer

Olga Grlic . . . . Cover Designer

Dylan Helstien . . . . Creative Services

Austin Adams . . . . Marketing

Brant Janeway . . . . Marketing

Angela Tabor . . . . Publicity

Jennifer Enderlin . . . . St. Martin's
                          Publishing Group President and Publisher

Anne Marie Tallberg . . . . St. Martin's
                          Griffin Publishing Director

And a special thank-you to the entire
Macmillan sales force!

ABOUT THE AUTHOR

Chris Lehane

LUCY LEHANE writes love stories about terrible people. Her interests include binge-watching, cheese and game nights with friends. Favourite vampires include Spike, Damon, Lestat, Nadja and Count von Count.